Saint Jack

Also by Paul Theroux

WALDO
FONG AND THE INDIANS
GIRLS AT PLAY
JUNGLE LOVERS
SINNING WITH ANNIE

Criticism
V. S. NAIPAUL

Saint Jack

a novel by

Paul Theroux

HOUGHTON MIFFLIN COMPANY BOSTON

1973

FIRST PRINTING   C

Copyright © 1973 by Paul Theroux
All rights reserved. No part of this work may be
reproduced or transmitted in any form by any means,
electronic or mechanical, including photocopying and
recording, or by any information storage or
retrieval system without permission in
writing from the publisher.

Portions of this novel originally appeared in
Playboy magazine and *Works in Progress*.

ISBN: 0-395-17118-0
Library of Congress Catalog Card Number: 72-12400
Printed in the United States
of America

For Anne, as always, with love
And to
good friends in twenty
tropical places

"Action will furnish belief, — but will that belief be the true one?"

— A. H. Clough, *Amours de Voyage*

1

IN ANY MEMOIR it is usual for the first sentence to reveal as
much as possible of your subject's nature by illustrating it in a
vivid and memorable motto, and with my own first sentence now drawing to a finish I see I have failed to do this!
But writing is made with the fingers, and all writing, even the
clumsy kind, exposes in its loops and slants a yearning deeper
than an intention, the soul of the writer flapping on the
clothespin of his exclamation mark. Including the sentence scribbled above: being slow to disclose my nature is
characteristic of me. So I am not off to such a bad start after
all. My mutters make me remember. Later, I will talk about
my girls.

I was going to get under way with an exchange which took
place one morning last year between Gopi and me. Gopi
was our *peon*—pronounced "pyoon," messenger, to dis-
tinguish him from "pee-on," the slave. He was a Tamil
and had a bad leg. He sidled into my cubicle. He showed
me two large damp palms and two discolored eyes and said,
"Mister Hing vaunting Mister Jack in a hurry-*lah*."

That summons was the beginning. At the time I did not

3

know enough to find it dramatic. In fact, it annoyed me. Though it seems an innocent request, when it is repeated practically every day for fourteen years it tends to swaddle one with oppression. That "hurry-*lah*" stung me more than the summons. Mr. Hing, my *towkay*, my boss, was an impatient feller. I was a sitting duck for summonses.

"No one tells Jack Flowers to hurry," I said, turning back to my blue desk diary. I was resolute. I entered a girl's name beside a circled day. He can whistle and wait, I thought, the bugger. "Gopi, tell him I'm busy."

Carrying that message made the *peon* liable to share the blame. I suspected that was why I said it — not a cheering thought. But I couldn't go straight up to Mr. Hing. Gopi left slowly, dragging his bad leg after him. When he was gone I slammed my diary and then, as if stricken with grief, and sighing on each rung, I mounted the narrow stepladder to Mr. Hing's office.

Mr. Hing, a clean tubby Cantonese, got brutal haircuts, one a week, the sort given to inmates of asylums, leaving him a bristly pelt of brush on top and the rest shaven white. He had high Chinese eyebrows and his smile, not really a smile, showed a carved treasure of gold teeth. His smile was anger. He was angry half the time, with the Chinese agony, an impulsive bellyaching Yin swimming against a cowardly Yang: the personality in deadlock. So the Chinese may gaze with waxen placidity into your face, or refuse to reply, or snort and fart when you want a word of encouragement. The secrecy is only half the story. In the other half they yell and fling themselves from rooftops, guzzle weed killer and caustic soda and die horribly to inconvenience their relatives, or gibber in the street with knives — Chinese fire drill. What kept Mr. Hing from suicide was perhaps the thought that he couldn't kill himself by jumping from the crenelated roof of his low two-story shophouse. The two opposing parts of his nature made him a frugal but obsessive

4

Part One

Part One

gambler, a tyrannical philanthropist, a tortured villain, almost my friend. He had a dog. He choked it with good food and kicked it for no reason — he may have kicked it because he fed it, the kindness making him cruel. When it ran away, which was often, Mr. Hing placed an expensive ad in the *Straits Times* to get the poor beast back. Mr. Hing was short, about my own age, and every morning he did exercises called burpees in his locked office. He had few pleasures. Until six in the evening, when he changed into striped pajamas and dandled his grandson on his knee, he wore an ordinary white shirt, an expensive watch, plain trousers, and cheap rubber sandals he kicked off when he sat cross-legged on his chair. He was seated that way the morning I entered his office.

He was slightly more agitated than usual, and the appearance of agitation was heightened by a black fan on a shelf moving its humming face from side to side very rapidly and disturbing the clutter of papers on his desk. Papers trembled and rose, and Mr. Hing clapped them flat as the fan turned away; then it happened again, another squall, another slap.

Mr. Hing's brother perched beside him in a crouch, his knees drawn up, his arms folded into the trough of his lap. He was wearing a T-shirt, the collar stretched showing his hairless chest, and large khaki shorts. I thought of him as Little Hing; he was skinnier and younger, and his youthful hungry face made him seem to me most untrustworthy. Together, their faces eight inches apart, staring at me from behind the desk, they resembled the pair of fraternal faces you see fixed in two lozenge-shaped frames on a square-shouldered bottle of Chinese patent medicine, Tiger Tonic, Three Legs Brain Fluid, or (Mr. Hing's favorite) Rhino Water. Big Hing was especially agitated and saying everything twice: "Sit down, sit down," then, "We got a problem, got a problem."

True Chinese speech is impossible to reproduce without

distraction, and in this narrative I intend to avoid the conventional howlers. The "flied lice" and "No tickee, no shirtee" variety is really no closer to the real thing than the plain speech I have just put in Big Hing's mouth. Chinese do more than transpose *r* and *l*, and *v* and *b*, and *s* and *sh*. They swallow most of their consonants and they seldom give a word an ending: a glottal stop amputates every final syllable. So what Big Hing really said was, "Shi' duh' " and "We go' a pro'luh' "; there is no point in being faithful to this yammering. Little Hing's English was much better than Big's, though Little spoke very fast; but when they were in the same room, Little didn't open his trap, except to mutter in Cantonese. That morning he sat in silence, his teeth locked together, the lowers jutting out, fencing the uppers with yellow pickets.

The conversation, I knew, would be brief, and the only reason Big Hing asked me to sit down was that I towered over the desk like a sweaty bear, panting with annoyance, my tattoos showing. My size bothered them especially. I was a foot taller than Big Hing, and a foot and a half taller than Little — when they were standing. I sat and sank into a chair of plastic mesh, and as I was sinking Big Hing started to explain.

A month before, he had been told that a man was coming from Hong Kong to audit our books. There was another Hing in Hong Kong, a *towkay* bigger than Big Hing, and the auditing was an annual affair. It was also an annual humiliation because Big Hing didn't like his accounts questioned. Still, it happened every year. At one time it was a sallow little man who always arrived ravaged from traveling deck class on a freighter; then, for a few years, a skeletal soul with a kindly smile and popping eyes, who hugged a briefcase — turned to suede by wear — to his starched smock with frog buttons. The auditors stayed for a week, snapping the abacus and thumbing the ledger; Big Hing sat close by, pouring tea, saying nothing. Last year it was a man called Lee, and he was the problem, though Big Hing didn't say so. All he said was: meet this man at the airport.

It was why Hing was agitated. He assumed Lee was Cantonese or at least Chinese. But he discovered, I never learned how, that Lee was an *ang moh,* a redhead. The *ang mohs* were my department. It was the reason I was employed by Hing — *Chop Hing Kheng Fatt: Ship Chandlers & Provisioners,* as the shop sign read. Hing was peeved that he was mistaken about the name, and furious that his books were going to be scrutinized by an *ang moh.* He beamed with anger and banged his fist down upon the fluttering papers, repeating Lee's name and my orders to meet him at the airport. I drew my own conclusions, and I was correct in every detail except the spelling, which was *Leigh.*

"My car's at the garage," I said. I was not being difficult. It was a noisy ten-year-old Renault with 93,000 miles on the clock. One wheel, the front right, had come unstuck from the chassis and made the front end shimmy at any speed, a motion that rubbed the tread from the tires. "I'll have to take a taxi."

"Can, can," said Big Hing.

Little Hing whispered something, staring at me, keeping his teeth locked, a coward's ventriloquism. For Little Hing I was the ultimate barbarian: my hair was once reddish, I am hairy, my arms are profusely tattooed — a savage, "just out of the trees," as Yardley used to say.

"Bus to airport, taxi to town," said Big Hing. That was Little's whispered suggestion.

It was a two-dollar taxi fare; the bus was forty cents. There was no direct bus. I hated sitting at an out-of-town bus shelter, in the heat, with twenty schoolchildren. But I said okay because I could see Big Hing's anger makes him determined that I should save one-sixty and know who was boss. I didn't start arguments I knew in advance I was going to lose. Big

7

Hing was my *towkay:* I couldn't win. But my dealings with him were small.

He counted out $2.40 from petty cash and looked at his watch.

"What time is his plane due in?" I asked.

Big Hing thought three-thirty; Little murmured in Cantonese, and I expected an amendment, but Big stuck to three-thirty and gave me the flight number. I went down to consult my bus guide.

So far it had been an unpleasant day, ruined first by the *peon* telling me to hurry and second by the command to take the bus all the way out to the airport. After looking at the bus guide I saw that several things were in my favor. I was right about there being no direct bus, but the 18-A Singapore Traction Company bus passed by Moulmein Green. I could have lunch at home for a change, and if I hurried, a quick nap. The transfer would have to be made on Paya Lebar Road — a stroke of luck: I could see if Gladys was available before continuing on the 93 to the airport. None of this would cost a penny extra; out of two humiliations I had rescued a measure of self-respect. And if Gladys was free and Leigh was interested I stood to make nine dollars. In any event, I was anxious to meet him. It was nice to see a new face, and an *ang moh*'s was more welcome than most. We were lonelier than we admitted to; after many years of residence in Singapore, we all went for the mail twice a day, even Yardley and Smale, who never got any.

This is the beginning of my story, and already I can see that it represents my fortunes more faithfully, in the haphazard recollection of a single morning's interruption, than if I had planned it as carefully as I once intended and began with the rumbling factual sentence I used to repeat to myself in the days when I believed my early life mattered, before I went away — about being born in the year 1918, in the North End of the city of Boston, the second child of two

8

transplanted Italians; and then the part about my earliest memory (the warm room, my wet thumb and velvet cushion, my father singing with the opera on the radio). There is no space for that here.

2

FOURTEEN YEARS AGO, lowering myself on a rope from the rusty stern of the *Allegro,* anchored then in the Straits of Malacca ("the financial straits," Yardley said), I did not think I was an old man — though if anyone had insisted I was old I would have believed him. Most people are willing to make fools of themselves with a little persuasion, and the question of age is answered by the most foolishness. Now I know that old and young make little difference: the old man talks easily to a child.

They say every age is more barbarous than the last. It is possible. If there is an error in the statement it doesn't matter, because the people who say this are either very young or very old, just starting out and with no experience, or musing in life's sundowner with false flickers of half-forgotten memories. The age, as they call it, is too big to see, but they have time on their hands: it is too early for one and too late for the other to worry about being wrong. What they don't know is that however awful the age is, it is placid and hopeful compared to a certain age in a man.

Fifty: it is a dangerous age — for all men, and especially

for one like me who has a tendency to board sinking ships. Middle age has all the scares a man feels halfway across a busy street, caught in traffic and losing his way, or another one blundering in a black upstairs room, full of furniture, afraid to turn on the lights because he'll see the cockroaches he smells. The man of fifty has the most to say, but no one will listen. His fears sound incredible because they are so new — he might be making them up. His body alarms him; it starts playing tricks on him, his teeth warn him, his stomach scolds, he's balding at last; a pimple might be cancer, indigestion a heart attack. He's feeling an unapparent fatigue; he wants to be young but he knows he ought to be old. He's neither one and terrified. His friends all resemble him, so there can be no hope of rescue. To be this age and very far from where you started out, unconsoled by any possibility of a miracle — that is bad; to look forward and start counting the empty years left is enough to tempt you into some aptly named crime, or else to pray. Success is nasty and spoils you, the successful say, and only failures listen, who know nastiness without the winch of money. Then it is clear: the ship is swamped to her gunwales, and the man of fifty swims to shore, to be marooned on a little island, from which there is no rescue, but only different kinds of defeat.

That was how I recognized Mr. Leigh, the man they sent from Hong Kong to audit our books. I knew his name and his flight number — nothing else. I waited at Gate Three and watched the passengers file through Health and Immigration. First the early birds, the ones who rush off the plane with briefcases, journalists and junior executives with Chinese girl friends, niftily dressed, wearing big sunglasses; then the two Chinese sisters in matching outfits; a lady with a little boy and further back her husband holding the baby and juggling his passport; a pop group with blank faces and wigs of frizzy hair, looking like a delegation from New Guinea, anxious to be met; the missionary priest with a goatee and a cheroot, addressing porters in their own language; a few overdressed ones, their Zurich topcoats over their arms. Lagging behind, a lady in a wheelchair about whom people say, "Lord, I don't know how she does it," a man with a big box, a returning student with new eyeglasses, and Mr. Leigh. I knew him as soon as I set eyes on him: he was the only one who looked remotely like me.

He was red-faced and breathless; and, unaccustomed to the heat, he was mopping his face with a hanky. He was a bit heavier than he should have been — his balance was wrong, his clothes too small. I waved to him through the glass doors. He nodded and turned away to claim his suitcase. I went into the men's room, just to look in the mirror. I was reassured by my hair, not white like Leigh's and still quite thick. But I wished I had more hair. My face was lined: my nap had made me look older. I was disheveled from the bus ride and looked more rumpled than usual because I had rolled my sleeves down and buttoned the cuffs. It was my tattoos. I hid them from strangers. Strangers' eyes fix on tattoos as they fix on scars in unlikely places. A person spots a tattoo and he has you pegged: you're a sailor, or you do some sort of poorly paid manual labor; one day you got drunk with your friends and they got tattooed, and to be one of the gang so did you. It did not happen this way with me, but that is the only version strangers know of a tattooing.

Mr. Leigh was just pushing through the glass doors as I came back from the toilet smoothing my sleeves. I said hello and tried to take his suitcase. He wouldn't let go; he seemed offended that I should try to help. I knew the feeling. He was abrupt and wheezing and his movements tried to be quick. It is usually this way with people who have just left a plane: they are overexcited in a foreign place, their rhythm is different — they are attempting a new rhythm — and they are not sure what is going to happen next. The sentence they have been practicing on the plane, a greeting, a quip, they know to be inappropriate as soon as they say it. Leigh said, "So they didn't send the mayor." Then, "You don't look Chinese to me."

I suggested a beer in the lounge.

"What time are they expecting me?" he asked. He had just arrived and already he was worried about Hing. I knew this man: he didn't want to lose his job or his dignity; but it is impossible to keep both.

"They weren't too sure what time your plane was coming in," I said. We both knew who "they" were. He put down his suitcase.

One reason I remember the first conversation I had with Mr. Leigh (or William, as he insisted I call him, but I found this more formal than Mister; he didn't reply to "Bill") is that I had the same conversation with every *ang moh* I met in Singapore. We were in the lounge having a beer, sharing a large Anchor; every few minutes the loud-speakers became noisy with adenoidal announcements of arrivals and departures in three languages. Leigh was still keyed up and he sat forward in his chair, taking quick gulps of beer and then staring into his glass.

I asked about the flight and the weather in — William being English, I attempted some slang — "Honkers." This made him look up from his glass and squint straight at me, so I gave up. And was it a direct flight? No, he said, it landed for fueling at Bangkok.

"Now *that's* a well-named place!" I said and grinned. I can't remember whether it got a rise out of him. I asked if he had a meal on the plane.

"Yes," he said, "perfectly hideous."

"Well, that food is always so damned hideous," I said, trying to sound more disgusted than him. The word stuck to my tongue. I wasn't telling the truth. I thought airplane food was very good, always the correct color and each course in its own little covered trough on the tray, the knives

13

and forks wrapped up and all the rest of the utensils in clean envelopes and in fitted slots and compartments. I had to agree the food was hideous. He was a guest, and I had plans for him.

The next thing I said to him was what I said to everyone who came through. I said it slowly, with suggestive emphasis on the right syllables: "If there's anything you want in Singapore, anything at all" — I smiled here — "just let me know and I'll see what I can fix up."

He replied, as most strangers did — but he was not smiling — "I'm sure you don't mean *anything.*"

"Anything." I took a drink of my beer to show I wasn't going to qualify the promise.

He mopped his face. "I was wondering — "

And I knew what he was wondering. The choice wasn't large, but people didn't realize that. A tout could follow a tourist on the sidewalk and in the space of a minute offer everything that tourist could conceivably want. The touts who didn't know English handed over a crudely printed three-by-five card to the man with a curious idle face. The card had half a dozen choices on it: blue movies, girls, boys, exhibition, massage, ganja — a menu which covered the whole appetite of longing. No new longings were likely, and the tout who breathed, "You want something special?" had in mind a combination based on the six choices.

Leigh was perspiring heavily. Vice, I was thinking: it sounded like what it was, it squeezed, expressing the grape of fantasy. Gladys was free. It was possible to stop off at her place on the way back from the airport — Leigh would appreciate the convenience — and I was going to say so. But it is a mistake to make explicit suggestions: I discovered that very early. If I suggested a girl and the feller wanted a boy he would be ashamed to admit it and the deal would be off. It was always wrong to offer an exhibition — like saying, "You can't cut the mustard but how about watching?" —

and if a person was thinking of having a go he would refuse if I suggested it. Most people thought their longings were original, but they weren't: they could only be one of six, or else a combination. Various as fantasy, but fantasy didn't allow for the irregular performance of man's engine. I knew the folly of expectation, and how to caution a feller against despairing of his poor engine and perhaps hitting his pecker with a hammer.

I sized up Leigh as he was blotting his cheeks and pulling at his collar, counting the whirring fans in the lounge. I took him to be an exhibition man, with a massage to follow — not an ordinary massage, something special, Lillian jumping naked on his spine. Intimacy, as the girls called it, or *boochakong*, to use the common Chinese term I preferred to the English verb, would still be a strong possibility, I was thinking. There was no such thing as impotence: it was successful as soon as money changed hands. It wasn't the money, but the ritual.

"What do you say?" I asked, as brightly as I could. Usually it wasn't so hard; when it was, it meant the feller was worried about asking for something I couldn't provide.

"Oh, I don't know," he said, and drew a deep breath. So I was wrong about the exhibition, and just as well, I thought; I hated those monkeyshines. I guessed Leigh was slightly bent; his particular crimp was a weakness for transvestites, of which, as is well known, there is a whole sorority in Singapore. Very few fellers admitted to this yen; they were the hardest ones to handle, but over the years I had seen how they reacted to the Chinese boys who in skirts were more winsome than girls. Middle age may be an emergence of this comfort, too, a fling at play-acting with a pretty boy, a reasonable occasion for gaiety, the surprise of costuming and merry vestments. If I detected the wish I took the fellers down to Bugis Street and steeered them over to the reliable ones, Tiny or Gina. Lucy had the operation which sometimes disappointed the fellers. Your bashful fruit pretended he was talking to a girl, but just so we knew where we stood I said, "Take Gina — he's a very nice feller." The client looked surprised and said, "You mean — ?" And then: "I might as well take him home — I'm too drunk to notice the difference," and going out would slip me ten dollars.

"What did you have in mind?" asked Leigh.

A very uncommon question. I was going to say nothing, just keep smiling in a willing fashion. But he looked as though he meant it and wouldn't tumble to my willingness.

I said, "I thought . . . if you were interested in anything illegal, hyah-yah, I might be able to — "

"Illegal?" said Leigh and put his hanky down. He leaned over and, puzzled and interested, asked, "You mean a prostitute?"

I tried to laugh again, but the expression on his face turning from puzzlement to disgust rattled me. It had been a mistake to say anything.

"No," I said, "of course not." But it came too late, my tardy denial only confirmed the truth, and Leigh was so indignant — he had straightened up and stopped drinking — that shame, unfamiliar as regret, tugged at my neck hairs. Through the glass-topped table in front of me I could see I was curling my toes and clawing at my sandals.

"Let's go," I said. "I'll call a taxi." I started to get up. I was hot; I wanted to roll up my sleeves, now damply stuck to my tattoos, revealing them.

"Flowers," he said, and narrowed his eyes at me, "are you a ponce?"

"Me? Hyah-mn! What a thing to say!" It was a loud hollow protest with a false echo. Prostitute, he had said, pimp, whore, queer, ponce — words people use to name the things they hate (liking them they leave them nameless, the human voice duplicating the suspicion that passion is unspeakable). "I'm a sort of pornocrat," I was going to

16

say, to mock him. I decided not to. His incredulity was a prompting for me to lie.

The waitress passed by.

Leigh said, *"Wan arn!"* greeting her in vilely accented Mandarin.

"Scuse me?" she said. She took a pad from the pocket of her dress, a pencil from her hair. "Anudda Anchor?"

"Nee hao ma," said Leigh. He had turned away from me and was looking at the girl. But the girl was looking at me. *"Nee hway bu hway —"*

"Mister," said the girl to me, "what ship your flend flom?"

Leigh cleared his throat and said we'd better be going. In the taxi he said hopelessly, "I was wondering if I might get a chance to play a little squash."

"Sure thing," I said, pouncing. "I can fix that up for you in a jiffy." *Squash?* He was wheezing still, and red as a beet. Carrying his suitcase to the taxi rank he kept changing hands and groaning, and then he put his face out the taxi window and let the breeze blow into his mouth, taking gulps of it the way dogs do in a car. He had swallowed two little white pills with his beer. He looked closely at his palms from time to time. And he wanted to play squash!

"What's your club, Flowers?"

We had agreed that I was to call him William if he called me Jack. I liked my nursery-rhyme name. Now I felt he was cheating.

"Name it," I said, and to remind him of our agreement I added, "William."

I had an application pending at the Cricket Club once, or at least the "Eggs," two elderly bald clients of mine, who were members, said I did. I had been trying to join a club in Singapore for a long time. Then it was too late. I couldn't apply for membership without giving myself away, for I often drank in the clubs and most of the members —

they knew me well — thought I had joined years before. There wasn't a club on the island I couldn't visit one way or another. I had clients at all of them.

"Cricket Club's got some squash courts, but the Tanglin's just put up new ones — you may want to have a look at those. There's none at the Swimming Club so far, though we've got a marvelous sauna room." I thumped his knee. "We'll find something, William."

"Sounds very agreeable," he said, pulling his head back into the taxi. He was calm now. "How do you manage three clubs? I'm told the entrance fees are killing."

"They *are* pretty killing," I said, using his dialect again, "but I reckon it's worth it."

"You're not a squash player yourself?"

"No," I said, "I'm just an old beachcomber — drinking's my sport, nyah!"

That made him chuckle; I was laughing too, and as I shifted on the seat I felt a lump in my back pocket press into my butt: two thick envelopes of pornographic pictures I had brought along just in case he asked. Their reminding pressure stopped my laughing.

The taxi driver tilted his head back and said, "Bloomies? Eshbishin wid two gull? You want boy? Mushudge? What you want I get. What you like?"

"Just a game of squash, driver, thank you very much," I said in a pompous fruity voice to this poor feller for the benefit of the horse's ass next to me. Then I smiled at William and tried to tip him a wink, but his head was out the window and he was blinking and gulping at the breeze and probably wondering what he was doing on that tedious little island.

3

I WALKED into a bar where they did not know me well and I could hear the Chinese whispers: "Who does that jackass think he is?" And then it ceased; my face made silence. It was not the face you expected in Ho's or Toby's or the Honey Bar, in the Golden Treasure or Loon's Tip-Top. Years ago I had not minded, but later my heart sank on the evenings all my regulars were tied up and I had to go into these joints recruiting. I got stares from round-shouldered youths sitting with plump hostesses; and the secret society members watched me — in Ho's the Three Dots, in the Honey Bar the Flying Dragons. There was no goblin as frightening as a member of a secret society staring me down. He first appeared to have no eyes, then the slits became apparent and I guessed he was peering at me from somewhere behind the slits. I never saw the eyes. The slits didn't speak; and it was impossible to read the face, too smooth for a message. I turned away and slipped the manager a few dollars to release the girl, and when I was hurrying out I heard growls and grunts I didn't understand, then titters. On the sidewalk I heard the whole bar crackle and explode into yelling laughter. Now they had eyes; but I was outside.

One night a thug spoke to me. He was sitting up front at the bar eating a cold pork pie with his fingers. He was wearing the secret society uniform, a short-sleeved shirt with the top four buttons undone, sunglasses — though it was dark — and his hair rather long, with wispy wing-tufts hanging past his ears. I didn't think he saw me talking to the manager, and after I passed the money over and turned to go the thug put his hand on my shoulder, and rubbing pork flakes into it, said gruffly, "Where you does wuck?"

I didn't answer. I hurried down the gloomy single aisle of the bar, past eerily lit Chinese faces. The thug called out, *"Where you wucking!"* That was in the Tai-Hwa on Cecil Street, and I never went near it again.

Who is he? they murmured in the Belvedere, the Hilton, the Goodwood when I was in the lobby flicking through a magazine, waiting for one of my girls to finish upstairs. I could have passed for a golf pro when I was wearing my monogrammed red knit jersey — the one with long sleeves — and my mustard-colored slacks and white ventilated shoes. No one knew I had a good tan because I worked for Hing, who refused to pay for taxis in town and who sent me everywhere, but always to redheads, with parcels. In my short-sleeved flowered batik shirt, with my tattoos displayed, they took me for a beachcomber with a private income or a profitable sideline, perhaps "an interesting character." Once, in the Pebble Bar of the Hotel Singapura, an American lady who was three sheets to the wind said I looked like a movie actor she knew, but she couldn't think of his name.

"What's your name?" she asked.

I smiled, to give her the impression that I might be that actor, said, "Take a guess, sweetheart," and then I left; leaving, I heard some hoots, from the gang of oil riggers who always drank there, and I knew who they were hooting at.

My appearance, this look of a millionaire down on his luck,

which is also the look of a bum attempting to be princely, was never quite right for most of the places I had to go. I was the wrong color in the Tai-Hwa and all the other Chinese joints — that was clear; at the Starlight, strictly Cantonese, they seated me with elderly hostesses and overcharged me. I was too dressy for the settler hangouts and never had enough money for more than one drink at the Hilton or Raffles, though I looked as if I might have belonged in those hotels. I certainly looked like a member of the Tanglin Club, the Swiss Club, the Cricket Club, and all the others where my chits were signed for me by fellers who liked my discretion. I was always welcome in the clubs, but that was a business matter. And they did not laugh at the Bandung: they knew me there.

In the taxi I mentioned the Bandung to Leigh; he didn't say no, but he thought we should stop at Hing's first — "Let's have a look at the *towkay*" was what he said. We got stuck in rush-hour traffic, a solid unmoving line of cars. There was an accident up front, and the cars were passing the wrecked sedan at a crawl to note down the license number so they could play it on the lottery. There was a bus in front of us displaying the bewildering sign *I Don't Know Why, But I Prefer Sanyo*. The local phrase for beeping was "horning," and they were horning to beat the band. We sat and sweated, gagging on the exhaust fumes; it was after five by the time we got to Hing's.

Little Hing was sitting in the shop entrance reading the racing form. He sat like a roosting fowl, his feet on the seat, his knees drawn up under his chin. Seeing us, he turned his bony face and bawled upstairs, then he locked his teeth and snuffled and paddled the air with his free hand, which meant we were to wait.

"Your Oriental politeness," I said. "He'll spit in a minute, probably hock a louie on your shoes, so watch out."

We had made Big Hing wait; now, to save face, he was making us wait. Hing spent the best part of a day saving face, and Yardley said, "When you see his face you wonder why he bothers."

Gopi, the *peon*, brought a wooden stool for Leigh, but Leigh just winced at it and studied Hing's sign: *Chop Hing Kheng Fatt: Ship Chandlers & Provisioners*, and below that in smaller assured script, *Catering & Victualling, Marine Hardware, Importers, Wholesale Drygoods & Foodstuffs, Licensed Agents, Frozen Meat*, and the motto, *"All Kinds of Deck & Engine Stores & Bonded Stores & Sundries."* "Sundries" was my department. The signs on the shops to the left and right of Hing, and all the other shops — biscuit-colored, peeling, cracked and trying to collapse, a dusty terrace of shophouses sinking shoulder to shoulder on Beach Road — were identical but for the owner's name; even the stains and cracks were reduplicated down the road as far as you could see. But there was something final in the decline, an air of ramshackle permanency common in Eastern ports, as if having fallen so far they would fall no further.

"What's your club in Hong Kong?" I asked.

"Just one, I'm afraid," he said. He paused and smiled. "The Royal Hong Kong."

"Jockey or Yacht?"

"Yacht," he said quickly, losing his smile.

Little Hing spat and went back to his racing form without bothering to see where the clam landed.

"Missed again," I said, winking at Leigh. "I've heard the Yacht Club's a smashing place," I said, and he looked at me the way he had when I said "Honkers." "You're in luck, actually. You have a reciprocal membership with the Tanglin here and probably a couple of others as well."

"No," he said, "I inquired about that before I came down. Bit of a nuisance, really. But there it is."

He was lying. I knew the Royal Hong Kong Yacht Club

and the Tanglin Club had reciprocal memberships and privileges; a member of one could sign bar chits at the other and use all the club's facilities. So he was not a member, and there we were standing on the Beach Road sidewalk, on the lip of its smelly monsoon drain, at the beck and call of a surly little *towkay* who had chosen to sulk upstairs, lying about clubs we didn't belong to. It made me sad, like the pictures hidden in my back pocket I would never admit to having: two grown men practicing lies, and why?

Big Hing came out in his pajamas and gave Leigh that secret society stare. Hing was not a member; he was a paid-up victim of the Red Eleven, who controlled Beach Road and collected "coffee money" for protection. The payment gave Hing a certain standing, for having victimized him the Red Eleven would stick by him and fight anyone who tried to squeeze him. Leigh handed over a letter, and we waited while Hing gnawed the sealing wax from the flap. He put on his old wire glasses and read the column of characters, then he smiled his angry eyeless smile and nodded at Leigh.

"I trust everything is in order," said Leigh to Hing.

It was a wasted remark; Hing was muttering to Little Hing, and Little replied by muttering into the racing form he held against his face.

"Where's our friend going to put up?" I asked.

"Booked at the Strand," said Big Hing. "Can come tomorrow." He picked up his grandson and bounced the trouserless little feller to show the interview was over.

The Strand Hotel was on Scotts Road, diagonally across the road from the Tanglin Club. As we were pulling into the Strand's driveway, under the arch with the sign reading *European Cuisine — Weddings — Parties — Reasonable Prices,* Leigh saw the Tanglin signboard and said, "Why don't we pop over for a drink?"

I let my watch horrify me. "God," I said, "it's nearly half past six. That place is a madhouse this time of day. Fellers having a drink after work. Look, William, I know a quiet little — "

"I'd love to have a look at those new squash courts of yours," he said. He hit me hard on the arm and said heartily, "Come *on*, Flowers, I'll buy you a drink." He gave his suitcase to the room-boy at the Strand, signed the register, and then clapped his stomach with two hands. "Ready?"

"I'll buy you a drink," said Leigh, but that was impossible because money was not allowed and only a member could sign chits. The brass plaque on the club entrance — MEMBERS ONLY — mocked us both. I looked for someone I knew, but all I could see were tanned long-legged mothers, fine women in toweling smocks, holding beach bags and children's hands, waiting for their *syce*-driven cars after a day at the club pool. They were eagerly whispering to each other, and laughing; the sight of that joy lifted my heart — I couldn't help but think they were plotting some trivial infidelity.

"The new squash courts are over there," I said, stepping nimbly past the doorman and bounding up the stairs.

"Drink first," said Leigh. "I'm absolutely parched." He was enjoying himself and he seemed right at home. He led the way into the Churchill Room, and "Very agreeable" he said, twice, as he looked for an opening at the bar.

The Churchill Room had just been renovated: thick wall-to-wall carpets, a new photograph of Winston, a raised bar, and a very efficient air-conditioning system. In spite of the cool air I was perspiring, a damp panel of shirt clung to my back; I was searching for a familiar face, someone I knew who might sign a drink chit. The bar was packed with men in white shirts and ties, some wearing stiff planter's shorts, standing close to the counter in groups of three or four, braying to their companions or sort of climbing over each other and waving chit pads at the barmen. Leigh was pushing ahead of me and I had just reached out to tap him on the shoulder and tell him I had remembered something important — my nerve had failed me so completely I could not think what, and prayed for necessity's inspiration — when I saw old Gunstone over in the corner at one of the small tables, drinking alone.

Gunstone was one of my first clients; he was in his seventies and came to Singapore when it was a rubber estate and a few rows of shophouses and go-downs. During the war he was captured by the Japanese and put to work on the Siamese Death Railway. He told me how he had buried his friend on the Burmese border, a statement like a motto of hopeless devotion, an obscure form of rescue, *I buried my friend.* He was the only client who took me to lunch when he wanted a girl, but he was also the cagiest, because I had to make all the arrangements for him and even put my own name on the hotel register. What he did with the girls, I never knew — I never asked: I did not monkey with a feller's confidence — but it was my abiding fear that one day Gunstone's engine was going to stop in a hotel room I had reserved, and I was going to have to explain my name in the register. I never saw Gunstone's wife; he only took her to the club at night and most of my club work was in the daytime.

"Jack," he said, welcoming me, showing me an empty chair. Good old Gunstone.

"Evening, Mr. Gunstone," I said. It was a servile greeting, I knew, but I could not see Leigh and I was worried.

Gunstone seemed glad to see me; that was a relief. I feared questions like, "Who are you and what are you doing here?"

"What'll you have?" asked Gunstone.

"Small Anchor," I said, and as Gunstone turned to find a waiter Leigh appeared with a drink in his hand.

"Chappie here wants your signature, Flowers," said Leigh.

I took the chit pad from the waiter and put it on Gun-
stone's table, saying "All in good time," then introduced
Leigh. Gunstone said, "Ever run into old So-and-So in
Hong Kong?" and Leigh said charmingly, "I've never had
the pleasure." Gunstone began describing the feller, saying,
"He's got the vilest habits and he's incredibly mean and
nasty and — " Gunstone smiled — "perfectly fascinating.
He might be in U.K. now, on leave."

"Do you ever go back to U.K.?" Leigh asked.

"Used to," said Gunstone. "But the last time I was
there they passed a bill making homosexuality legal. I
said to my wife, 'Let's get out of here before they make the
blasted thing compulsory!' "

Leigh laughed. "I meant to ask you, Flowers," he said,
"are you married?"

"Nope," I said. Leigh went on talking to Gunstone. Once,
and it was at the Tanglin Club, I used to fix up a certain
feller with girls. The feller was married and I eventually
got friendly with the wife, and "She's ever so nice," I
said to the feller. On the afternoons when he had one of
my girls I visited his wife at their house in Bukit Timah and
had no fear that he would show up. But there were children;
she hollered at them and sent them out with the *amah*.
She was very sweet to me, a moment after she had cuffed
the children. One afternoon I was in the Bandung. I had
agreed we should meet, but I realized I was late, delaying over
a large gin. She was waiting; I was waiting; I did not want
to go. It was like marriage. I went on drinking, and lost
her.

"I must be going," said Gunstone. He pulled the chit
pads over and signed them. He said, "I scratch your back,
you scratch mine."

"Tomorrow," I said, and winked.

"Lunch," said Gunstone. "The usual time, what?"

"Sounds frightfully hush-hush," said Leigh.

To Gunstone I said, "We were just leaving, too," which made it impossible for Leigh to object. It was unfair to do this, but I was sore: Leigh's two gin slings were going to cost me a whole afternoon of waiting in the lobby of a hotel, cooling my heels and worrying about Gunstone's engine.

Yardley was telling his joke about the Irishman and the love-starved gorilla as we entered the Bandung. We walked over to the bar and, perversely I thought, Yardley delivered the punch line to Leigh, " 'One thing more, sair,' says O'Flannagan to the zoo keeper, 'If there's any issue — any issue at all — it's got to be raised a Roman Catholic.' "

They started to laugh — Yates, Smale, Frogget, and loudest of all and closing his eyes with mirth, Yardley himself. I smiled, though I had heard it before. Leigh wasn't amused; he said, "Yes, well." That was his first mistake in the Bandung, not laughing at Yardley's joke. Yardley, an old-timer, had been drinking in the Bandung for years, and one day when Yardley was out of the room Frogget said, "Yardley *is* the Bandung." Every bar had a senior member; Yardley was ours. Frogget, a large shy feller, balding but not old, was Yardley's ape. Frogget — Desmond Frogget — ate like a horse, but he was sensitive about his weight; it was considered impolite to remark on the amount of food Frogget ate, the platters of noodles he hoovered up. Frogget could not have been much more than thirty-five, but the ridiculous man had that English knack of assuming elderly biases and a confounding grumpiness that made him seem twice his age. He regretted the absence of clipper ships, he remembered things that happened before he was born and like other equally annoying youths who drank at the Bandung started sentences with "I always" and "I never."

"Don't believe we've met," said Yardley, putting his hand out to Leigh.

Leigh hinted at reluctance by frowning as he offered his

27

hand, but the worst offense was that after he said his name he spelled it.

"Been in Singapore long?" asked Smale. Smale was a short, ruddy-faced man whose squarish appearance gave the impression of having been carpentered. He carried a can of mentholated cigarettes with him wherever he went. He was working the cutter on the lid as he asked Leigh the question.

"No," I said, "he just — "

"To be precise," said Leigh in a prissy voice, and checking his watch, "four hours and forty-five minutes."

"We like to be precise around here," said Yardley, nudging Frogget. "Don't we, Froggy? I mean, seeing as how we're all on the slag heap of life, it's a bloody good thing to know the time of day, what Froggy?"

"I always wear my watch to bed," said Frogget.

"You come down from K.L.?" Yates asked, seeing Yardley getting hot under the collar.

"Hong Kong," said Leigh, stressing the *Hong* the way residents do. He looked around the room, as if trying to locate an exit.

The Bandung was a huge place — in its prime a private house with an elegant garden, birdbath, and sundial and intersecting cobblestone paths. But the garden had fallen to ruin and the trellises had broken under the weight of vines which had become thick, leaning on and pinching the frail trellis ladders. I liked the garden in this wild state, the elastic fig trees strangling the palms, the roots of the white-blossomed frangipanis cracking the stone benches and showing knuckles between the cobblestones. And the vines, now more powerful than the trellises that had once supported them, needed no propping; they made a cool leafy cavern from the walled front entrance to the verandah, where there were pots of orchids hanging from wires, with gawking blossoms and damp dangling roots.

28

The bar itself stood in what was once a vast parlor, colored glazed tiles on the floor and a ceiling so high there were often some confused swallows flying in circles near the top. The windows were also large and Yardley said a swarm of bees flew in one day, passed over the heads of those drinking at the bar, and flew out the other side without disturbing a soul. The adjoining room we called the "lounge," where there was a jumble of rattan furniture, a sofa, the piano Ogham used to play, and little tables and potted palms. No one sat there except the barman, Wallace Thumboo, when he was totting up the day's chits at midnight, sorting them into piles according to the signatures. I was seeing the Bandung now with Leigh's eyes, and I could understand his discomfort, but I didn't share it.

"Could use a coat of paint," Leigh said. "Do I smell cats?" He wrinkled his nose.

"I was in Hong Kong a few years back," said Yardley. "My *towkay* sent me up to get some estimates on iron sheeting. I was supposed to stay for a month, until the auction, but after two days I came back. Couldn't stick the place. They treated me like dirt. Told the *towkay* the deal was up the spout. Ever been to Hong Kong, Froggy?"

Frogget said yes, it was awful.

"What's the beer like?" Smale asked Leigh.

"My dear fellow," said Leigh, "I haven't the remotest idea."

That annoyed everyone, and Yardley said, "Got a right one 'ere." At that point I wasn't sure who I disliked more — Yardley for being rude to Leigh, or Leigh for spelling his name and saying "I haven't the remotest idea" to what was meant as a friendly question. The next thing Leigh said put me on Yardley's side.

"Flowers," said Leigh sharply, ignoring the others, "I thought you said we could get a drink here."

This magisterial "Flowers," in front of my friends. Frogget grinned, Smale winked and raised his glass to me, Yates frowned, and Yardley smirked as if to say, "You poor suffering bastard" — all of this behind Leigh's stiffened back.

I knocked for Wally and ordered two gins. Leigh wrapped his hanky around his glass and drank disgustedly. It may have been anger or the heat, but Leigh was reddening and beads of sweat began percolating out of his face. Ordinarily, Yardley would have behaved the same as Gunstone and said, "Ever run into old So-and-So in Kowloon?" which might have brought Leigh around. Or he would have told his story about the day the swarm of bees flew through the window, and if he was in a good mood he would have embellished it by imitating the bees, running from one side of the room to the other, flapping his arms, and buzzing until he was breathless.

"Bit stuffy in here," Smale said.

Yardley was looking at Leigh. Leigh seemed unaware that he had nettled Yardley. Yates said he had to go home and Yardley said, "I don't blame you."

"Say good night to Flowers," said Frogget.

"*Mister* Flowers to you, Froggy," I said.

Yates left, saying good night to everyone by name, but omitting Leigh. Leigh said, "Tiffin time — isn't that what they call it here?"

Yardley had not taken his eyes off Leigh. I thought Yardley might sock him, but his tactic was different. He told his McCoy joke, the one he always told when there was a woman in the bar he wanted to drive out. It concerned four recruits being interviewed for the army. The sergeant asks them what they do for a living and the first one, saying his name's McCoy, mutters that he's a cork sacker ("puts the cork into sacks, you see") ; the next one, also a McCoy, is a cork soaker ("soaks it in water, you understand") ; the third McCoy is a coke sacker ("sacks coke for a dealer in fuel") ; and the last one, a mincing feller in satin tights, says that he's the real McCoy. Yardley told it in several accents, lengthening it

30

with slurs and pauses ("What's that you say?"), and obnoxiously set it in Hong Kong.

Leigh made no comment. He ordered a gin for himself, but none for me.

"You giving up the booze, Jack?" said Smale, who noticed.

"A double, Wally," I said.

Yardley giggled. "I must have my tiffin," he said.

"Tiffin time, breh-heh," said Frogget.

"Take care of yourself, Jack," said Yardley, and left with Frogget shambling after him.

"I think I'll go whore hopping," said Smale in a thoughtful voice. He pressed down the lid of his cigarette can and said, "Say, Jack, what was the name of that skinny one you fixed me up with? Gladys? Gloria?"

I pretended not to hear.

"Give me her number. God, she was a lively bit of crumpet." He stared at Leigh and said, "She does marvelous things to your arse."

"Ask Wally," I said.

"It was like being dead," said Smale, still addressing Leigh. He grinned. "You know. Paradise."

Wally was polishing glasses at the far end of the bar, smiling at the glasses as he smiled at the counter when he wiped it and at the gin bottle when he poured. Wally said, "What you want, Mr. Smale? You want mushudge?" He nodded. "Can."

"Aw hell," said Smale. "Maybe I should forget it. I could have another double whiskey, toss myself off in the loo, and go down to the amusement park and play the pinball machines. What do you think?" He leered at me, then snorted and sloped off.

Leigh did not say anything right away. He climbed onto a barstool and dabbed at the perspiration on his upper lip with his finger. He looked at his finger, and feelingly, said, "How do you stand it?"

It made me cringe. It happened, this moment of worry

31

when, hearing a question that never occurred to me, I discovered that I had an answer, as once in the Tai-Hwa on Cecil Street, a stranger wearing dark glasses asked, "Where you does wuck?" and I remembered and was afraid.

4

IN MY CUBICLE, irritably dialing a third hotel, I heard Gopi coming. Then, in Singapore, disability determined the job; Gopi, a cripple, was a *peon* from birth. He could be heard approaching by the sigh-shuffle-thump of his curious bike-riding gait. One leg was shorter than the other, and the knee in that rickety limb bent inward, collapsing into the good leg and making Gopi lean at a dangerous angle as he put his weight on it. A long step with his good leg checked his fall, and that was how he went, heaving along, dancing forward, swaying from side to side, like the standing dance of a man pumping a bike up a steep hill.

Some years ago a horse named Gopi's Dream ran an eight-furlong race at the Singapore Turf Club. I was not a member of that club, but two dollars got me into the grandstand with the howling mob; and it was there that I spent at least one afternoon of every race meeting. I had just arrived and was getting my bearings when I saw that the horse I had picked for the first race had been scratched. There were poor odds on all the others except Gopi's Dream, and the logic of choosing this horse was plain to me. I put ten dollars on him to win, though my usual bet was a deuce on a long shot to place, bolstered by a prayer, which I screamed into my hands as the ponies leaped down the homestretch. I told myself that half the bet was Gopi's Deepavali present. Gopi's Dream won, as all horses do when the logic is irrefutable, and it paid two hundred dollars; half I put away for Gopi, the rest I lost in the course of the afternoon.

The next day I took Gopi to a shop over on Armenian Street and had him fitted for a brace and a boot with a five-inch sole. He was a bit rocky on it at first, but soon he got the hang of it and instead of his cyclist's swaying he learned a jerking limp, dragging the enormous boot and clumping it ahead of him and then chasing it with the other leg. The brace clinked and the boot gave out long twisting squeaks. The odd thing was that although he walked fairly straight he walked much more slowly, perspiring and pulling and swinging the boot along.

He stopped wearing the apparatus. He told me in Malay that it was "biting" his leg and that it was at the cobblers being put right. After a week I asked him about it; he started wearing it — two days of clinks and squeaks, then he stopped. I asked why. It was biting. The brace was a greater affliction than the limp, a cure more painful than the ailment; the incident cured me of certain regrets.

"All full up," the voice was saying to me over the phone. Gopi peddled over and I slammed the receiver into its cradle.

"Hupstairs," said Gopi, pointing his slender finger to indicate that Leigh was in Hing's office. He clamped his tongue at the side of his mouth and scribbled in an invisible ledger to show he had seen Leigh writing. Then he asked me about Leigh: Who was he? Where was he from? Did he have children? Was he a Eurasian?

I told Gopi what I knew and asked what time Leigh had arrived.

"Seven-something."

That was news. As an eager new employee at Hing's, with the hunch that if I did a good job I had a chance for promotion, I used to come in at seven-something, too. By the time Hing rolled in I was already in a sweat, saying "Right you are, Mr. Hing," and "Just leave it to me." There was no promotion. I asked for Christmas off; Hing said, "I am Buddhist, but wucking on Besak Day, birthday of Buddha, isn't it?" I started to come in at eight-something and never said "Leave it to me," and after I made a go of my enterprise it was ten before I showed my face. I would not be promoted, but neither would I be sacked: he could never have gotten another *ang moh* for what he paid me. In the acceptance of this continuing meekness, the denial of any ambition, was an unvarying condition of enduring security and the annual promise of a renewed work permit. It was an angle, but it cost me my pride. When someone at a club bar or hotel lounge said, "Go on, Jack, have another one," I was happy; I had the satisfaction of having earned my reward. The reminder that the drink would never have been offered if I hadn't had a girl in tow was something that didn't worry me unless a feller like Leigh woke up my scrupling with, "How do you stand it?" A feller who lived in Singapore and knew me would never have asked that. The real question was not how but why. My answer would have unstrung him, or anyone.

Leigh was eager to please Hing — that was plain. He had not found out it was no use. And who was he, this accountant from Hong Kong? A clerkly fugitive, laying low after an incautious embezzlement in London? Sacked by a British bank for interfering with a woman in Fixed Deposits, or for incompetence; and like many *ang mohs* in the East, seeking cover in a Chinese shop, consoling himself with clubby fantasies and the fact that he was too far away to be of concern, an alien at a great distance, the bird of passage

35

who mentioned from time to time when things got rough that there was always Australia? He had lied about his clubs — the first time anyone had tried that on me — but so had I, three times over. It could not be held against him.

The feeling I had for him was an inward clutching at self-pity. There was so much I could have told him if only he had been friendly and stopped calling me Flowers. Go away and save yourself, I wanted to say; I could have watched him do that and watching him given myself hope. I had my girls; I knew the limits of employment; I had faith in extraordinary kinds of rescue, miraculous recoveries; I knew a thing or two about love. What was his alternative? I decided to watch him closely, this version of myself; his nervy question still rankled, and pity prevented me from asking him the same. He was not aware of how much I knew.

Seeing me engrossed, Gopi left, shoulders heaving. His arms did not swing or give him motion. They dangled uselessly as he pedaled. He was a small man, and sometimes I believed that without him I would have floundered.

I dialed another hotel for Gunstone and got another refusal. That was the last of his Victoria Street favorites. It was nearly lunchtime, so I called the Belvedere. I was at the airport, I told the receptionist, and did they have an air-conditioned double room for one night?

"All our rooms — we got eight hundred plus — they are all air-conditioned," she said.

"That's very nice," I said, and made the reservation. "If Hing asks," I told Gopi, leaving him holding the can as usual — but who except the meekest man would hold it? — "tell him I'm down with the flu."

Since it was going to be lunch at the Tanglin, then off to the Belvedere, I thought I'd better change my duds.

"Why the black suit?" Gunstone asked.

"My others are at the cleaners," I said, still rolling "I've just come from a funeral" around on my tongue. He would have asked who died, or perhaps have been spooked by the announcement. I had the fluent liar's sense of proportion and foresight. Gunstone was calmed.

Lunch was the Friday special, my favorite, seafood buffet. I followed Gunstone, taking the same things he did, in the same amounts, and I soon realized that I was heaping my plate with oysters and prawns, which I liked less than the crab and lobster Gunstone took in two small helpings. I put some oysters back and got a frown from the Malay chef.

At the table I said, "I hope I haven't boobed, Mr. Gunstone, but I've fixed you up at the Belvedere this afternoon."

He stabbed a prawn and peeled off the shell and dunked the naked finger of pink meat into a saucer of chili paste. "Don't believe we've ever been to the Belvedere before, have we, Jack?"

"The other places were full," I said.

"Quite all right," he said. "But I ate at the Belvedere last week. It wasn't much good, you know."

"Oh, I know what you mean, Mr. Gunstone," I said. "That food is perfectly hideous."

"Exactly," said Gunstone. "How's your salmon?"

I had not started to eat. I took a forkful, smeared it in mayonnaise, and ate it. "Delicious," I said.

"Mine's awful," he said, and he pushed his salmon to the side of his plate.

"Now that you mention it," I said, "it *does* taste rather — "

"Desiccated," said Gunstone.

"Exactly," I said. I pushed my salmon over to the side and covered it with a lettuce leaf. I was sorry; I liked salmon the way it tasted out of a can.

"Lobster's pretty dreadful, too," said Gunstone a moment later.

I was just emptying a large claw. It was excellent, and

37

I ate the whole claw before saying, "Right again, Mr. Gunstone. Tastes like they fished it out of the Muar River."

"We'll shunt that over, shall we?" said Gunstone. He moved a lobster tail next to the discarded salmon.

I did the same, then as quickly as I could ate all my crab salad before he could say it was bad. I gnawed a hard roll and started on the oysters.

"The prawns are a success," he said.

"The oysters are — " I didn't want to finish the sentence, but Gunstone was no help " — sort of limp."

"They're cockles, actually," said Gunstone. "And they're a damned insult. Steward!" A Malay waiter came over. "Take this away."

Demanding that food be sent back to the kitchen is a special skill. It is done with *panache* by people who use that word. I admired people who did it, but could not imitate them.

"Yours, *Tuan?*" asked the waiter.

"Yes, take it away," I said sadly.

"Want more, *Tuan?*" the waiter asked Gunstone.

"If I wanted more would I be asking you to remove that plate?" Gunstone said.

The waiter slid my lunch away. I buttered a hard roll and ate it, making crumbs shower down the front of my suit.

"That steward," said Gunstone, shaking his head. "The most intelligent thing I ever heard him say was, 'If you move your lump of ice cream a bit to the right, *Tuan,* you will find a strawberry.' God help us."

I laughed and brushed my jacket. "Still," I said, "I wouldn't mind joining this club."

"You don't want to join this club," said Gunstone.

"I do," I said, and saw myself lying in the sun, by the pool, and one of those tanned long-legged women whispering urgently, "Jack, where have you been? I've been looking everywhere for you. *It's all set.*"

"Why, whatever for?"

"A place to go, I suppose," I said. The Bandung's only publicity was the matchboxes Wallace Thumboo had printed with the slogan, *There's Always Someone You Know at the Bandung!*

Gunstone chuckled. "If they can pronounce your name you can join."

"Flowers is pretty easy."

"I should say so!"

But Fiori isn't, I thought. And Fiori was my name, Flowers an approximation and a mask.

"Now," said Gunstone, looking at his watch, "how about dessert?"

Gunstone's joke: it was time to fetch Djamila.

The old-timers, I found, tended to prefer Malays, while the newcomers went for the Chinese, and the Malays preferred each other. The Chinese clients, of whom I had several, liked the big-boned Australian girls; Germans were fond of Tamils, and the English fellers liked anything young, but preferred their girls boyish and their women mannish. British sailors from H.M.S. *Terror* enjoyed fighting each other in the presence of transvestites. Americans liked clean sporty ones, to whom they would give nicknames, like "Skeezix" and "Pussycat" (the English made an effort to learn the girl's real name), and would spend a whole afternoon trying to teach one of my girls how to swim in a hotel pool, although it was costing them fifteen dollars an hour to do it. Americans also went in for a lot of hugging in the taxi, smooching and kidding around, and sort of stumbling down the sidewalk, gripping the girl hard and saying, "Aw, honey, whoddle ah do?" Later they wrote them letters, and the girls pestered me to help them reply.

Djamila — "Jampot," an American feller used to call her, and it suited her — was very reliable and easy to contact. She was waiting by the Hongkong and Shanghai Bank with my trusty suitcase as we pulled up in the taxi. I hopped out and opened the door for her, then got into the front seat and put the suitcase between my knees. Djamila climbed in with Gunstone and sat smiling, rocking her handbag in her lap.

Smiling is something girls with buck teeth seldom do with any pleasure; Djamila showed hers happily, charming things, very white in her broad mouth. She had small ears, a narrow moonlit face, large darting eyes, and heavy eyebrows. A slight girl, even skinny, but having said that one would have to add that her breasts were large and full, her bum high and handsome as a pumpkin. Her breasts were her virtue, the virtue of most of my Malay girls; unlike the Chinese bulbs that disappeared in a frock fold, these were a pair of substantial jugs, something extra that moved and made a rolling wobble of her walk. That was the measure of acceptable size, that bobbing, one a second later than the other, each responding to the step of Djamila's small feet. Her bottom moved on the same prompting, but in a different rhythm, a wonderful agitation in the willowy body, a glorious heaving to and fro, the breasts nodding above the black lace of the tight-waisted blouse, the packed-in bum lifting, one buttock pumping against the other, creeping around her sarong as she shuffled, showing her big teeth.

"Jack, you looking very smart," said Djamila. "New suit and what not."

"I put it on for you, sweetheart," I said. "This here's Mr. Gunstone, an old pal of mine."

Djamila shook his hand and said, "Jack got nice friends."

"Where's that little car of yours, Jack?" Gunstone asked.

"It packed up," I said. "Being fixed."

"What's the trouble this time?"

"Suspension, I think. Front end sort of shimmies, like Djamila but not as pretty."

"It's always the way with those little French cars. Problems. It's the workmanship."

The taxi pulled up in front of the Belvedere. The doorman in a top hat and tails snatched the door open and let

Gunstone out. I handed over the suitcase; it was a good solid Antler, a sober pebbly gray, filled with copies of the *Straits Times* and an R.A.F. first-aid kit, a useful item — once we had to use the tourniquet on a Russian seaman, and the little plasters were always handy for scratches.

"You should get yourself a Morris," said Gunstone at the reception desk.

I could not answer right away because I was signing my name on the register and the clerk was welcoming me with a copy of *What's On in Singapore.* I was not worried about being asked about Gunstone and Djamila; anything is possible in a big expensive hotel, and the accommodating manager will always smile and say he remembers you. In the elevator I said, "Yes, your Morris is a good buy."

"I like Chevy," said Djamila.

The elevator boy and the bellhop stared at her. My girls looked fine, very pretty in bars and on the street, but in well-lighted hotels they looked different, not out of place, but prominent and identifiable.

"I hate these American cars," said Gunstone.

"So do I," I said. "Waste of money."

"Nice and big," said Djamila. She gave a low throaty laugh. Most of my girls had bad throats: it was the line of work, all those germs.

"Here you are, sah. Seven-o-five," said the bellhop. He followed us in and swung the suitcase over to a low table; I could hear the newspapers shift inside. He started his spiel about the lights and if there's anything you want, but I interrupted him, pressing fifty cents into his hand, and he took off.

"Your lights," I said, discovering the switch and turning them all on. I went around the room naming appliances and opening doors, as the bellhop would have done if I had given him a chance. "Your TV, your washroom, window blinds, radio —" switching that on I got a melody from *Doctor Zhivago.* "I think everything is in order."

"You couldn't do better than a Morris," said Gunstone. He came over to me and said, "What's she like?" in a whisper.

"Very rewarding," I said. "Very rewarding indeed."

Djamila was sitting on the edge of the large double bed, removing her silver bracelets. She did it with dainty grace, admiring her arm and showing herself her fingernails as she pulled each bracelet past them.

Gunstone, on a stuffed chair, sighed and twisted off one of his shoes. He had pulled off a sock and was intently poking the limp thing into the empty shoe, pushing at the balled-up sock with his trembling finger, when I said: "I'll leave you two to get on with it. Bye for now."

The elevator boy, seeing the feller he had just deposited on that floor, looked away from me, at the button he was punching, and I could tell from the movement of his ears and a peculiar tightening of a section of scalp on the back of his head that he had summed up the situation and was grinning foolishly. I felt like socking him.

"What's your name?"

"Tony-*lah*," he said. A person sobers up when he has to tell a stranger his name.

"Here you are, Tony." I handed him a dollar. "Don't blab," I said. "Nobody likes a blabber."

That dollar would have come in handy, and I could have saved it if I had gone down the fire stairs, which was what I usually did. But seven flights of dusty-smelling unpainted cement was more than a man my age should tolerate. A little arithmetic satisfied me that I could afford one drink; in the Belvedere lounge-bar the *hors d'oeuvres* were free.

Avoiding the lobby, I nipped into the lounge, found a cool leather armchair, and sat very happily for a few minutes reading *What's On* and looking up every so often to admire the décor. Yardley and the rest did not think much of the new Singapore hotels — too shiny and tacky, they said, no character at all. Character was weevils in your food, metal folding chairs, and a grouchy barman who insulted you as he overcharged you; it was a monsoon drain that hadn't been cleared for months and a toilet — like the one in the Bandung — located in the middle of the kitchen. Someday, I thought, I'm going to reserve a room at the Belvedere and burrow in the blankets of a wide bed — the air conditioner on full — and sleep for a week. The ground floor of the Belvedere was Italian marble and there was a chandelier hanging in the lobby that must have taken years to make. I was enjoying myself in the solid comfort, sipping my gin, looking at a seashell mural on the lounge wall, periwinkles spilling out of conches, gilded sea urchins and fingers of coral; but I became anxious.

It was not my habitual worry about Gunstone's engine failing. It was the annoying suspicion that the seven or eight tourists there in the lounge were staring in my direction. They had seen me come in with Gunstone and Djamila and like Tony they had guessed what I was up to. The ones who weren't laughing at me despised me. If I had been younger they would have said, "Ah, what a sharp lad, a real operator — you've got to hand it to him"; but a middle-aged man doing the same thing was a dull dirty procurer. I tried to look unruffled, crossing my legs and flicking through the little pamphlet. Recrossing my legs I felt an uncommon breeze against my ankles: I wasn't wearing any socks.

How could I be so stupid? There I was in the lounge of an expensive hotel, wearing my black Ah Chum worsted, a dark tie and white shirt and shoes my *amah* had buffed to a high gloss — and sockless! That was how they knew my trade, by my nude ankles. I wanted to leave, but I couldn't without calling attention to myself. So I sat in the chair in a way which made it possible for me to push at the knees of my pants and lower my cuffs over my ankles. I tried to convince myself that these staring tourists didn't matter — they'd all be on the morning flight to Bangkok.

I lifted my drink and caught a lady's eye. She looked

away. Returning to my reading, I sensed her eyes drift over to me again. You never knew with these American ladies; they made faces at each other in public, sometimes hilarious ones, a sisterly foolishness. The other people began staring. They were making me miserable, ruining the only drink I could afford. The embarrassment was Leigh's doing; the stranger had called my vocation "poncing."

"Telephone call for Bishop Bradley . . . Bishop Bradley . . ." The slow demanding announcement came over the loud-speaker in the lounge, a cloth-faced box on the wall above a slender palm in a copper pot. No one got up.

Two ladies looked at the loud-speaker.

It stopped, the voice and the hum behind it; there was and expectant pause in the lounge, everyone holding his breath, knowing the announcement would start again in a moment, which it did, monotonously.

"Bishop Bradley . . . Telephone call for Bishop Bradley . . ."

Now no one was looking at the loud-speaker.

I had fastened all the buttons on my black suit jacket. I stood up and turned an impatient face to the repeated command coming from the cloth-faced box. I swigged the last of my gin and with the eyes of those people upon me, strode out in my clerical-looking garb in the direction of the information desk. I knew I had made them sorry for staring at my sockless feet, for judging my action at the desk, and *There goes the bishop,* they were saying.

Outside I walked up and down Orchard Road until Gunstone and Djamila appeared, all the while blaming Leigh for this new behavior of mine, embarrassment and fumbling shame making me act strangely. His shadow obscured my way: I wanted him to go.

5

It was early lighted evening, that pleasant glareless time of day just before sunset; the moon showed in a blue sky — a pale gold sickle on its back — and it was possible to stroll through the mild air without hunching over and squinting away from the sun. It was the only hour when the foliage was not tinged with hues of sickly yellow; trees were denser, green, and cool. All the two-story Chinese houses set in courtyards along Cuppage Road had their doors and green shutters open for the breeze, and there was a sense of slowed activity, almost of languor, that the sight at dusk of men in pajamas — the uniform of the peaceloving — produces in me.

A formation of swallows dived into view, pivoted sharply like bats, and then chased, lurching this way and that, toward the brightest part of the sky, where a reddening millrace of cloud poured this brightness into a subdued rosy wash. The palms towering above the Bandung did not sway — they never did in Singapore — but I could hear the papery rattle of the fronds shaking, hearing a coolness I couldn't feel. To a northern-born American, the palm tree was when I was growing up, a graceful symbol of wealth: it suggested lush

45

Florida, sunny winter vacations, certain movie stars and long days of play, white stucco hotels and casinos on wide beaches, and fresh fruit all year round; fellers had fun under nature's parasol. I looked up at the Bandung's palms, a tree I no longer associate with fun, so as to avoid looking at the top of the stockade wall enclosing the garden; on top of the wall glass shards were planted to discourage intruders and the sight of these bristling never failed to make my pecker ache.

I crunched down the cobblestone path, under the tunnel of vines, in the comfortable damp of the freshly watered garden; the sun had dropped behind the roof of the Bandung and was now dazzling at the back door, shooting brilliant gold streaks through two rooms, along the ground floor on the gleaming tiles. My jacket sat well on me for the first time that day, and with Gunstone's envelope of cash in my breast pocket, I was cool and happy.

But I knew what I was in for: I quailed when I heard Yardley's angry whoop of abuse echo in the big room. I paused near the wicker chairs on the verandah, and for a hopeless fluid moment I wished there was somewhere else I could go. It wasn't possible. A man my age, for whom a bar was a habit and a consolation — a reassurance of community that could nearly be tender — a man my age didn't drink in strange bars; that meant an upsetting break in routine; my friends interpreted absence as desertion, and they did not forgive easily. It would have seemed especially suspicious if I had avoided the Bandung after being responsible for bringing Leigh there the previous evening. Leigh had intruded and disturbed Yardley — Yardley's last joke was proof of that. The blame was mine and an explanation was expected of me. I had come prepared to denounce Leigh.

Yardley saw me and stopped whooping. Frogget was beside him; Smale, Yates, and Coony were at the bar, and over in an armchair drinking soybean milk and absorbed in the *Reader's Digest* sat old Mr. Tan Lim Hock. Mr. Tan, a retired civil servant, helped the regulars at the Bandung with their income tax — "He can skin a maggot," Yardley said. He was a rather tense man whom I had seen smile only twice: once, when he saw what Hing paid me ("Is this *per mensem* or *per annum?*" he asked) , and once — that day in 1967 — when China exploded her H-bomb.

I crossed the tiles and ordered a gin. Yardley's defiant silence, and the sheepishness on the faces of the rest, told me what I had expected: that Leigh was the subject of the abusive shouts.

"What's cooking?" I said.

"Are you alone?" asked Yardley. Yates and Coony looked at him as if they expected him to continue, but all he said when I told him I was alone was, "Wally nearly got pranged this afternoon. Isn't that right, Wally? Got a damned great bruise on his arm. Show us your bruise again, Wally, come on."

Wally, at the center of attention, was uncomfortable. "Not too bad," he said, smiling at his bandaged elbow.

"That's not what you told me!" said Yardley. He turned to me. "Poor little sod nearly got killed!" Yardley was maddened; ordinarily, Wally's injury would not have mattered to him — he might even have mocked it — but Yardley was in a temper, and his anger about Leigh, which I had deflected by barging in, had become a general raging. It was at times like this that he called Frogget "Desmond" instead of "Froggy" (and Frogget didn't object: he had attached himself to Yardley and like Wally simplified his loyalty by surrendering to abuse for praise) ; and it was only in anger that Yardley remembered I was an American.

"It's these bloody taxis," said Yates — the "bloody" was for Yardley's benefit. Yates was a quiet soul, the only one of us who did not work for a *towkay*. He got what were called "perks," home leave every two years, education and family allowances, and could look forward to a golden handshake and one hundred cubic feet of sea freight.

"No, it's not," said Yardley. "It's these jumped-up bastards who come here and act like they own the road." He stared at me. "You know the kind, don't you, Jack?"

"I see them now and again," I said.

"Who was it, Wally? Was it a Chink that ran you down?"

Mr. Tan Lim Hock was ten feet away; he chose not to hear.

"European," said Wally, blinking and gasping at his own recklessness. "He didn't hit me, I fell. Assident."

"He *hit* you, you silly shit," said Yardley. "I knew it was a European, and I'll bet he doesn't live in Singapore either. No sir, not *him*. Wouldn't dare. Take someone like that friend of yours, Jack — "

Yardley began blaming Leigh for Wally's bruise. Not so incredible: a month earlier, in a similar series of associations, after he had been overcharged by the Singapore Water Board on an item marked "sewer fee," he flung the crumpled bill in Wally's face and said, "There's no end to the incompetence of you fuckers." Now, Yardley worked himself up into such a lather that soon he was saying — ignoring Wally and the bruise — "That pal of yours, that shifty little bastard would run down the lot of us if we gave him half a chance, I can tell you that. If Jack keeps bringing him in here I'm going to stay home — nothing against you, Jack, but you should know better. Wally, for God's sake look alive and give me a double."

"Let me explain," I said. They didn't know the half of it; I could tell them Leigh's lie about his club, the airport story about "What ship your flend flom?" and how he had suggested we go see Hing before having a drink ("Arse licker!" Yardley would have cried). But I flubbed it before I began by saying, "William arrived yesterday, and where else — "

"*William?*" Yardley looked at me. "You call that little maggot *William?* Well, I'll be damned." He shook his head. "Jack, don't be a sucker. Even bloody Desmond can see that bugger's jumped-up, and he knows you're a Yank so he can get away with telling you he's governor general — *you* won't know the difference. Listen to me. I'm telling you he's so shifty the light doesn't strike him."

"I hear he's a nasty piece of work," said Coony.

"He's all fart and no arse," said Smale, who then mimicked Leigh, saying, "I haven't the remotest idea."

"He'd try the patience of a bloody saint," said Yardley.

"Why don't you lay off him," I said, surprising myself with the objection.

"Jack likes him," said Yardley. "Don't he, Desmond?"

"Yeah," said Frogget, turning away from me and rubbing his nose which in profile was a snout. "I fancy he does."

"I don't," I said, and although I had planned a moment earlier to denounce Leigh, I hated myself for saying it. When I first saw Leigh at the airport I had an inkling — a tic of doubt that made me want to look into a mirror — of how other people saw me. Now I understood that tic, and whatever I might say about Leigh did not matter: I could prove my dislike to these fellers at the bar facing me, but there was no way I could make myself believe it. It was not very complicated. Middle age is a sense of slipping and decline, and I suppose I had my first glimpse of this frailty in Leigh, the feeling of the body growing unreliable, getting out of control in a mournfully private way — only the occupier of the body could know. Once, *I* might have said, "He's all fart and no arse," but hearing it from Smale was a confirmation of my fear. The ridicule involved me — it was fear, and I was inclined now to defend the stranger, for hearing him ridiculed I knew how others ridiculed me; defending him was merciful, but it also answered a need in myself by providing me with a defense.

It was so simple. But the peril of being over fifty is, with anger's quick ignition, the age's clinging to transparent deceptions. We let others confirm what we already know, and we get mad because they say it; what appears like revelation

49

is the calling of a desperate bluff: the young wiseacre who, starting his story, says, "This feller was really old, about fifty or sixty — " drives every listener over fifty up the wall. We knew it before he said it. What is aggravating is not that the wiseacre knows, but that he thinks it's important and holds it against us. Our only defense is in refusing to laugh at his damned joke.

So: "He's not here," I said, "and it's not fair to talk behind his back."

"Look who's talking about being fair!" said Yardley. He had overcome his colicky anger and was laughing at me. "Who is it that imitates the maggot skinner when his back is turned?"

It was true; I did. When Mr. Tan left the bar I sometimes did an imitation of him with his *Reader's Digest* and bottle of Vimto soybean milk. I looked over and was glad to see that Mr. Tan had gone home; Yardley's "Chink" had done it. My other routines were Wally polishing glasses, Frogget's shambling, and Yardley, drunk, forgetting the punch line of a joke. My imitations were not very accurate, but my size and panting determination made the attempt funny. Mimicry reassures the weak, and the envious fool takes the risk as often as the visionary who mocks the error and leaves the man alone; I did not like to be reminded by my brand of mimicry.

"I'm turning over a new leaf," I said.

"By wearing a suit?" Smale asked.

Of course. I had forgotten I was wearing a suit. That bothered them most of all. They were sensitive about fellers who dressed up and made a bluff of the success they felt was denied everyone because it was denied them.

"I had to go to a funeral," I said. I took off my jacket and rolled up my shirt-sleeves. I knew instantly what Yardley's next words would be.

He said: "Don't tell me your friend's packed it in!"

"That'd be a ruddy shame," said Smale.

"Let's drop it, shall we?" I said. After all my indignant sympathy that was the only rebellion I could offer.

Then Leigh walked in.

I heard Gopi's characteristic trampling of the cobbled path in the garden, his whisper, and Leigh's, "Ah, yes, here we are," and my heart quickened.

"Long time no see," said Yardley.

Leigh brightened; but Yardley was beckoning to Gopi and ordering Gopi a drink. "How you doing?" said Yardley, putting his arm around the *peon*.

"*There* you are," said Leigh. I winced at the demonstration of pretended relief. Leigh glanced at the others and said, " 'd evening" and "M'ellow."

"Go on," said Yardley, "drink up! There's a good chap."

Gopi had a whiskey in his hand. He drank it all and at once his eyes glazed, his face went ashen and matched his caste mark.

"Leave him alone," I said. "Gopi, don't drink if you're not in the mood."

"He's going to be sick," said Coony.

"I like this little chap's company," said Yardley. It was his revenge on Leigh. "Have another one?"

Gopi nodded, but he was not saying yes. He covered his face with a hanky and pedaled to the door. Outside, in the garden, he became loud, hawking and spitting.

"The call of the East," said Smale.

Gopi groaned, and dragged himself away.

"That was mighty nice of you," I said to Yardley.

"He'll be all right," Yardley muttered, and turned away, saying, "Now, where was I?" to Frogget and Smale.

"How are you doing?" asked Leigh.

"Anyone I can," I said.

"That clerk of yours very kindly showed me the way here. Poor chap's got a sort of gammy leg, hasn't he, and I was a bit

sorry he had to — " Leigh was still talking about Gopi's lameness, but he was not looking me in the eye. He stared at my tattoos, the ones on my left arm, and in particular at the long blue crucifix crowned with a circle of thorns dripping inverted commas of blood onto my wrist. I pressed my right to my side as soon as I saw him fasten on the left.

"He's a wonderful feller," I said. "Minds his own business." I reached for my drink and when I lifted it his gaze lifted until it met my own. He looked tired. He had been hard at work all day, probably sitting in that low chair in Hing's office, out of range of the fan's blowing, while Hing looked on and slapped at papers on his desk. Leigh's eyes were watery and his hair was stuck to his head with sweat; the floridness of his face, which had looked like ruddy good health the day before, was not a solid color, but rather many little veins and splotches. I looked at him as at a picture in a newspaper that goes insubstantial with closeness, the face blurred to a snowfall of dots.

"How do the accounts look?" I asked, handing Leigh a tumbler of gin.

"Bit ropey," said Leigh. "Any of the pink stuff?"

Wally shook some drops of Angostura into the gin.

"That'll put lead in your pencil," I said.

"Best to put it in the glass before the gin and work it around the sides," said Leigh. He wrapped the glass in his hanky, said, "Cheers," and drank.

"I don't mind telling him to get knotted," Yardley was saying.

"Bit ropey," Leigh repeated, smacking his lips. "We'll sort it out, though if you ask me, your *towkay*'s missing a few beads from his abacus."

"He'll drive you out of your gourd," I said.

"Funny little thing, isn't he? I can't understand a word he says."

"What about your *towkay* — in Hong Kong?" I asked.

"Him!" Leigh gathered his features solemnly together and said, "In actual fact . . . he's a cunt."

Yardley heard and smiled, and I wondered for a moment whether the obscenity would redeem Leigh. It didn't. Yardley continued to talk to the fellers on my right, and sometimes to me; Leigh spoke only to me. I was, awkwardly, in the middle, a zone of good humor. There was no way out of it; to skip off with Leigh would mean the end of my drinking at the Bandung; the desertion would prohibit my return. Soon Yardley was saying less and less to me, and Leigh growing quite talkative on his third drink.

" — God, sometimes I hate it," Leigh said. "One thinks one is going to the tropics and one finds oneself in the Chinese version of Welwyn Garden City. The call of the East indeed — your friend over there was right. That fantastic hoicking puts me off my food, it really does. Still, it won't be much longer."

"How long do you plan to stay in Hong Kong?"

"My dear fellow," said Leigh, "not a moment longer than is absolutely necessary."

In different words, for fourteen years I'd said the same thing to myself; it was an ambiguous promise, and when I said it, it sounded like never. But Leigh's sounded like soon.

"Margaret — my wife — Margaret's got a magnificent cottage picked out. In Wiltshire — you know it? Fantastic place. When I go all broody about the Chinese, Margaret looks at me and says, 'We're halfway to Elmview' — that's the name of the cottage. That cheers me up. And then I don't feel so bad about — "

The name depressed me; it sounded like the name of an old folks' home, and I imagined an overheated parlor, a radio playing too loud, an elderly inmate snoring in an armchair, another in a frilly apron busying himself with a dustpan and brush, and a young heavy nurse patiently feeding a protesting crone who was wearing a blue plastic bib and batting the spoon away with her hand. Just saying the name lifted Leigh's spirits; he was still talking about the cottage.

" — thought of doing a little book about my experiences. Call it *Hong Kong Jottings* and pack it with sampans and chatter from the club, that sort of thing. I see myself at Elmview on a spring morning, in the front room, sun splashing through the window, working on this book. In longhand, of course. Outside I can see masses of bluebells and a green meadow." He sighed. "An old horse out to pasture."

"It sounds — " I could not think of another way of saying it — "very agreeable."

"You know," he said, "I've never set foot in that cottage. I saw it from a motorcar; Margaret pointed it out from the road. It was raining. We had a ploughman's lunch in the village — beautiful old pub — and went back to London that same afternoon. But it's as if I've been living there my whole life. I can tell you the position of every stick of furniture, every plate, how the sun strikes the carpet. I can see the tea things arranged on the table, and there's that — " he sniffed — "curious stale smell of cold ashes in the grate."

Yardley used to say, "Everyone in the tropics has a funkhole," and Leigh had told me his; his description had taken the curse off the name — the place was happy, a credible refuge. I had my own plans. I had never told a soul; I had kept my imaginings to myself and added little details now and then over the years. Maybe I had had one gin too many, or it might have been my triumphant feeling over that Bishop Bradley business. Whatever it was — it might have been Leigh's candor magnetizing mine — I drew very close to him and whispered, "It's an odd thing, isn't it? Everyone imagines a different funkhole. Take mine, for example. You know what I want?"

"Tell me," said Leigh, sympathetically.

"First, I want a lot of money — people don't laugh at a feller with dough. Then I want a yacht that you can sleep on and a huge mansion with a fence or a wall around it and maybe a peacock in the garden. I'd like to walk around all day in silk pajamas, and take up golf and give up these stinking cheroots and start smoking real Havana cigars. And that's not all — "

Leigh gave me an awfully shocked look; it rattled me so badly I stuttered to a halt and finished my drink in a single gulp. He thought I was mocking him. The dream of mine, the little glimpse of fantasy that had widened into the whole possible picture I saw every day I spent on that island, saving my sanity as I obeyed Hing or turned my girls out or sorted pornographic pictures on the kitchen table in my house in Moulmein Green, hopeful and comforting in its detail, making me resourceful — that to him was mockery.

He said, "Are you taking the mickey out of me?"

There was no way I could explain that I was perfectly serious. I saw it all coming to me quickly, like a jackpot I imagined myself winning: "Just a minute," I would say to the fellers at the bar, and while everyone watched I would put a coin — say my last — into a one-arm bandit, yank the lever and watch the whirr become a row of stars as the machine exploded and roared, disgorging a shower of silver dollars.

An old horse out to pasture, he had said; I had not giggled — at that or the bluebells. I believed it because he did. But my version of Elmview, my own funkhole (deep-sea fishing in a silk robe and a velvet fedora, with a cigar in my teeth) made him mad. And what bothered me most was that I could not tell whether he felt mocked because my imaginings were grander than his or because they sounded absurd and he doubted them. I would not have minded his envy, but his doubt would have made my whole plan seem inaccessible to me by encouraging my own doubt.

His grim expression made me say what I at once regretted: "I guess it sounds pretty crazy."

He did not hear me. Behind me, Yardley was horsing

around, bawling a joke: " '*Organ*,' she says. '*That's* no organ, breh-heh! Looks more like a *flute* to me!' "

"I take it Singapore's not a terribly expensive place to live," said Leigh.

"That's a laugh," I said. "It's probably more expensive than Hong Kong!"

"I'm quite surprised," he said, lifting his eyebrows. He took a sip of his drink. "Then the salaries here aren't very, um, realistic."

"They're not too bad," I said. I even laughed a little bit. But I stopped laughing when I saw what he was driving at. "You mean Hing?"

He nodded and gave me the tight rewarded smile of a man who has just tasted something he likes. He said, "You've got an *amah's* salary."

"You've got the wrong end of the stick," I said. "If you think I bank on — " But I was ashamed, and flustered — and angry because he still wore that smile. He had spent the day in that upstairs cubicle examining my salary. What could I say? That Gunstone had a few hours before thanked me with an envelope of cash? That I was welcome in any club in Singapore, and was snooker champion of one (unbeaten on the table at the Island Club), and knew a sultan who called me Jack and who had introduced me as his friend to Edmund de Rothschild at a party? That once, on Kampong Java Road, where I had my own brothel, I cleared a couple of thousand after pilferage and breakage was settled? That Edwin Shuck of the American embassy had told me that if it had not been for me Singapore would never have been used as a base for the GIs' "R and R" and Paradise Gardens would not have existed? That I had *plans?*

I hated him most when he said, with a concern that was contemptuous patronage, "How do you manage?"

My elbows were on the bar, my head in my hands. Far off on a green ocean I saw a yacht speeding toward me with

56

its pennants snapping in the breeze. A man in a swivel chair on the afterdeck had his feet braced on the gunwales and was pulling at a bending rod. Just behind him a lovely girl in a swimsuit stood with a tray of drinks and — I knew — club sandwiches, fresh olives, dishes of rollmop herring, and caviar spread on yellow crackers. The fish leaped, a tall silver thing turning in the sun, whipping the line out of the water. The yacht was close and I could see the man now. It was not me; it was no one I knew. I released my fingers from my eyes.

"Flowers," said Leigh. Why was he smiling? "How about a drink at the club?"

My girls were fairly well known at the Bandung — "Jack's fruit flies," Yardley called them — but no one there had any knowledge of my club work, and how I came straight from the Churchill Room or the Raffles Grill to the Bandung like an unfaithful husband home from his beguiling mistress's arms. I tried to whisper, "Maybe later."

Leigh looked beyond me to the others. "Does this establishment," he said, "have a toilet?"

"In the kitchen," said Coony, glad for a chance to say it.

Wally pointed the way.

"Does this establishment have a toilet?" said Smale. He guffawed. I wondered if Leigh could hear.

"Calls it a toilet," said Yardley. "He knows it's a crapper, but he calls it a toilet. That's breeding, you understand."

Frogget went yuck-yuck.

"What's this club he's talking about?" asked Yardley suspiciously.

I said I didn't have the remotest idea.

"You sound more like him every day," said Yardley.

"Knock it off," I said.

"Don't be narked," said Smale. "He's your mate, ain't he?"

"He hasn't bought anyone a drink yet," said Coony. "I could tell he was a mean bastard."

57

"Did you hear him rabbiting on?" asked Smale.

"I liked the part about him having tea in the pasture," said Frogget. "That shows he's around the twist."

They had heard. They had been talking the whole time but they had caught what Leigh had said about Elmview — a distorted version of it. I had whispered, confiding my hopes; they could not have heard me. But why had I weakened and told Leigh? And who would *he* tell? He was out of the room; I wanted him to stay out, never to come back, and for his engine to gripe and stop his mouth.

"He's a pain in the neck," I said, at last.

"Been in the bog a little while," said Smale. "What do you suppose he's doing in there?"

"Probably tossing himself off," said Frogget.

"You're a delicate little feller," I said.

No one said anything for a little while, but it was not what I had said to Frogget that caused the silence. We were waiting for the flush, which you could hear in the bar. The only sounds were the fans on the ceiling and the murmuring of Wally's transistor. We were drinking without speaking, and looking around in the way fellers do when they have just come into a bar; Leigh might have crept back without pulling the chain.

"So he's doing your *towkay*'s accounts," said Yardley. It was a meaningless remark, but for Yardley an extraordinary tone of voice: he whispered it.

"It's a very fiddly sort of job," said Yates after a moment. "You really have to know what's what."

"Takes ages to do those sums," said Smale. "Our accountant told me some days he looks at all those numbers and feels like cutting his throat."

"You have to pass an exam," said Coony, staring toward the kitchen. "To be an accountant. It's a bugger to pass. I know a bloke who failed it five times. Bright bloke, too."

Yardley called Wally, who was holding his radio to his ear

the way a child holds a seashell for the sound. He ordered
drinks and when Wally set them up Yardley handed me two
gins and a bottle of tonic water. "Pink one's for your pal,"
he said. He glanced toward the kitchen.

"I wouldn't mind living in Wiltshire," Smale said. He
said it with reverent hope, and we continued talking like this,
in whispers. I had not realized just how long Leigh had been
gone until I saw that the ice in his pink gin had melted and
my own glass was empty.

I climbed down from the barstool and hurried into the
kitchen. The toilet door was ajar, but Leigh was not inside.
He was sitting on a white kitchen chair, by the back door,
with his head between his knees.

"William," I said, "are you okay?"

He shook his head from side to side without raising it.

"Get up and walk around a bit. It's cool out back. The
fresh air — can you hear me? — the fresh air will do you a
world of good. Can you get up?"

He groaned. The back of his neck was damp, the sick
man's sweat made his hair prickle; his ears had gone white. I
knew it was his engine.

"He sick-*lah*," said Wally, appearing beside me with the
radio squawking in his hand.

"Will you shut that fucking thing off!" I screamed. I do
not know why I objected or swore. "Get a doctor, and
hurry!"

Wally jumped to the phone.

Yardley and the others came into the kitchen as I was helping Leigh up. Leigh's face had a white horror-struck expression — wide unmoving nose holes — that of a man drowning
slowly in many fathoms of water. I had seen these poor devils hoisted out of the drink: their mouths gaped open and
they stared past you with anxious bugging eyes, as if they
have acquired phenomenal sight, the ability to see far, and
see at that great distance something looming, a throng of ter-

rors. Leigh looked that way; he seemed about to whisper rather than scream. He was breathing: I saw a flutter in his throat, and a movement like a low bubble rise and fall in the declivity of his shoulder.

We carried him into the lounge, stretched him out on the sofa, and put pillows under his head. I took off his watch; it had made white roulettes on his wrist, perforations that wouldn't go away. He looked paler than ever, more frightening in the posture of a corpse. But the worst part was when his legs came alive — just his legs, like a man having a tantrum — and his kicking heels made an ungodly clatter on the bamboo armrest of the sofa.

"Christ," said Coony, stepping back. Smale and Frogget clamped their hands on his ankles and held them down. The clattering stopped, but the silence after that weird noise was much worse.

I was conscious of standing there with my tattooed arms hanging at my sides, not doing a blessed thing, and I heard a voice, Yardley's, saying, "See that tatty sofa over in the lounge near the piano? That's where Jack's mate from Hong Kong packed it in. It was the damnedest thing — "

I turned to shut him up. But he was not talking; he was standing, expressionless, holding Leigh's drink, the pale pink gin in which all the ice had melted. He seemed to be offering it to Leigh and though he held the tumbler in two hands it was shaking.

Leigh stared past us, at that looming thing very far off we could not see. I memorized his astonishment. It made us and the Bandung and everything on earth small and unimportant, not worth notice, and we were — for the time Leigh was on the sofa — as curious and baffled as those people on a city sidewalk who pass a man looking up at the sky and look up themselves but are made uneasy because they can't see the thing they know must be there.

6

THAT WAS how, in a manner of speaking — by the act of dying — Leigh had the last word; though toward the end we tried to take back the things we had said. I have a memory of the six of us dancing around that green sofa in the badly lighted lounge, before the doctor came and took him away, frantically attempting ways to revive him, to coax him back to life so that we could have another chance to be kind to him — or perhaps so that he could amend his last words, which had been "Does this establishment have a toilet?" to something if less memorable, more dignified.

Our reviving methods were the ineffectual kind we had learned from movies: lifting his eyelids (why? did we want to see the eye or not?); plumping his pillow; unbuttoning his shirt; pouring cold water over his face with the Johnnie Walker pitcher; fitting an ice bag on his head like a tam-o'-shanter, and lightly slapping his cheeks while asking persistent questions — "Where does it hurt?" and "Can you hear me?" — to which there were no replies.

The doctor sensibly put a stop to this. "How did he get so wet?" he asked as he knelt and swiftly tinkered with Leigh's chest and shone a light in his eyes. He held Leigh's wrist various ways and said, "It's too late." It sounded like a reproach for what I had whispered to Leigh — "Maybe later."

"A lot *he* cares," said Smale, muffling what he had said with his hand and backing away from the doctor.

"Is it all right to smoke?" asked Coony. But he had already lit one, which was smoldering half-hidden in his cupped fingers.

"One of you will have to come along with me," said the doctor, ignoring Coony's question. The doctor was Chinese, and I think what Smale held against him was his unclinical appearance; he was wearing a bright sports shirt and Italian sandals.

Yardley and the others turned to me and became very attentive and polite, as to the next of kin, offering me the considerate sympathy they had lavished on William, as they had started calling him when he was on the sofa and, most likely, dead. We wore long faces — not sad because we liked him, but mournful because we hated him. Coony put his hand on my shoulder and said, "Are you okay, Jack?"

"I'll be fine in a minute," I said, becoming the grieving person they wanted me to be.

"If there's anything we can do," said Yates.

I put on my suit jacket and fixed my tie. I was dressed for a death, buttoning the black jacket over my stomach.

"What are you going to tell his wife?" asked Yardley.

I stopped buttoning. "Won't the hospital tell her?" It had not occurred to me until Yardley mentioned it that I would have to break the news to Leigh's wife.

"They'll get it all wrong," said Smale. He held my sleeve and confided, "They'll make it sound bloody awful."

"Don't tell her it happened here," said Coony quickly. "Say it happened somewhere else."

"During the day," said Smale. "A sunny day."

"But in the shade," said Coony, "of a big Angsana tree. In

the Botanical Gardens. While he was — " Coony hit his fist against his head.

"While he was having a good time with the rest of us," said Yardley. He looked from face to face.

There was a long silence. The doctor was at the bar speaking on the telephone to the hospital.

"Near the bandstand," said Frogget. "Maybe he tried to climb that hill. And it was too hot. And his ticker gave out."

"We told him to stop," said Yardley, sounding convinced. "But he wouldn't listen to us. 'Have it your way,' we said. So off he went — "

"I'll think of something," I said, cutting Yardley off. I didn't like this.

It had all fallen to me. He was mine now, though I had tried several times to disown him. I had not wanted him; I had disliked him from the moment he asked, "Flowers . . . are you a ponce?" And his triumphant contempt: "How do you stand it?" and "How do you manage?" It was as if he had come all that way to ask me those questions, and to die before I could answer.

The doctor clicked Leigh's eyes shut, moving the lids down with his thumbs; but the lids refused to stick and sightless crescents of white appeared under the lashes. We carried him to the doctor's Volvo and folded him clumsily into the back seat. I sat beside him and put my arm around him to keep him from swaying. He nodded at every red light, and at the turning on River Valley Road his head rolled onto my shoulder.

"How long have you been in Singapore?" the doctor asked. It was a resident's question. I told him how long. He did not reply at once; I guessed I had been there longer than him. He drove for a while and then asked when I would be leaving.

"Eventually," I said. "Pretty soon."

"Haven't I seen you at the Island Club?"

"Yes," I said. "I go there now and then, just to hack around."

"What's your handicap?"

"My handicap," I said. "I wouldn't repeat it in public."

The doctor laughed and kept driving. Leigh slumped against me.

In my locked bedroom on Moulmein Green, late at night and so dog tired after driving one of my girls back to her house from a hotel that I collapsed into bed without pulling my pants off or saying my prayers, I had imagined death differently — not the distant horror of the drowning man, but the sense of something very close, death crowding me in the dark: a thing stirring in a room that was supposed to be empty. The feeling I got on one of those nights was associated in my mind with the moment before death, the smothering sound of the cockroach. A glossy cockroach, motionless, gummed to the wall by the bright light, goes into action when the light is switched off. It is the female which flies and its sound is the Chinese paper fan rapidly opening and closing. This fluttering dung beetle in the black room is circling, making for you. You listen in the dark and hear the stiff wings beating near your eyes. It is going to land on your face and kill you and there is nothing you can do about it.

I did not imagine a moment of vision before death, but quite the reverse, blindness and that fatal *burr* of wings. Leigh's eyes were not completely closed, the lids were ajar and the sulfurous streetlamps on Outram Road lit the gleaming whites. In the General Hospital Leigh peered past the orderly who pinned an admission ticket to his shirt — number eighty-six, a lottery number for Mr. Khoo — and turned out his pockets: a few crumpled dollars, a withered chit, some loose change, a wallet containing calling cards, a picture of Margaret, a twenty-dollar Hong Kong note, and a folded receipt from the Chinese Emporium on Orchard Road. This went into a brown envelope.

"We'll need a deposit," said the nurse.

I took out Gunstone's envelope, *Singapore Belvedere,* and handed over fifteen dollars. *How do you manage?*

"Please fill up this form," she said.

The form was long and asked for information I could not provide without Leigh's passport. So with the matron's permission I went back to the Strand by taxi, told the desk clerk that Leigh was dead, and picked up the passport. "It seems like only yesterday that he checked in," the desk clerk said; he assured me that he would take care of everything. By the time I was back at the hospital, copying Leigh's full name, home address, nearest relation, race, and age — he was a year younger than me; the pen shook in my hand — Leigh was staring out of the chilly morgue drawer; after the autopsy he looked much the same, though unzipped, he fixed on that distant thing with the single eye the autopsy left him.

I had forgotten Leigh's suitcase. After the certificate of death had been made out I picked up the case at the Strand, and at my insistence the taxi driver detoured past the Bandung. As we went past I could see lights burning and Yardley, Frogget, Smale, and the others at the bar, like lost old men, vagrants huddled around a fire late at night, sharing a bottle, afraid to go to bed.

It was after midnight. I did not have the heart to wake up Leigh's wife and get her out of bed to tell her she was a widow. I locked my door, put a match to the mosquito coil, and knelt beside it. The mosquito coil, lighted to suffocate the gnats and drive the cockroaches away, smoked like a joss stick. I blinked in the fumes and tried to pray; the first words that came to me were, *Is this all?*

The next day I awoke as if after a binge, with that feeling of physical and mental fragility, exposure, distraction — the knowledge of having done something shameful which refuses to be summoned up: of having revealed my closest secret which now everyone knew except me! And then I remembered Leigh, not as a corpse; it was an uncharitable intrusive thought, something connected with the smile he wore when he had asked, "How do you manage?" A picture of his dead face followed.

So more as an act of penance than out of any curiosity, I opened his suitcase and picked through it. Each thing I found made me sad; nothing was concealed. There were tags and labels on the case, the traveler's campaign ribbons, KHAO YAI MOTOR LODGE, HOTEL BELA VISTA — MACAU, and the luggage tag from the airline with the destination lettered SIN. Here was a sock with a hole in the toe, a pathetic little sewing kit, some salt tablets, a packet of Daraprim, very wrinkled pajamas with a white-piping border, his human smell still upon them. In a paper bag from the Chinese Emporium there were a set of screwdrivers, a new shaving brush, some Lucky Brand razor blades. There was a wrapped parcel of batik cloth from another shop, probably a present for his wife, and stuck to the parcel were two receipts for the cloth, but giving different prices, the lower faked price to fool the customs official in Hong Kong and avoid a few dollars' import duty. At the bottom of the case was a detective novel with a grisly title that described Leigh's own death, an eerie coincidence italicizing the improbable fraud of one, the pitiful condition of the other. He was in the morgue drawer, and here was his poor bundle of effects: this was all.

I dressed, practicing how to tell his wife what had happened. The suitcase caught my eye; I opened it again and sorted through it quickly, lifting everything out a second time and shaking the clothes. There was no money in it! I had told the desk clerk at the Strand he was dead, but only later picked up the suitcase. After I had left with the passport they had gone up to his room and robbed him.

The phone crackled; Hing fretted beside me; Gopi watched. I said, "Listen carefully. Yesterday I was with your husband at the Botanical Gardens. Wait a minute — listen. It was a beautiful day — "

It was a suffocating day, producing the feverish symptoms of a fatal illness in me. I had picked up my car at the garage, we had all met at the mortuary, and we followed behind the hearse — polished and sculpted like an old piano — attempting funereal solemnity by keeping our faded elderly cars in file, my chugging Renault, Yardley's blue Anglia, Hing's Riley (he sat in the back seat with Little; a Malay drove), Mr. Tan and Wallace Thumboo in an old Ford Consul, Yates in his boxy Austin, and the others trailing, impossible to see in my rear-view mirror. We hit every red light, getting hotter and sicker at each stop, and we lost the hearse (I could see Yardley irritably pounding his palm against the steering wheel) at one junction when it speeded up and ran on the yellow.

Gladys was with me. I had guessed in advance that only men would be there, and that didn't seem right. Also, I had to drop her off at a hotel immediately afterward, an appointment of long standing I had only noticed that morning in my desk diary. Gladys was fanning herself absent-mindedly as I drove, and quickly against her chin at stoplights, making that fluttering I dreaded, the papery burr of beating cockroach wings. I told her to knock it off. That and the heat oppressed me. We were not in sunlight, but sweating in the mid-morning Singapore veil of dim steam that makes a gray tent of the slumping sky and nothing on the ground solid. There was nothing worse, I was thinking, than a cremation on a hot day in the tropics. It had all the inappropriateness of a man puffing on a pipe in a burning house. I vowed that I would spare myself that fate.

The crematorium off Upper Aljunied Road was a yellow building, with a chimney instead of a steeple, on a low hill, in a treeless Chinese cemetery, a rocky weedy meadow of narrow plots, stone posts as grave markers, figured like milestones turned on a lathe, an occasional angel, and worn cement vaults with peeling red doors, set in scorched hillocks: a whole suburb of trolls' huts, clustered there in the kind of chaotic profusion that matched their lives, sleeping families on shophouse floors, and now, head to toe, beneath those posts and stones. Here and there was a high vault with a roof, fenced in from the others, the graveyard equivalent of a *towkay*'s mansion, which might almost have borne a nameplate, *The Wongs, Chee's Tower*, or *Dunroamin*. All this was hazy in the steamy air and when I looked back, obscured by the dust cloud our procession of cars was raising on the road that wound up to the crematorium. The chimney was not smoking. Some distance away, in the middle of the cemetery, a ghostly white-shirted party with umbrellas open stood slightly bowed before a vault mound. They could have been praying, but they weren't. Stooping reverentially, they began to let off firecrackers.

"Can't they stop those little bastards?" said Yardley, rushing up to me after we parked. Our dust cloud descended, sifting down on us. He looked at Gladys and suppressed another curse. "We can't have that nonsense going on during the service."

The Chinese mourners were lighting packets of fifty with the fuses knotted. The noise carried in steady burps; there were flashes and delayed bangs.

"Bloody — " Yardley turned and stalked away growling.

"To amaze the gods," Gladys said. "Very lucky to have big noise. Also can make devils piss off."

The other fellers came over to us.

"Are you okay, Jack?" asked Coony.

"I hope it doesn't rain," said Smale, leaning back and squinting at the sky.

We looked at him.

"It'd ruin it," he said nervously. "Wouldn't it?" Was he

68

thinking of the fire that could be doused, or was it that fear of excessive gloom that fellers associate with rain at funerals?

"It won't rain until October," said Yates.

The two Hings were in white, their terrifying color of mourning, white cotton suits and straw hats, carrying umbrellas, looking wretched. Mr. Tan wore a black tie. Because of the appointment, Gladys wore a bright green dress and carried a large handbag; her face was a white mask with wizard's eyes. Big Hing cracked his umbrella open, shook it, and walked in oversized shoes toward the building, holding the umbrella upright, but bouncing it as he walked. The rest of the Chinese followed him.

I asked the hearse driver what we were supposed to do. He said four of us were to carry the coffin into the chapel; the priest would take care of the rest. I objected to the word "priest" to describe an effeminate Anglican cleric of perhaps thirty, blushing in the heat, his cheeks pink, and wringing his hands by the crematorium door; in his white smock-like surplice he eyed Gladys disapprovingly, like a spinsterish intern about to check her for the clap. I beckoned to Yardley and the others and said, "Look alive."

I had known most of them for fourteen years; I had drunk with them nearly every night at the Bandung. Only that. I had never seen them all together, assembled in daylight away from the Bandung. So I was seeing them for the first time. They were strangers who knew me. The bad light of the Bandung had been kind to Yardley's liverish pallor, a tropical sallowness in an unlined face; Frogget looked bigger and hairier, and his tie was frayed; Yates I noticed had freckles, and his glasses had slipped down his nose from his perspiring; Smale's hair was reddish — I had always thought of it as brown; Coony's hair was combed straight back, the shape of his head, and his lower lip, which always protruded when his mouth was shut, was dry for once. None of them was standing straight; they were self-conscious in their suits, in unfamiliar postures, and Yardley's leaning — one shoulder higher than the other — made him appear unwell.

It might have been the old-fashioned rumpled suits I had never seen them wear, dark gray or black, wrinkled, smelling of moth balls and spotted with mildew like soup stains: an old ill-fitting suit makes the wearer seem shy. The wrinkles were not in the usual places, the consequence of sitting or reaching, but were in unlikely places, across the chest of the jacket, pinches on the back and sleeves, drawer folds, creases from storage, the cuffs bunched up; the trousers were more faded than the jackets and this mismatching together with the seediness of the suits reminded me of something Yates had once whispered at the Bandung. "Tell me, Jack," he said, "don't we look like the legion of the lost?"

It seemed disrespectful to smoke near the crematorium, so we were all more edgy than usual. The hearse driver and his assistant slid the coffin out and Yardley, Frogget, Smale, and myself carried it across the dusty compound to the entrance where the rest stood behind the cleric. I thought I heard Yardley mutter, "He's damned heavy," but he might have said, "It's damned heavy." It was. I was afraid we might drop it. The others had been up drinking the night before and I had not been able to sleep. I knew they were worried about dropping it too, because they were carrying it much too fast.

"Wally," I said.

Wally stood blocking the door, looking inside, with his back to us.

"Wally!" I said again. He didn't hear. His square head was turned away. My hands were growing moist and slipping on the chrome fixture I was holding, and I snapped, "Move it or lose it!"

He jumped out of the way, and we proceeded inside and unsteadily down the aisle, panting, the six busy overhead

70

fans in the room of folding chairs mocking our forced solemnity with practical whirrs. We placed the coffin on a high wheeled frame at the front of the room and took our seats with the others.

After a few moments Yardley leaned over and asked, "What's the drill?"

I shrugged. It was my first cremation, and in that bare room of steel chairs, the only ornaments the photographs of the President and his wife, I could not imagine what was going to happen. We sat expectantly, the chairs squeaking and clanking. Hing loudly cleared his throat, so loud it made me want to spit, and as one person's hacking inspires another's, particularly in a still room, soon Smale and Coony were at it, coughing in shallow growls. Outside, the *poop-poop* of firecrackers continued; and beside me Gladys began beating her fan, scraping it against her chin. The cleric walked up the aisle, his starched surplice rustling. The coughing stopped; now there were only the fans, the chair squeaks, and the distant firecrackers.

"Fellow brethren," he said, looking at us with uncertainty and distaste; he clung to his Bible, holding it chest high, and nodded at everyone individually with his pink flushed face — making suspense. He took a breath and began. His sermon was the usual one, but he was young enough and had delivered it few enough times to make it sound as if he believed it: life was short and difficult, a testing time loaded with temptations; and he pictured God as the all-seeing bumptious neighbor, rocking irritably on his celestial porch and passing judgment. He talked about our weaknesses and then concentrated on Leigh's soul, which he addressed with great familiarity. The worst religions, I was thinking, rob you of your secrets by reminding you that you're all in the same sinking boat; harping on your sameness and denying you fancies and flesh and blood and visible hope, they reduce you to moaning galley slaves, manacled to a bloody

71

oar, puking in a sunless passage and pulling blindly toward an undescribed destination; and constantly warning you that you might never arrive. "Believe in God," the cleric was saying, and I thought, Yes, that's easy, but does God believe in me? I liked my religion to be a private affair ashore, a fire by a stone, a smoky offering; one necessary at night, the light giving the heavens fraternal features to surprise me with the thrill of agreeable company. It was to make the authority of ghosts vanish by making holiness a friendly human act and defining virtue as joy and grace as permission granted.

" — to judgment," the cleric was saying, and as he spoke he jerked around several times to nod at Leigh's coffin, as if Leigh was listening as long as his corpse was whole, and needed only combustion to get him to paradise. "We are all of us sinners, wallowing in the flesh," the cleric said. Gladys stopped fanning herself. She sniffed and began to cry; and I hoped she was not planning to repent and back out of the appointment at the Palm Grove. She was the only person weeping; the Hings were impassive and pale, Mr. Tan and Wally limply crestfallen; Yardley and the others were sweating, but the sweat ran like tears and wet their faces and was almost like grief.

My face was streaming, too, but I wasn't crying; my thoughts were too confused for that. Leigh, alive, had reminded me of myself, and his death warned me about my own — a warning so strong it made me ignore his death for part of the time. But I was also thinking: Now he can't tell anyone about my plans, my silk pajamas and cigars; and I felt childish relief mingled with adult sadness that he was out of the way. When the engines stop on a ship in mid-ocean the whole ship ceases to vibrate and it makes a silence so sudden after three weeks of continual noise that you think your heart has stopped and you wonder for seconds if you're dead. After those seconds you understand mortality, and the silence that terrified you is a comfort. Leigh's death affected me that way, and at the cremation I felt peaceful. It seemed better that he was going to be reduced to ashes — a corpse made small and poured into a little pot was not a corpse; it was so tiny and altered you couldn't reasonably weep over it. Cremation simulated disappearance; it really was like flight, a movement I knew well. Bodies decaying underground made people cry, but a dozen pots on a shelf, a bottled family, were uncharacteristic relics of the forgettable dead, who might have simply skipped off and left their urns behind, one apiece. Burning, as the cleric hinted — and here I agreed — was like deliverance; it was only bad on a hot day.

My thoughts stopped coming: the cleric had stopped talking. There was a clatter at the door; a scrape; a shuffle-thump, shuffle-thump. The cleric stared. We all turned. Gopi was cycling in, his shoulders heaving, making his sleeves flap. His eyes were big from the physical effort of his pedaling, and his shirt was stuck in a dark patch to his back. He took a seat at the front, alone, and he watched the coffin as if it was a magician's box.

The cleric, who might have thought Gopi was going to interrupt with Hindu wailing, quietly resumed, "Let us pray."

We knelt on the stone floor. Gopi had to look back to see how it was done. I was anxious for him, balanced on that wobbly knee; he managed by steadying himself on the chair next to him.

A sound of enormous wheezing filled the room as we stood; it was not ours. A clapped-out harmonium had begun asthmatically to breathe "Jerusalem" at the back of the room. Yardley and the others seemed glad to have a chance to sing, and they did so with the hoarse gusto they gave the obscene songs Frogget started at the Bandung on Saturday nights. Frogget had a fine voice, higher than one would have expected from a feller his size and (Gopi and Gladys were both

73

weeping for Leigh — why?) all the voices rang in the room, echoing on the yellow walls and drowning the fans, the fire-crackers, and even the woofing harmonium with the hymn.

> *And did those feet in ancient time*
> *Walk upon England's mountains green?*

We gave the lines in the last part — *Bring me my bow of burning gold, Bring me my arrows of desire* — the sahib's emphasis, trilling the *r* in the command resolutely.

The cleric walked over to the coffin and sprinkled it and prayed out loud. I started thinking of the man out back, stoking the fire like a fry cook in clogs, stirring the coals in a black kitchen, sweating worse than we were and wiping his face on his shoulder, banging his poker on the furnace door to slam the hot ashes from the tip. What burial customs.

It was over. The cleric flung his arms into the sign of the cross, a novice's flourish of sleeves, and blessed us and said, "Amen." The coffin was rolled out of the room through a rear door and we all went out to our cars.

"You ready?" I asked Gladys.

Her tears had dried. She looked at me. "This short time or all day?"

Before I could answer Yardley was beside me asking, "You coming along? We're going for a drink. The day's a dead loss — no sense going to work."

"I'll be there in a little while," I said, and seeing Hing leaving, smiled and waved him off. Hing's face was tight; he was unused to the lecturing at Christian services and might have expected the brass band, the busloads of relatives, the banners and pennants and cherry bombs that saw a Chinese corpse to the grave.

"Short time," said Gladys. "Where I am dropping?"

I did not reply. Yardley and Frogget faced the sky behind me. I turned to look. Smoke had started from the chimney, a black puff and ripples of stringy heat, then a gray column

74

unimpeded by any breeze shooting straight up and enlarging, becoming the steamy air that hung over the island. Despair is simple: fear without a voice, a sinking and a screamless fright. We watched in silence, all of us. Coony ground his cigarette out and gaped; then, conscious that we were all watching the smoke, we looked away.

"Who's paying for this?" Yardley asked.

"I am," I said, and felt sad. But when I got into the little car with Gladys and started away, throwing the shift into second gear, I felt only relief, a springy lightness of acquittal that was like youth. I was allowed all my secrets again, and could keep them if I watched my step. It was like being proven stupid and then, miraculously, made wise.

Part Two

1

FOR AS LONG as I could remember I had wanted to be rich, and famous if possible, and to live to the age of ninety-five; to eat huge meals and sleep late out of sheer sluttishness in a big soft bed; to take up an expensive but not strenuous sport, golf or deep-sea fishing in a fedora with a muscular and knowledgeable crew; to gamble with conviction instead of bitterness and haste; to have a pair of girl friends who wanted me for my money — the security was appealing: why would they ever leave me? All this and a town house, an island villa, a light plane, a fancy car, a humidor full of fat fragrant cigars — you name it. I guessed it would come to me late: fifty-three is a convenient age for a tycoon; the middle-aged man turning cautious and wolflike knows the score, and if he has been around a bit he can take the gaff. It did not occur to me that it might never happen.

Being poor was the promise of success; the anticipation of fortune, a fine conscious postponement, made the romance, for to happen best it would have to come all at once, as a surprise, with the great thud a bag of gold makes when it's plopped on a table, or with the tumbling unexpectedness of thick doubloons spilling from the seams of an old wall you're tearing apart for the price of the used wood. One rather fanciful idea I'd had of success was that somehow through a fortuitous mix-up I would be mistaken for a person who resembled me and rewarded with a knighthood or a country estate; it was as good as admitting I did not deserve it, but that it was far-fetched made my receptive heart anticipate it as a possibility. It might, I thought, be a telephone call on a gray morning when, fearing bad news, I would hear a confident educated voice at the other end say, "Brace yourself, Mr. Flowers, I've got some wonderful news — "

Wonderful news in another fantasy was a letter. I composed many versions of these and recited them to myself walking to the 8-A bus out of Moulmein Green in the morning, or killing time in a hotel lobby when a girl was finishing a stunt upstairs, or dealing out the porno decks, or standing on the Esplanade and staring at the ships in the harbor.

One started like this:

Dear Mr. Flowers,
    It gives me great pleasure to be writing to you today, and I know my news will please you as much . . .

Another was more direct:

Dear Flowers,
    I've had my eye on you for a long time, and I'm very happy to inform you of my decision concerning your future . . .

Another:

Dear Jack,
    I am asking my lawyer to read you this letter after my death. You have been an excellent and loyal friend, the very best one could hope for. I have noted you in my will for a substantial portion of my estate as a token thanks for your good humor, charity, and humanity. You will never again have to think of . . .

Another:

Dear Sir,
   Every year one person is singled out by our Foundation to be the recipient of a large cash disbursement. You will see from the enclosed form that no strings whatever are attached . . .

Another:

Dear Mr. Flowers,
   The Academy has entrusted to me the joyful task of inform-ing you of your election. This carries with it as you know the annual stipend of . . .

There were more; I composed as many as thirty in an af-ternoon, though usually I stuck to one and phrased it to per-fection, working on it and reciting every altered declaration of the glorious news. The last was long and rambling; it was only incidentally about money, and it began, *My dar-ling . . .*

No man of fifty-three wants to look any more ridiculous than his uncertain age has already made him, and I am well aware that in disclosing this fantastic game I played with myself, the sentences above, which prior to a few moments ago had never been written anywhere but in my head, much less typed under the embossed letterheads I imagined and pushed through the mail slot of my semidetached house on Moulmein Green — I am well aware that in putting those eager ("Brace yourself") openings in black and white I seem to be practicing satire or self-mockery. The difficulty is that unchallenged, squatting like trepanned demons in the padded privacy of an idle mind, one's lunatic thoughts seem tame and reasonable, while spoken aloud in broad daylight to a stranger or written before one's own eyes they are the extravagant ravings of a crackpot. *You know what I want?* I said to Leigh, and told him, and was made a fool by his look of shock; I should have kept my mouth shut, but how was I to know that he was not the stranger who would say,

81

"I've got some good news for you, Flowers." He might have thought I was mad. Madness is not believing quietly that you're Napoleon; it is demonstrating it, slipping your hand inside your jacket and striking a military pose. He might have thought I was crude. But the beginner's utterance is always wrong: I used to stand in Singapore doorways and hiss, "Hey bud" at passers-by.

Crude I may have been, but mad never; and I would like to emphasize my sanity by stating that even though I dreamed of getting one of those letters (*It gives me great pleasure* . . .) I could not understand how I would ever receive one, for I imagined thousands, paragraph by glorious paragraph, but I never mentally signed them, and none, not even the one beginning *My darling*, bore a signature. Who was supposed to be writing me those letters? I hadn't the faintest idea.

The letters were fantasy, but the impulse was real: a visceral longing for success, comfort, renown, the gift that could be handled, tangible grace. That momentary daydream which flits into every reflective man's mind and makes him say his name with a title, *Sir* or *President* or *His Highness* — everyone does it sometimes: the clerk wants a kingship, it's only natural — this dubbing was a feature of my every waking moment. I wasn't kidding; even the most rational soul has at least one moment of pleasurable reflection when he hears a small voice addressing him as *Your Radiance*. I had a litany which began *Sir Jack, President Flowers, King John,* and so forth. And why stop at king? *Saint Jack!* It was my yearning, though success is nasty and spoils you, the successful say, and only failures listen, who know nastiness without the winch of money. If the rich were correct, I reasoned, what choice had they made? Really, was disappointment virtue and comfort vice and poverty like the medicine that was good because it stung? The President of the United States, in a sense the king of the world, said he had the loneliest job on earth; where did that leave a feller like me?

The theatrically convulsed agony of the successful is the failure's single comfort. "Look how similar we are," both will exclaim: "We're each lonely!" But one is rich; he can choose his poison. So strictly off my own bat I gave myself a chance to choose — I would take the tycoon's agony and forego the salesman's. I said I wanted to be rich, famous if possible, drink myself silly and sleep till noon. I might have put it more tactfully: I wanted the wealth to make a free choice. I was not pleading to be irresponsible; if I was rich and vicious I would have to accept blame. The poor were blameless; they could not help it, and if they were middle-aged they were doubly poor, for no one could see their aches and no one knew that the middle-aged man at that corner table, purple with indigestion, thought he was having a heart seizure. That man will not look back to reflect unless he has had a terrible fright that twists his head around. Characteristically, he will look back once, see nothing, and never look back again. But Leigh and his hopeless last words gave me such an awful shock that driving out of the crematorium with Gladys I took a long look back — with the recent memory of imagining what my own last words might be, *Is this all?* mumbled in a hot room — and thought of nothing but what had brought me to Singapore, and the sinking ships I had boarded since then.

It was a bumboat. I jumped off the *Allegro* and there I was, sitting at the stern of a chugging bumboat, making my way toward Collyer Quay. It might have been cowardice; in me, cowardice often looked like courage by worrying me into some panicky act. I ran, and it looked like pursuit; but it wasn't that — it was flight.

The bumboat touched the quay. The Chinese pilot pressed a finger in salute to the hanky that was knotted around his head like a tea cosy.

Having learned the trick of survival and reached a ripe old age, most fellers can look back on their lives and explain the logic of everything they've done, show you the pattern of their movements, their circlings toward what they wanted and got. Justifying their condition, they can point without regret to the blunt old-type exclamation marks of their footprints, like frozen ones in snow, and make sense of them. If the footprints are a jumble and some face in retreat the feller might say with a wild accompanying cackle that he had his shoes on backward and appeared to be walking away as he advanced. The explanation is irrefutable, for old age itself is a kind of arrival, but I could not say — being fifty-three in Singapore — that I had arrived anywhere. I was pausing, I thought, and there was no good reason for any of my movements except the truthful excuse that at the time of acting I saw no other choice. The absence of plot or design inspired my forlorn dream that magically by letter I would become a millionaire. My life was a pause; I lived in expectation of an angel.

My vision was explicit, and no guilt hampered it; I wished away the ego of my past — I would not be burdened by my history. But I had a fear: that I might turn out to be one of those travelers who, unnerved by the unconscious boldness of their distance — the flight that took them too far — believe themselves to be off course and head for anything that resembles a familiar landmark. Only, up close, they discover it to be a common feature of a foreign landscape on which identical landmarks lie in all directions. They chase these signs, their panic giving the wheeling chase some drama, and very soon they are nowhere, travelers who never arrive, who do not die but are lost and never found, like those unfortunate Arctic explorers, or really any single middle-aged feller who dies in a tropical alien place, alone and among strangers who mock what they can't comprehend, the hopeful man with the perfect dream of magic, burned to ashes one hot day and negligently buried, who was lost long before he died.

2

THE BUMBOAT touched the quay. I vaulted to the stone steps and almost immediately, in a small but ingenious way, became a hustler. The word is unsuitable, but let it stand. It was an aspect of a business I understood well, for over the previous eleven months, soothed by Mothersill's Pills, I had been crossing and recrossing the Indian Ocean in the *Allegro*, and at every port, from Mombasa to Penang, I had been appointed by the captain to perform a specific job for extra pay; that is, to take on supplies by contacting the ship chandler. I enjoyed doing this; it gained me admittance to a friendly family ashore, Ismailis in Mombasa, Portuguese in Beira, an Indo-French one in Port Louis, Parsees in Bombay. It was an entry into a world as mysterious for the sailor as the sea is for the landsman, the domestic life, drama in dry rooms that lay beyond the single street of seamen's bars, the frontier that barricades harbors from their cities. At each port the ship chandler was our grocer, butcher, dhobi, fishmonger, hardware man; he would supply anything at short notice, but I believe that at Hing's in Singapore — after I jumped ship — I could take credit for introducing a new

85

wrinkle to one of the world's most versatile professions. Later it was taken up by other ship chandlers and Singapore became a port in which even a large vessel could make a turnaround in six hours without the crew mutinying.

I look back and see a wild August storm, known in Singapore as a Sumatra: a high wind blows suddenly from the west and the sky gathers into unaccountable blackness, a low heavy ceiling, night at noon, the cold rain sheeting horizontally into the surf. That day I was standing in the wheel house of a rocking launch. It was warm and sunny when we left the quay, but fifteen minutes out the sky darkened, the cabin door banged, and rain began hitting the glass with a sound like sleet; we bolted the doors and breathed the engine fumes. Stonelike waves, each dark one with streaming ribbons of oil on its bumpy edges and topped with a torn cap of lacy froth, slammed into the starboard side of the launch, making the same boom as if we had run aground. I hung onto a canvas strap and wiping the steam off the back window put my nose to the moaning glass.

We were towing a forty-foot lighter, the sort used for transporting bales of raw rubber; Chinese decorations were painted on the bow, evil white and black eyes, green whiskers, and a red dragon-fang mouth. The painted face with its scabrous complexion of barnacles rose and fell, gulping ocean, and the canvas cover, a vast pup tent pitched over the lighter, was being lashed by the wind; our towrope, now loose as the lighter leaped at us, now tight as it plunged and dragged, was periodically wrung of water, which shot out in a twist of bubbly spray as it stretched tight. A grommet on the corner of the canvas tarp tore free, and the tent fly burst open, unveiling our cargo, twenty-three smartly dressed Chinese and Malay girls, their scared white faces almost luminous in the gloom of the quaking shelter; they were huddled on crates and kegs, their knees together, holding their plastic handbags on their heads.

The visibility, what with the fog and rain and steamed-up windows, was very poor, and I had the impression we were thrashing in the open ocean, for no ships and not even the harborside could be made out. It was just after tiffin; no wharf lights were on. It was fearfully dark and cold, and I was dizzy from the cabin fumes. We might have been in the South China Sea.

"More to port," I shouted to Mr. Khoo, showing him a circle I had drawn on the Western Roads of my harbor chart.

"No," he said, and spun the wheel starboard.

"Don't give me that!" I said, and went for him. The launch bucked and threw me to the floor. I could feel the launch turning, slowed by the weight of the lighter, and just under the whistling wind the screams of my girls. Mr. Khoo was taking us back.

I had seen seamen fight below decks during storms on the *Allegro*; it was something that made me want to strap on a life vest and hide near the bridge, like a child in a slum running from his quarreling parents. My fear was of seeing people enclosed by a larger struggle swept away and dying in a hammer lock. The storms encouraged fighting, and the fighting seemed to intensify the storm.

"Give me the wheel like a good feller," I said to Mr. Khoo.

Mr. Khoo threatened me with a sharp elbow and held tight to the wheel. The wipers were paralyzed on the window; I swayed and tried to see.

"Do you know what this is costing me!" I shouted.

"Cannot," said Mr. Khoo, refusing to look at me.

"Drop the anchor, then," I said. "I'll do it."

I unbolted the door and stepped into the wind. Up ahead, the rusty brown silo of a ship's stern loomed, a light flashed, and I made out the name, *Richard Everett, Liverpool*.

"Oh boy, there she is!"

Mr. Khoo gave a blast on the horn; he was crouched at the wheel. He looked up at the freighter, twisting his head. I stayed on deck, waving to faces framed by yellow bonnets. It was too rough to use the ladder; some men in slickers and boots were pushing a cargo net over the side.

The launch still pitched. Mr. Khoo worked the lighter close by circling the launch around and nudging it against the side of the *Richard Everett*, and I had the satisfaction in a storm during which other lightermen waited at the river mouth by Cavanagh Bridge, of seeing my girls hoisted up, three at a time in the hefty cargo net, all of them soaked to the skin, fumbling with collapsed umbrellas and shrieking at the gale. The crane swung them on board and lowered them into the hold. There was a cheer, audible over the storm and wind, as the cargo net descended.

I went up myself with the last load of girls and to the sound of steel doors slamming in the passageway, had a brandy with the first mate, and played a dozen hands of gin rummy; the light softened in the porthole and then the sun came out. He paid me fifteen dollars a girl. He had asked for them on consignment, but I insisted on a flat rate. Two hours later, in sparkling sunshine, we were on our way. I rode in the lighter with the girls. We took down the canvas roof and May played a transistor radio one of the seamen had given her. Some of the girls put up their umbrellas, and they all sat as prim as schoolteachers on a Sunday outing. Junie wore a sailor hat. We cruised slowly back, enjoying the warmth and the light breeze, and docked at Pasir Panjang behind a palm grove — I could not risk arriving at Collyer Quay or Jardine Steps with that cargo.

It was not my first excursion. I had been doing it for several months, usually small loads. Sometimes only two in a sampan rowed out from Collyer Quay to an old tanker, the girls disguised as scrubwomen in faded *sam-foos*, with buckets and brushes and bundles of old rags, to fool the harbor police. I had always made it a practice — I was the first in Singapore, perhaps anywhere, to do so — to have a girl along with me when I delivered groceries and fresh meat and coils of rope, just in case. The girl was always welcome, and came back exhausted.

The storm made me; it became known that I was the enterprising swineherd who took a lighterful of girls out at the height of a Sumatra that swamped a dinghy of Danish seamen that same day. A week later a crewman on the *Miranda* buttonholed me: "You the bloke that floated them pros out to the *Everett?*"

I told him I was, and stuck out my hand. "Jack Flowers," I said. "Call me Jack. Anything I can do for you?"

"You're a lad, you are," he said admiringly, and then over his shoulder, " 'ey, Scrumpy, it's *'im!*"

I rocked back and forth, smiling, then took out my pencil and clownishly licked the lead, and winked, saying, "Well, gentlemen, let's see what we can scare up for you today . . ."

The Sumatra had come sudden as a bomb, darkly filling the sky, outraging the sea, pimpling it with rain like lead shot, wrinkling it and snarling it into spiky heaves. I never let on that it hit us when we were halfway to the *Richard Everett* or that I had put my last dollar into releasing those girls and hiring the launch and lighter, and that to have turned back — no less perilous than going forward — would have disgraced me and ruined me irrecoverably. If we had sunk it would have been the end, for none of the twenty-three girls knew how to swim. I had not known the extent of the risk, but it was a venture — probably cowardly: I was afraid to lose my money and scared to turn back — that had tremendous consequences. The mates on the *Miranda* were the first of many who praised me and gave me commissions.

And Hing's business boomed.

I had known Hing long before I jumped ship. The Allegro was registered in Panama, but her home port was Hong Kong. We were often in Singapore, and the only occasion in eleven months we left the Indian Ocean was to take a cargo of rubber to Vancouver. I thought of jumping ship there, and nearly did it, except that beyond Vancouver and the cold wastes of Canadian America I saw the United States, and that was the place I was fleeing.

Hing was the first person I thought of when I developed my plan for leaving the *Allegro*. At the time he seemed the kindest man. I always looked forward to our stops in Singapore, and Hing was glad of our business. Just a small-time provisioner, delivering corn flakes to housewives at the British bases and glad for the unexpected order of an extra pound of sausages, he worked out of his little shop on Beach Road; Gopi packed the cardboard cartons, and Little Hing took the groceries around in a beat-up van. We were not dealing with Hing then. Our ship chandler was a large firm, also on Beach Road, just down from Raffles Hotel. One day, checking over our crates of supplies, I saw some secondhand valves wrapped in newspaper that I felt were being palmed off on me.

"We didn't order these," I said.

The clerk took them out of the crate. He dropped them on the floor.

"Where are the ones we ordered?"

The clerk said nothing. The Chinese mouth is naturally grim; his was drawn down, his nether lip pouted; his head, too large for the rest of his body, had corners, and looked just like a skull, not a head fleshed out with an expression, but in contour and lightness, the sutures and jaw hinges visible, a bone with a flat skeletal crown. This feller's head, ridiculously mounted on a scrawny neck, infuriated me.

"Where," I repeated, "are the ones we ordered?"

He swallowed, setting his Adam's apple in motion. "Out of stock."

"I thought as much. So you gave us these. You're always doing that!" I almost blew a gasket. "We're going to be at sea for the next ten days. What if a valve goes? They aren't going to be any good to us, are they?" I wanted him to reply. "*Are they?*"

Anger takes some responsive cooperation to fan blustering to rage. He would not play; the Chinese seldom did. Some fellers accused the Chinese of harboring a motiveless evil, but it was not so. Their blank look was disturbing because it did nothing to discourage the feeling that they meant us harm. The blankness was blankness, a facial void reflecting a mental one: confusion. If I had to name the look I would call it fear, the kind that can make the Chinese cower or be wild. The clerk cowered, withdrawing behind the counter.

I kicked the crate and stamped out of the shop. Next door Hing was smiling in the doorway of his shop. I was immediately well disposed to him; he was reliably fat and calm, and he had the prosperous, satisfying bulk, the easy grace of a trader with many employees.

"Yes?"

Apart from a few wooden stools, a calendar, an abacus, bills withering on a spike, and on the wall a red altar with a pot full of smoldering joss sticks, the shop was empty of merchandise. Little Hing was carrying groceries from the back room, Gopi was ramming them into a crate.

"I need some valves," I said. Then, "Got?"

He thought I was saying "bulbs," but we got that straight, and finally, after I described the size, he said, "Can get."

"When?"

"Now," he said, calling Little over. "You want tea? Cigarette? Here — " He shook a cigarette out of a can. "Plenty for you. Don't mention. Come, I light. Thank you."

He had the valves for me in twenty minutes, and that was how we started doing business with Hing. The next time the *Allegro* called at Singapore, Hing had put up his ship chandler's sign. There was nothing he could not get; he had a genius for winkling out the scarcest supplies, confirming the claim he printed on his stationery, *Provisions of Every De-*

scription Shall Be Supplied at Shortest Notice. And every time I called on him with my shopping list he took me out to dinner, a roast beef and Yorkshire pudding feed at the Elizabethan Grill, or a twelve-course Chinese dinner with everything but bears' paws and fish lips on the table.

It was simple business courtesy, the ritual meal. I was buying a thousand dollars' worth of provisions and supplies from him; for this he was paying for my dinner. I was an amateur. I thought I was doing very well, and always congratulated myself as, lamed by brandy, I staggered to the quay to catch a sampan back to the *Allegro.* I only understood the business logic of "Have a cigar — take two," when it was too late; but as I say, I started out hissing, "Hey bud" from doorways along Robinson Road. I was old enough to know better.

During one of the large meals, Hing, who in the Chinese style watched me closely and heaped my plate with food every five minutes, leaned over and said, "You . . . wucking . . . me." His English failed him and he began gabbing in Cantonese. The waitress was boning an awed steamed *garupa* that was stranded on a platter of vegetables. She translated shyly, without looking up.

"He say . . . he like you. He say . . . he want a young man . . ."

"*Ang moh,*" I heard Hing say. "Redhead."

The waitress removed the elaborate comb of the fish's spine and softened Hing's slang to, "European man . . . do very good business for European ship. European people . . . not speak awkward like Chinese people. And he say . . ."

Hing implored with his eyes and his whole smooth face.

I was thirty-nine. At thirty-nine you're in your thirties; at forty, or so I thought then, you're in the shadow of middle age. It was as if he had whispered, "Brace yourself, Flowers. I've had my eye on you for a long time . . ." I was excited. The Chinese life in Singapore was mainly noodles and children in a single room, the noise of washing and hoicking.

It could not have been duller, but because it was dull the Chinese had a gift for creating special occasions, a night out, a large banquet or festive gathering which sustained them through a year of yellow noodles. Hing communicated this festive singularity to me; I believed my magic had worked, my luck had changed with my age; not fortune, but the promise of it was spoken. I saw myself speeding forward in a wind like silk.

Three weeks later, I walked into Hing's shop. He shook my hand, offered the can of cigarettes, and began clacking his lighter, saying, "Yes, Jack, yes."

Little Hing came over and asked for the shopping list, the manifests and indents.

"No list," I said, and grinned. "No ship, no list!" I had turned away to explain. "From now on I'm working for the *towkay*."

Behind me, Big Hing was screwing the lid back on to the can of cigarettes, and that was the only sound; the tin lid caught and clicked and rasped in the metal grooves, and was finally silent.

Big Hing was grave, reflectively biting his upper lip with his lower teeth. He banged the cigarette tin onto the trestle table, making the beads on the abacus spin and tick. He became brisk. He led me to my cubicle, two beaverboard partitions, without a ceiling, narrow as a urinal, and he shot the curtain along its rod, jangling the chrome hoops. I climbed onto the stool and put my head down. I did not turn around. I knew the *Allegro* had sailed without me.

3

THE SECOND TIME I met Hing, when I was still buying for the *Allegro* and thought of him as a friend, he took me to an opium parlor, a tiny smoke-smeared attic room off North Bridge Road. It was one of the stories I told later in hotel bars to loosen up nervous fellers whom I had spotted as possible clients. I had expected the opium parlor to be something like a wang house filled with sleepy hookers relaxing on cushions; I was not prepared for the ghostly sight of five elderly addicts, dozing hollow-eyed in droopy wrinkled pajamas, and two equally decrepit "cooks" scraping dottle out of black pipes. The room was dark; a single shutter, half-open, gave the only light; the ceiling panels seemed kept in place by the cobwebs that were woven over the cracks between the panels and the beams they dangled from. The walls were marked with the cats' paws of Chinese characters. There were some scarred wooden furniture, broken crates and stools, and low cots and string beds with soiled pillows where the derelict men slept with their mouths open. A very old woman in wide silk trousers and red clogs drank coffee out of a condensed milk tin and watched me. It was an atmosphere only an opium trance could improve. I anxiously sucked one pipeful; none of the skinny dreamers acknowledged me, and we left. In front of the opium parlor, where Hing's Riley sat, a parking attendant, a round-faced girl in a straw hat and gray jacket, was writing out a ticket. Hing saw the joke immediately, and we both laughed: the parking ticket at the opium den. I embellished it as a story by increasing the overtime parking fine and glamorizing the dingy room, giving it silk pillows and the addicts youth.

The opium parlor was Hing's idea. He had convinced me that I could ask anything of him; he said, "Singapore have everything," and he wanted a chance to prove it. Faced by variety, my imagination was confounded; I chose simple pleasures, outings, walks, the Police Band concerts at the Botanical Gardens, fishing from the pier. Hing made suggestions. He introduced me to Madam Lum and her chief attraction, Mona, a girl with the oddest tastes, whom I used to describe truthfully to fellers, saying, "She's not fooling — she really likes her work, and everyone comes back singing her praises!" Hing took me to the "Screw Inn," a little bungalow of teen-age girls off Mountbatten Road, and he taught me that yellow-roofed taxis were the tip-off: more than two parked together in a residential area indicated a brothel close by. At Hing's urging I had my first taste of the good life: a morning shave, flat on my back at the Indian barbershop on Orchard Road (Chinese barbers used dull razors — the sparse Chinese beard was easy to scrape off) ; a heavy lunch at the Great Shanghai, followed by a nap and a massage by a naked Chinese girl who sat astride me and kneaded my back and who afterward invited another girl into the room so that the three of us could fool for the whole afternoon. After tea, both girls gave me a bath and we went for a stroll; I walked them to a bar, had a last drink, then early to bed with a novel — the sequence of a lovely exhausting day, which gave me a stomach full of honey and the feeling that the skin

I wore was brand new. Hing paid the bills. He had few pleasures himself, and he wasn't a drinker. What he liked were big Australian girls in nightclubs who stripped to the buff and then got down on all fours and shook and howled like cats. He understood food; he taught me the fine points of ordering Szechwan meals, the fried eels in sauce, the hot-sour soup, poached sea slugs, steamed pomfret, and crisp duck skin that was eaten in a soft bun. He gave me bottles of gin-seng wine, which he claimed was an aphrodisiac tonic, and on the appropriate festival, a whole moon cake wrapped in red paper. He said he was glad I wasn't British, and why wasn't I married, and how did I like Singapore?

All this time I was his customer; the ritual friendship ended when I became his employee, and at 600 Straits dollars a month I was treated as a difficult burden, crowding his shop with my bulk, wasting his time, eating his money. He stopped speaking to me directly, and if the two of us were in the shop alone he assumed a preoccupied busy air, rattling scraps of paper, pretending to look for things, banging doors, groaning, saying his commercial rosary on his abacus. He spoke to me through his dog; my mistakes and lapses got the dog a kick in the ribs. I thought I might be promoted, but I learned very early that no promotion would come my way. The job interested me enough so that I could do it without any encouragement from Hing. For Hing to thank me, something he never did, would have been an admission on his part of dependency, a loss of face: civility was a form of weakness for him. I understood this and took his rudeness to be the gratitude it was. We had no contract; after our verbal agreement Hing arranged a visa for me which allowed me to stay in Singapore as long as I worked for him. This was convenient (the bribe came out of his pocket), but limiting: if he fired me the visa would be canceled and I would be deported. He needed me too much to fire me, but I knew that to remind him of this would be to ask for a sacking, for that was the only way he could demonstrate I wasn't needed.

But I was. A year on the *Allegro* and all the calls we had made at Singapore had acquainted me with most of the other vessels and skippers who called regularly, and I knew many of the fellers in the Maritime Building who managed the shipping lines. The advantage I had, which Hing had hinted at, only dawned on me later: I was white. The rest of the ship chandlers in Singapore were either Indian or Chinese. As a paleface in the late fifties in Singapore I drank in clubs and bars where "Asians," as they were called, were not allowed. Largely, I drank in these places because I was not welcome in the Chinese clubs, and I didn't like the toddy in the Indian ones. It offended me that I was forced to drink with my own race — later, I would not do otherwise: I couldn't relax with fellers of other races — but in the end, this simple fact of racial exclusiveness landed Hing with many contracts for supplying European ships. I was learning the ropes: Chinese and Indians transacted all their business in offices, Europeans did it in clubs and used their offices as phone booths.

A club, even a so-called exclusive one, was easy to enter but hard to join. The doormen were Malays or Sikhs, and I had learned how to say "How's every little thing, brother?" in Malay and Punjabi. In any case, they would not have dared to turn an *ang moh* away; and as for signing the drink chits, I had a number of match tricks and brain twisters that I'd spring on anyone drinking alone. The loser had to sign for the drink. I never lost.

"Just in from Bangkok," I'd say. "Feller up there showed me a cute gimmick. You've probably seen it. No? Well, you put six matches down like this, make a little sort of circle with them. There. Now — I wonder if I've got that right? I'm a real jerk when it comes to these tricky things. What you're supposed to do is rearrange five matches without disturbing — "

After I explained, I'd say, "Loser signs, okay?" and the drink would be as good as mine. That was a British con.

Americans were easier. "Bet you can't name the twelve apostles," or "Whose picture's on the hundred?" or "What's the capital of Maine?" secured my drinks with Americans, and with a drink in my hand I could stay in a club bar for hours, making up stories, chatting, or telling jokes that appealed to the listener's prejudices by confirming them. There were not many Chinese jokes, apart from the funny names, of which I had a long list, culled from the Singapore telephone directory ("Pass me the phone book, Ali; my friend here doesn't believe Fook Yew and Wun Fatt Joo really live in Singapore"). There were many good Indian jokes, and these always went down well. I told Englishmen the joke about the Texan who's accused of sodomizing animals. "Cows, pigs, mules," says his accuser, a girl he wants to take home. She goes on, "Sheep, dogs, cats, chickens — " The Texan interrupts in annoyance: "What do you mean, *chickens?*"

Americans were always bowled over by the story of the Englishman whose pecker is accidentally cut off. After a painful month he finally decides to see a doctor, who says he knows how to sew the thing back on. "Just hand it over and I'll see to it straightway." The Englishman slaps his pockets, says, "I've got the damned thing here somewhere," and gives the doctor a huge cigar. "This is a cigar," says the perplexed doctor, and "My word," says the Englishman, "I must have smoked my cock!"

Sometimes I clowned around, like making a great show of ordering cherries in brandy, simply to say, "To tell the truth, I hate these cherries, but I like the spirit in which they're given!" So, even without the match tricks and brain twisters, someone was always buying me a drink and saying, "You're a card." And in clubs where I was not a member, fellers said, "We haven't seen you lately — missed you at the film show," and "Don't forget the A.G.M. next week, about time we tackled that gatecrashers' clause"; eventually, a feller would ask, "Say, Jack, what's your line of work?"

"Me? I'm in ship chandling." I never said I was a water clerk.

"Odd, that," would be the reply.

"I know exactly what you mean," I'd say. "But the way I figure it, this business could use a little streamlining. Methods haven't changed since Raffles's time, and by God neither have some of the groceries they're flogging, from the taste of them! Shops haven't been swept in years, bread's as hard as old Harry, weevils in the rice — mind you, I've got nothing against our Asiatic brothers. It's just as you say, they work like dogs. On the other hand, your Indian is never really happy handling meat — but you can't hold their religion against them, can you?"

"One can't, I suppose. But still — "

"And your Chinese ship chandler — he'll give you a turd and tell you it's an orchid. Shall I tell you what I saw one day in a Chinese shop? This'll kill you — "

The feller would be agreeing with me and putting his oar in from time to time. I'd tell my valve story and he'd cap it with a better and terrifying one about defective life jackets or wormy provisions, all the while working up the indignation to change ship chandlers.

My most effective selling ploy, which I used just before mealtimes, when conversations always got around to food, was my English breakfast. This never failed. The English, I had discovered, had a weakness for large breakfasts; it might have had a literary source — a Dickens character having a beefsteak with his tea — or a tradition begun on those cold mornings when the Thames used to freeze over, or war rationing. Whatever the reason, it was an inspired way of getting a contract.

I hit on this a few months after I began ship chandling in Singapore, with a feller from the Victoria Shipping Lines. It was on the verandah of the Singapore Cricket Club, on a Saturday just before tiffin. The feller was sitting beside me

99

in a wicker chair and we were watching some ladies bowling on the grass. This form of bowling was exactly like the Italian game *bocce*, which my father played in an alley in the North End every Sunday afternoon. It was the only game I knew well, and I was commenting on the ladies' match to the feller on my right. "Gotta have more left-hand side . . . Not enough legs on that one . . . Kissed it . . . Never make it . . . She's out for blood — it's going like a demon — " The ladies took a rest. I turned to the feller and said, "Seems there was this Texan — "

"Very amusing," he said, when I finished, his understatement contradicting the honking laughter he couldn't suppress. "Have a drink?"

"*Thank* you."

"Actually, I'm hungry," he said. "No time for breakfast this morning. Ruins the day, don't you find?"

"Absolutely," I said. "That's what I try to tell these skippers I deal with. Give a seaman a slap-up breakfast and he'll do a fair day's work. Cut down on his lunch, but don't ever tamper with that breakfast of his!"

"My idea of a really topnotch breakfast is kippers, porridge oats, eggs, and a pot of tea — hot and strong." He smacked his lips.

"You're forgetting your fruit juice — juices are *very* important. And choice of cereals, some bubble and squeak, huge rashers of bacon, or maybe a beefsteak and chips, stack of toast, hot crumpets, marmalade. Boy!" The feller was nodding in agreement and swallowing. "It's a funny thing, you know," I went on. "These ship chandlers don't supply fresh juice — oh, no! Course the fresh is cheaper and the fruit grows locally. They give you this tinned stuff."

"You can taste the metal."

"Sure you can!"

"Potatoes make a nice breakfast," he said, still swallowing.

"Hashbrowns — fry 'em up crisp and hot and serve them with gouts of H. P. Sauce."

"I'm famished," he said, and looked at his watch.

"Me too," I said. "I wouldn't mind a big English breakfast right this minute. I envy the seamen on some of the ships I supply."

"All the same," he said, "it sounds an expensive meal."

"Not on your nelly," I said, and quoted some prices, adding, "I buy in bulk, see, so I can pass the savings on to the customer. I still make a profit — everyone gains."

"It sounds frightfully reasonable."

"And that's not all — "

Our drinks arrived, and the ladies resumed their bowling. The feller said, "I'm just the teeniest bit browned-off with my own chandler. What did you say was the name of your firm?"

I explained Hing's name on my card by saying he was a partner who came in handy when we were dealing with Chinese accounts — I'd known him for years. "Like I say, we're an unusual firm." I winked. "Think about it. We'll see your men get a good breakfast. Oh, and if there's anything *else* you require — *anything at all* — just give me a tinkle and I'll see what I can scare up. Cheers."

He rang the next day. He offered me a chandling contract for three freighters, a couple of tankers, and two steamships of modest tonnage that did the Singapore–North Borneo run. At the end of the conversation he hesitated briefly and murmured, "Yesterday, um, you said *anything*, didn't you?"

"You bet your boots I did."

"Um, I was wondering if you could help me out with something that's just cropped up this morning. One of our freighters is in from Madras. Crew's feeling a bit Bolshie about going off tomorrow to the Indonesian ports. We'd like to cheer them up a bit, um, give them a bit of fun without letting them ashore. Are you in the picture?"

"Leave it to me," I said. "How many guys are you trying to . . . amuse?"

101

"Well, it's the *Richard Everett*. She's got, say, twenty-three able seamen, and — "

"You've come to the right man," I said. "How about a coffee? I'll explain then."

"*Lunch*," he insisted, pleased. "At the club. And thanks, thanks awfully."

4

AT THAT PERIOD in my life, my first years in Singapore, I enjoyed a rare kind of happiness, like the accidental discovery of renewal, singing in my heart and feet, that comes with infatuation. It was true power: mercy and boldness. I felt brave. I didn't belittle it or try to justify it, and I never wondered about its queer origin. I was converted to buoyancy, and rising understood survival: the surprise of the marooned man who has built his first fire. I had turned forty without pain, and until Desmond Frogget came I was the youngest drinker in the Bandung.

The Bandung was a lively place: freshly painted, always full, with free meat pies on Saturdays and curry tiffin on Sundays, and a Ping-Pong table which we hauled out to work up a thirst. A stubby feller named Ogham used to play the piano in the lounge, jazzy tunes until midnight and finishing up with vulgar and patriotic songs. I can see it now on a Saturday night, the room lit by paper lanterns rocked by the fans, Wally in a short white jacket and black tie shaking a gin sling, the main bar heaving with drinkers, all of them regulars, and me in my white cotton suit and white shoes, wearing the flowered open-neck shirt that was my trademark, and Ogham in the lounge playing "Twelfth Street Rag." Some feller would lean over and say to me, "Oggie could have been a professional, you know, but like he says, that's no life for a man with a family."

Ogham pounded the piano at the Bandung and never introduced us to his family, and after he left Singapore there were various explanations of where he had gone. Some said to a London bank, but Yardley sneered, "He was a lush. He got the sack and three months' *gadji* and now he's in Surrey, mending bicycles." For Yardley no fate was worse. With Ogham gone I hacked around sometimes with the *Warsaw Concerto,* hitting a sour note at the end of an expertly played passage to be funny, but some fellers said I was being disrespectful to Ogham and I had to stop. Later, an old-timer wandering back through the lounge from the toilet in the kitchen would glance at the piano and say, "Remember Oggie? I wonder what happened to him. Christ, he could have turned professional."

"Oggie didn't know whether his arsehole was bored or punched," Yardley would reply, believing Ogham to be a deserter. "He got the sack and three months' *gadji* and now he's in — "

The day Ogham left he got very nostalgic about a particular towpath he had played on as a child; he bought us all a drink and reminisced. I had never seen him so happy. We listened at the bar as he took a box of matches and said, "The gasworks was over here," and put a match down, "and the canal ran along what we used to call the cut — here. And — " The scene was repeated with the others, the memory of a picnic or tram ride re-enacted at the bar before their ships sailed.

Many of the regulars at the Bandung started to leave. It was getting near to Independence, and over a drink, when a feller said he was going home you knew he meant England

and not his house in Bukit Timah. So the Bandung emptied. On a side road at the city limit, it was too far off the beaten track for the average tourist to find it, and what tourists there were in those days came by ship. I spent most of my free time hustling in bars in the harbor area, places a tourist with a few hours ashore might wander into, or in the cut-price curio shops in Raffles Place. I had earned enough money in my first year to be considered a big spender in the Bandung, and to rent a large yellow house on River Valley Road, with three bedrooms and a verandah supported by solid white pillars, shaded by chicks the size of sails on a Chinese junk. As a bachelor I lived in one room and allowed the other rooms to fall into disuse. I had two gray parrots who pecked the spines off all my books, a dozen cats, and an old underemployed *amah* who played noisy games of mahjong with her friends in the kitchen, often waking me at three in the morning as they shuffled the mahjong tiles, a process they called "washing the tiles." The *amah* had made the bed and fixed breakfast enough times to know that I was not practicing celibacy, and she was continually saying that as a "black and white" she was trained to care for children, a hint that I should get married. She sized up the girls I took home and always said, "Too skinny! You not like hayvie! Yek-yek!"

I believed that I would marry a tall young Chinese girl, with a boy's hips and long crow-black hair and a shining face; and I'd take her away, the hopeful mutual rescue that was the aim of every white bachelor then in the East. I did not give up the idea until later, when I saw one of these marriages, the radiant Chinese girl, shyly secretive, easily embarrassed, transformed into a crass suburban wife, nagging through her nose about prices in a monotonous voice, with thick unadventurous thighs, a complaining face, and at her most boring and suburban, saying to exhausted listeners in perfect English, "Well, we Chinese — " I had the idea of marriage; as long as I postponed the action, romance was

105

possible for me, and I was happy. Any day, I expected to get the letter beginning, *"Dear Mr. Flowers, It gives me great pleasure to be writing to you today, and I know my news will please you —"* Or perhaps the other one, starting, *"My darling —"*

My brief, unrewarding enterprises, evenings calling out "Hey bud" to startled residents walking their dogs, afternoons sailing two fruit flies dressed as scrubwomen (greasy overalls covering silk cheongsams) to rusty freighters — these were over. The *Richard Everett* episode and the notoriety that followed it singled me out. Fellers rang me up at all hours of the night, asking me to get them a girl, and one of my replies — delivered at four in the morning to an importuning caller who said he hoped he hadn't got me out of bed — became famous: "No," I had said, "I was up combing my hair." In the harbor bars I was "Jack" to everyone, and I knew every confiding barman by name. What pleasure it gave me, knocking off early at Hing's, to go home and put on my white shoes and a clean flowered shirt and then to make my rounds in a trishaw, a freshly lit cheroot in my teeth, dropping in on the girls, in bars or massage parlors, to see how many I could count on for the evening. The wiry trishaw driver pumped away; I sat comfortably in the seat with my feet up as we wound through the traffic. The sun at five o'clock was dazzling, but the bars I entered were dark and cool as caves. I would stick my head in and say in a jaunty greeting to the darkness, "Hi girls!"

"*Jaaaack!*" They would materialize out of booths, hobble over to me on high heels, and favoring their clawlike fingernails, hug my big belly and give me genial tickling pinches in the crotch. "Come, Jack, I give you good time." "Me, Jack, you like?" "Touch me, baby."

"You're all flawless," I'd say, and play a hand of cards, buy them all a drink, and move on to a new bar. Many of the girls were independent, not paying any secret society protection money. I called them "floaters" because when they weren't floating around looking for a pickup I was literally floating them by the dozen out to ships in the harbor. A great number of them who hung around the bars on Anson Road — The Gold Anchor, Big South Sea, Captain's Table, Champagne Club, Chang's — came to depend on me for customers. They were using me in the same way as Hing, to get Europeans, who didn't haggle and who would pay a few dollars more. The Chinese were after the *ang moh* trade, and it seemed as if I was the only supplier. I could get white tourists and sailors for the girls as easily as I got the club members who were in the shipping business for Hing. The floaters along Anson Road and the Hing brothers were not the only ones who depended on me; the British servicemen at Changi, the sailors from H.M.S. *Terror*, the club members and tourists depended on me as well: the Chinese who sought the *ang mohs* were in turn being sought by the *ang mohs*, and both, ignorant of the others' hunting, came to me for introductions — finding me they found each other.

But the girls in the wharf-area bars forfeited all their Chinese trade when they were seen holding hands with a paleface. After that, they were tainted, and no Chinese would touch them or notice them except to bark a singular Cantonese or Hokkien obscenity, usually an exaggeration of my virility ("So the redhead's got a big doo-dah!"), meant as a slur on the girls for being lustful, and on me for a deformity not in the least resembling the little dark bathplug most Chinese consider the size of the normal male organ.

I was resented by most of the Chinese men in the bars; they accused me, in the oblique way Hing had, of spoiling the girls. The occupation of a prostitute they saw as a customary traditional role, an essential skill. But pairing up with red-haired devils made the girls vicious — it was an abnormality, something perverse, and the Chinese men considered these girls of mine as little better than the demon-

107

women in folk stories who coupled with dogs and bore hairy babies. And that was not all. The men also had that little-country grievance, a point of view Yardley and the old-timers shared, about rich foreigners butting in and sending the prices up. Neither accusation was justified: the girls (who nearly always hated the men they slept with) were improved by their contact with Europeans, quiet undemanding men, unlike their sadistic woman-hating counterparts in the States. The men were instructive, curious, and kind, and wanted little more than to sail home and boast that they had spent the night with a Chinese whore in Singapore. And as for the prices going up — after a decade of inflation, when the price of a haircut doubled, cigarettes increased five times, and some house rents — my own, for example — went up by 200 per cent, the price of a short time with massage stayed the same, and an all-nighter cost only an extra three-fifty. Until Japanese cameras flooded the market, a night in bed with one of my girls was the only bargain a feller could find in Singapore.

The Chinese men would not listen to reason. *"Boochakong just now cost twenty-over dollar-lah,"* they complained. I felt loathed and large. Some simply didn't like my face or the fact that I was so pally with Chinese girls. I have already mentioned the secret-society member, the Three Dot in the Tai-Hwa who asked me threateningly, "Where you does wuck?" Another brute, late one night, took a swing at me in the parking lot of the Prince's Hotel. He came at me from behind as I was unlocking my car — Providence made him stumble; and later the Prince's manager, who to a Chinese eye might have looked like me — they can't tell *ang mohs* apart, they say, and don't find it funny — was found in a back alley with his throat cut and his flowered shirt smeared with blood. Karim, the barman, said his eyes had been ritually gouged. I had to choose my bars carefully, and I made sure my trishaw driver was a big feller.

Still, I was making money, and it delighted me on sunny

108

afternoons to have a cold shower, then make my rounds in a well-upholstered trishaw, chirping into dark interiors, "Hi girls!" and to say to a stranger in a confident whisper, "If there's anything you want — *anything at all* — " and be perfectly certain I could supply whatever he named.

Being American was part of my uniqueness. There were few Americans in Singapore, and though it was the last thing I wanted to be — after all, I had left the place for a good reason — the glad-hander, the ham with the loud jokes and big feet and flashy shirts, saying "It figures" and "Come off it" and "Who's your friend?" and "This I gotta see," it was the only role open to me because it was the only one the people I dealt with accepted. It alerted them when I behaved untypically; it looked as though I was concealing something and intended to defraud them by playing down the Yankee. In such a small place, an island with no natives, everyone a visitor, the foreigner made himself a resident by emphasizing his foreignness. Yardley, who was from Leeds, but had been in Singapore since the war — he married one of these sleek Chinese girls who turned into a suburban dragon named Mildred — had softened his Leeds accent by listening to the BBC Overseas Service. He put burnt matches back into the box (muttering, "These are threppence in U.K.") and cigarette ash in his trouser cuffs and poured milk in his cup before the tea. The one time I made a reference to the photograph in the Bandung of the Queen and Duke ("Liz and Phil, I know them well — nice to see them around, broo-reh-ah!"), Yardley called Eisenhower — President at the time — "A bald fucker, a stupid general, and half the time he doesn't know whether he wants a shit or a haircut." Consequently, but against my will, I was made an American, or rather "The Yank." When America was mentioned, fellers said, "Ask Jack." I exaggerated my accent and dropped my *Allegro* pretense of being Italian. I tried to give the impression of a cheerful rascal, someone gently ignorant; I claimed

109

I had no education and said, "If you say so" or "That's really interesting" to anything remotely intelligent.

It was awfully hard for me to be an American, but the hardest part was playing the dumb cluck for a feller whose intelligence was inferior to mine. The fellers at the Bandung reckoned they had great natural gifts; Yates, in his own phrase "an avaricious reader," would say, "I'm reading Conrad" when he was stuck in the first chapter of a book he'd never finish; Yardley pointed to me one night and said, "I wouldn't touch an American book with a barge pole," and Smale ended every argument with, "It all comes down to the same thing, then, don't it?" to which someone would add, "Right. Six of one and half a dozen of the other." They were always arguing, each argument illustrated by anecdotes from personal experience. That was the problem: they saved up stories to tell people back home; then, realizing with alarm that they probably weren't going home, wondered who to tell. They told each other. Stories were endlessly repeated, and not even the emphasis or phrases varied. The silent fellers in the Bandung were not listening; they were waiting for a chance to talk.

I was the only genuine listener — the inexperienced American, there to be instructed. But the funny thing was, I had a college education and almost a degree. It was no help in the Bandung to say a bright truth, for even if someone heard it he was incapable of verifying it. And on the job it created misunderstandings. I recall meeting an Irish seaman on one of my "meat runs," as my ferrying of girls into the harbor was called. Hearing his brogue I said, "I'm crazy about Joyce," and he replied, "That skinny one in the yellow dress?" I said, "You guessed it!" and he went over and pinched her sorry bottom through a fold in her frock. Later he thanked me for the tip-off. He was right and I was wrong: education is inappropriate to most jobs, and it was practically an impertinence to the enterprises of the feller whom an Indian ship chandler on Market Street described as "having a finger in every tart."

It was on the GI Bill; I was thirty-five, a freshman. I always seemed to be the wrong age for whatever I was doing, and because of that, paying dearly for it. But I was not alone. Older students were a common sight in every university in the late forties and fifties, army veterans from the Second World War and then Korea, wearing faded khaki jackets with the chevrons torn off, the stitch marks showing, and shoes with highly polished toes. My inglorious war — a punctured eardrum put me behind a desk in Oklahoma — ended in 1945. I came home expecting a miracle letter (*Dear Jack, It's good to hear you're home and I have some fabulous news for you . . .*), but nothing happened. I helped my father in the tailor shop, blocking hats and putting tickets on the dry cleaning, and sometimes doing deliveries. My uncle said, "There's good money in printing," so I joined a linotype school, which I quit soon after. "They're crying out for draftsmen" and "A good short-order cook can name his salary" sent me in other directions.

I was reading a great deal — the serious paperback was having its vogue in the early fifties (they were thought to be somewhat salacious: "He's just reading a paperback" was considered mockery) — and I was encouraged by the biographical notes, less frequent today, which listed the previous occupations of the author on the back cover. "Jim Sidebottom has had a varied career," they'd begin, and go on to list twenty back-breaking jobs. I imagined my own biographical note: "After his discharge from the U.S. Army, where he reached the rank of corporal, John ("Jack") Fiori worked as a hat blocker in his father's tailor shop, and then in succession as a printer, draftsman, short-order cook, bartender, dishwasher, lifeguard, baker, and fruit seller. He has always considered fiction to be his chief aim, and has this to say about

111

the present novel: 'I believe that mankind struggled from the sea to — ' " It was a good biographical note, enhanced by an imagined photograph of me smoking a cigarette over a typewriter. I smoked. I bought a typewriter and learned to use it. I typed my biographical note. But that was all: there was no book. I had nothing to write. I knew nothing beyond my name and the face I practiced. I didn't understand danger or regret; a book was an extensive biographical note.

Twenty years later William Leigh turned up and asked me urgent questions, and died with a foolish sentence on his lips before I could reply; and I burned him to dust. So this memoir was provoked. Writing a book is a splendid idea, but it was not mine. My notion was simpler, just a picture of my experienced face and the list of jobs that made the face that way. This memoir is not the book or the work I imagined; it was urged upon me, like a complicated, necessary enchantment I did little to inspire, made mostly of terror, which forced me to learn, laboriously, to conjure: an imprecise trick, half accident, half design, begun as a deliberate memory ("Mister Hing vaunting Mister Jack . . .") and completed by the kind of magic that to discover thoroughly is to fail at.

I thought I could learn at college. It was my only reason for going. I found myself among a few earnest veterans and many fresh-faced kids. The older fellers never flunked out, but at the same time never excelled, resenting being lectured to and corrected by educated fellers the same age or younger, draft dodgers or fairies with leather elbow patches, whom they could only nag with the reply, "I'll bet you don't even know how to clean a gun!" The ones on the GI Bill lived with their harassed wives and children in gray Nissen huts, referred to as "married quarters." Most of the older fellers were economics majors or engineers (the pocketful of pens, the slide rule in a scabbard) and had too much homework on their hands to take an interest in the college routine. Besides, they had problems at home, and so they treated their education as a job, being punctual and tidy, carrying creased lunch bags, and keeping regular hours. I saw them in the student union salting a hard-boiled egg and underlining a physics book.

Some, of whom I was one because I was unmarried and majoring in English, were accommodated by the fringe people, the art majors, would-be poets, weekend winos, hangers-on, and hitchhikers. That was the enterprise then, saying, "Aw shit, I gotta bust out" and hitchhiking in sweat shirts across the country, aiming for California or Mexico, and staying drunk the whole way by gagging down whole bottles of Tokay or Muscatel. These fellers would show up with stories of their travels ("I met this beautiful sad old man in Denver, and he says to me . . .") and some poems about America which they'd shout, taking swigs out of a can of beer. The writers they respected had all been deck hands on freighters, and going to sea was the height of their ambition. Some hung around the Seafarers' International Union in Brooklyn, hoping for a job, but few of them succeeded — they were too young and not strong enough for the work. They talked about Zen Buddhism, Ezra Pound, the atom bomb, mystical experiences. There was a little marijuana around, but the big kicks were in drinking three bottles of terpin hydrate cough syrup or washing down a can of nutmeg with a glass of milk. Or getting drunk like Dylan Thomas; or trying to grow a beard.

It was my beard that gained me entry. I had stopped shaving when I worked the night shift at the bakery and still had it the day I shambled in to register for classes. It was bright red, cut square across the bottom. They complimented me on it and I explained its redness by saying that Vivaldi's hair was the same color.

I suppose I should have kept to myself, but I had been doing that joylessly for ten years, and I liked the company, the spirit of careless romance in the younger kids. People called them "beatniks," already a dated word then, but they thought of themselves as "the folk." I moved into the top floor of a coffee shop, and generally I stuck close to them, proving my friendship the only way I knew, buying beer for them, lending them money, trying to set them straight on Ezra Pound, who was a fake poet but a genuine fascist; and I kept my hot eyes on the long-haired girls who strummed guitars and wrote poems in black sweaters and dancers' tights. I wrote poems, too, unfashionable rhyming ones:

> Is that the wind? I asked my friend,
> That shakes the trees and makes them bend?

In a group of six or seven grim-looking undergraduates I was the big bearded one in army fatigues, older than the others and trying to look inconspicuous; and more than likely there would be a small pale girl next to me, who couldn't stand her parents. "When you were my age," she would say, and go on cracking my heart, bending my ear.

It did not last long. My reading only trained me to read better. What I wrote sounded like what I read: "A cold dark November in my soul," I'd write, and then furiously cross it out, or again and again, "I was born in the year 1918, in the North End of the city of Boston, the second child of two transplanted Italians — " Then half a chapter about childhood fears — not the informed apprehension of the adult, but the impatient uncertainty of the little boy who was always made to wait, who thought he might die in his bed if the lamp was switched off and whose pleasures were his thumb, and the minutes after confession and the time spent in a slate urinal, pissing with one hand and eating an ice-cream sandwich with the other. To sit down and write *Chapter One — Childhood* was to begin a book rather than a story, a bold guarantee against ever finishing it. My character's name was Jack Flowers, not John Fiori. A first-love

114

chapter and an army chapter loomed, and Jack was going to discover the simplicity of love and the surprise of wealth. If the book succeeded I would write another about success; if it failed, about failure. The fellers in the coffee shop asked me what my book was about. I said, "It's about this guy who's trying to write a book — "

Writing bored me, and it sickened me in my attic to be staring at a white sheet of paper ("Chapter One") while the sun was shining outside and everyone else was at play, for every word I wrote seemed a denial of the complex uniqueness I could see just outside the window. My descriptions reduced what lacy trees and grass I could see to sorry props on the page, and my characters were either brutes or angels, too extreme and simple to be human. Still, fiction seemed to give me the second chances life denied me.

But there were other difficulties. In my short time as a student the artistic fringe people switched from getting drunk to getting high. I could cope with alcohol, but drugs baffled me, and I didn't even know that the pills I was taking to get my weight down, little heart-shaped orange tablets, were a kind of pep pill.

"John," a girl said, seeing me swallow one, "what's that?"

I was too embarrassed to explain that they had been prescribed to reduce my waistline. They killed my appetite: skinny fellers had more girl friends. I said, "It's just a tablet. I don't even know the name — "

"Dexedrine," she said. "Fantastic."

"You want one? Here, take a dozen."

"Cool." She swallowed three.

"You won't want any lunch," I said.

"Crazy." She shuddered.

That amused me. Handing out these reducing tablets won me the girl friends I had hoped to get by being thin. Briefly, I was happy. But happiness is a blurred memory of sensational lightness; fear and boredom leave me with a remembrance of particular details. I recall the discomfort: squatting or sitting cross-legged on the floor, listening to long poems by nineteen-year-olds beginning, *I have seen . . .* — getting cramps behind my knees, my back aching — *And I have seen . . .* I made myself sick on that sweet wine ("Look out, John's barfing!") and they talked about Zen, rejection slips from quarterlies with names like *The Goatsfoot,* ban-the-bomb, Ezra P. I would be dying for a hot bath. I admired their resilience; they could stay up all night gabbing, eating nothing but Dexedrines and cough syrup; I'd say, "Hell, I hate to be a party-pooper, but — " and crawl off to bed, hearing *And I have seen* — all the way to my room. The next morning I'd see them stretched out on the floor, paired up but still chastely in their clothes, and all of them sleeping in their shoes.

They invented a past for me. I deserved it; I had not told them a thing about myself. They intended flattery, but the stories were truly monstrous: "You've got a wife and kids somewhere, haven't you?" a girl whispered to me in my attic, candid in the dark after love. Another, rolling over, said, "Do anything you want to me — I know you're a switch hitter." I was a genius; I was a deserter; I was shell-shocked; I was a refugee; I sometimes took a knife to bed; the Germans tortured me. The stories were too ridiculous to deny, the truth too boring to repeat. I had grown to like the kids; I did not want to disappoint them. I used to make the eyes of those lovely girls bright by saying, "If I laid you once I'd turn you into a whore."

It ended badly. The coffee shop was in a residential area, and the late nights the kids spent discussing music and poetry were interpreted by the neighbors as sex orgies. We got strange phone calls, and visits at odd hours from well-dressed men. The police raided us. I say "raided." Two cops opened the door and said, "We've had a complaint about you."

"Let's see your search warrant," I said. It seemed a good gambit, but they weren't buying it.

"Out of the way, fatso," they said, pushing past me. They went upstairs, rousing people and saying, "Nothing here," and "Okay in here." Soon they were back in the hall, surrounded by angry poets and pretty girls.

One cop showed me his white glove. The palm was filled with Dexedrines. "Whose are these?"

They weren't mine. I had stopped taking them, though I still passed them around. I said, "Mine."

"No, they're not," said a girl named Rita. "Those are mine."

"They're his," said the cop, "so shut up."

"Anyway, what's the problem?" I said. "I take these things to kill my appetite. I got a weight problem."

"You got a problem, fella," the cop said, "but it ain't no weight problem. Better come along with us."

Rita screamed at him.

In the squad car the cop driving said, "We know all about you and those kids. You should be ashamed of yourself."

I was charged with possessing drugs without a prescription, procuring drugs for a minor, and on hearsay, on charges of fornication, bigamy, homosexuality, and petty theft. My trial would be in three weeks. Bail was steep, but the coffee shop fellers and some sympathetic faculty members started a fund and bailed me out; they told me I was being victimized.

Jumping bail was easy; the only loss was the money. I took a Greyhound bus to Los Angeles, and leaving everything including my name, flew to Hong Kong and signed on the *Allegro*. It was not despair; it was the convenience of flight, an expensive exit that was possible because it was final. I had no intention of going back. It would have been bad for my heart, and I'm using that word in its older sense.

117

And: "Flowers," said the skipper of the *Allegro*, reading my name from the crew list. He made a mark on the paper. "Age — thirty-eight. Single. No identifying marks or scars." He looked up. "Your first contract, I see. Know anything about oiling?"

"No," I said, "but I don't think it would take me long to learn."

"What *can* you do?"

"Anything," I said. "I suppose you've heard this one before, but what I really wanted to do was write."

"Take that pencil," the skipper said.

"This one?" I selected one from a pewter mug on his desk.

"And that pad of paper."

The letterhead said, *Four Star Shipping Lines.*

"Write," he said.

"Shoot," I said.

"Carrots, eighty pounds," he said. "White flour, two hundred pounds. Fresh eggs — "

5

A YEAR LATER, nimble in my soft white shoes, I was guiding a deeply tanned cruise passenger in his club blazer through the low sidewalk corridors of Singapore back lanes. It was night, dark and smelly in the tunnel-like passageways, and quiet except for the occasional snap of mahjong tiles and the rattling of abacus beads — no voices — coming from the bright cracks in burglar doors on shophouse fronts. Some shops, caged by protective steel grates, showed Chinese families sitting at empty tables under glaring bulbs and the gazes from the walls of old relations with small shoulders and lumpy heads in blurred brown photograph ovals — the lighted barred room like an American museum-case tableau of life-size wax figures depicting Chinese at night, the seated mother and father, ancestral relics, and three children's little heads in a coconut row at the far edge of the table. Sikh watchmen huddled, hugging themselves in bloomers and undershirts on string beds outside dark shops; we squeezed past them and past the unsleeping Tamil news vendors playing poker in lotus postures next to their shuttered goods cupboards. Here was a Chinese man in his pajamas, crouching on a stool, smoking, clearing his throat, watching the cars pass. Farther along, four children were playing tag, chasing each other and shrieking in the dark; and under a street-corner lamp, a lone child tugged at an odd flying toy, a live beetle, captive on a yard of thread — he flung it at us as we passed and then pulled it away, laughing in a shy little snort.

"Atmosphere," murmured the feller.

"You said it." There was a quicker way to Muscat Lane, but that took you over uncovered sidewalks, past new shops, on a well-lighted street. The atmosphere was an easy detour.

"It's like something out of a myth."

"Too bad the shops are closed," I said. "One down this way has bottles filled with dead frogs and snakes — right in the window. Frog syrup. Sort of medicine. The mixture — two spoonfuls three times daily. Hnyeh!"

"You seem to know your way around."

"Well, I live here, you see."

"Funny, meeting someone who actually *lives* in a place like this," said the feller. "I'm glad I ran into you."

"Always glad to help out. You looked a bit lost," I said. I had met him in the Big South Sea, and all I had said — it was my new opening — was "Kinda hot."

"By the way, it's not very far from here."

"Wait," he said, and touched my arm. "Is that a rat?"

A smooth dark shape, flat as a shadow, crept out of the monsoon drain and hopped near a bursting barrel.

"Just a cat," I said. "Millions of them around here." I stamped my foot; the rat turned swiftly and dived back into the drain. "A small pussy cat."

"I've got a thing about rats." There was a child's fearful quaver in his voice.

"So do I!" I said, so he would not be embarrassed. "They scare the living daylights out of me. Feller I know has doz-

120

ens of them in the walls of his house. They scratch around at night — "

"Please."

"Oh, sorry," I said. "Not to worry. Take a left — mind your head."

We passed under a low black archway into Sultana Street; a darkened shophouse smelling gloriously of cinnamon made me slow down to take a good whiff of the sweet dust in the air. Then we turned again into an alley of wet cobblestones where there was no sidewalk, Muscat Lane.

"I never would have found this place alone," the feller said behind me, and I could tell by his voice that he had turned to look back. He was nervous.

"That's what I'm here for!" I said, trying to calm him with heartiness. "I just hope they're not all asleep." I stopped at an iron gate, the only opening in a high cement wall, burglar-proofed with rows of sharp iron crescents instead of broken glass bristles. The house had once belonged to a wealthy Muslim, and the iron gate was worked in an Islamic design. Across the alley, four yellow window-squares in the back of a shophouse illustrated the night: a Chinese man and wife faced each other in chairs at one; above them a schoolboy, holding a fistful of his hair, wrote at a desk; next to him, an old man looked into a mirror, scraping his tongue with a stick; and in the yellow window under the old man's an old lady nuzzled an infant.

"It's night," said the feller, "but it's so hot! It's like an oven."

A padlock chained to the bars held the gate shut. I was rapping the lock against a bar.

"Yes?" A dim face and a bright flashlight appeared at the side of the gate.

"Mr. Sim, is that you?"

"Jack," said Mr. Sim.

"Yeah, how are they treating you? I thought you might be

in the sack. Look, have you got a girl you can spare?"

"Got," said Mr. Sim.

"Good, I knew I could count on you. But the thing is, we're in kind of a rush — my friend's ship is leaving in the morning — "

"Six-twenty," said the feller anxiously, still glancing around.

" — and he doesn't want one too old," I said. The feller's instruction meant he wanted one younger than himself; that was simple — he was over sixty, and no hooker downtown was over thirty. I went on to Mr. Sim, "And she has to be nice and clean. They're clean, aren't they? The feller was asking about that."

"Clean," said Mr. Sim.

"Fine," I said. "So can we come in and have a look-see?"

"Can," he said. He undid the chain and swung the gate open. "Come in, please."

"A red light," said the feller. "Appropriate."

"Yes, sir, appropriate all right!" I said, stepping back. "After you."

He was mistaken, but so pleased there was no point in correcting him. The red light was set in a little roofed box next to the door. It was a Chinese altar; there was a gold-leaf picture inside, a bald fanged warrior-god, grinning in a billowing costume, wearing a halo of red thunderbolts. He carried a sword — a saint's sword, clean and jeweled. A plate of fresh oranges, a dish of oil, and a brass jar holding some smoking joss sticks had been set before it on a shelf. The feller had seen the light but not the altar. It was just as well: it might have alarmed him to know that the girls prayed and made offerings to that fierce god.

"Cigarette?" asked Mr. Sim, briskly offering a can of them. "Tea? Beer? Wireless?" He flicked on the radio, tuned it to the English station, and got waltz music. "I buy that wireless set — two week. Fifty-over dollar. Too much-*lah*. But — !" He clapped his hands and laughed, becoming hospitable — "Sit! Two beers, yes? Jack! Excuse me." He disappeared through a door.

"So far, so good," said the feller, fastidiously examining the sofa cushion for germs before he sat down and looked around.

He seemed satisfied. It was what he expected, obviously the parlor of a brothel, large, with too much furniture, smelling of sharp perfume and the dust of heavy curtains, and even empty, holding many boisterous ghosts and having a distinct shabbiness without there being anything namably shabby in it. The light bulb was too small for the room, the uncarpeted floor was clean in the unfinished way that suggested it was often very dirty and swept in sections. It was a room which many people used and anyone might claim, but in which no one lived. The calendar and clock were the practical oversized ones you find in shops; the landscape print on the wall and the beaded doilies on the side tables looked as if they had been left behind rather than arranged there, and they emphasized rather than relieved the bareness. The room was a good indicator of the size and feel of the whole house, a massive bargelike structure moored at Muscat Lane. Outside, the date 1910 was chiseled into a stone shield above the door; the second-floor verandah had a balcony of plump glazed posts — green ones, like urns; the tiled roof had a border of carved wooden lace, and barbed wire — antique enough to look decorative — was coiled around the drainpipes and all the supporting columns of the verandah.

The feller sniffed: he knew where he was. In the room, as in all brothel rooms, a carnal aroma hung in the air, as fundamental as sweat, the exposed odor from the body's most private seams.

"Ordinarily," I said, "Mr. Sim wouldn't have opened up for just anyone. Like I say, he knows me. They all do. Not that I'm bragging. But it's the convenience of it."

"I'm very grateful to you," he said. He was sincere. The

house on Muscat Lane was a classic Asian massage parlor and brothel. If it had been a new semidetached house on a suburban street he would not have stayed. But when he spoke there was the same nervous quaver in his voice as when he had spied the rat. He was trembling, massaging his knees.

That made half the excitement for a feller, the belief that it was dangerous, illegal, secretive; the bewildering wait in a musky anteroom, swallowing fear in little gulps. A feller's fear was very good for me and the girls: it made the feller quick; he'd pay without a quibble and take any girl that was offered; he'd fumble and hurry, not bothering to take his socks off or get under the sheet. Fifteen minutes later he'd be out of the room, grinning sheepishly, patting his belt buckle, glancing sideways into a mirror to see whether he was scratched or bitten — and I'd be home early. I disliked the fellers who had no nervous enthusiasm, who sat sulkily in chairs nursing a small Anchor, as gloom-struck and slow as if they were at the dentists, and saying, "She's too old," or "Got anything a little less pricy?"

"I wonder what's keeping your friend," said the feller, leaning over to look through the door. The movement made him release one knee; that leg panicked and jumped.

"He'll be along in a jiffy," I said. "He's probably getting one all dolled up for you."

"I was going to ask you something," the feller said. "The purser on the ship said there were pickpockets here. People in Singapore are supposed to be very light fingered."

"You don't have to worry about that," I said.

"I was just asking," he said. "The purser lost a month's salary that way."

"It happens, sure," I said. "But no one can take that fat pig-skin thing you cart around."

"How did you — ?" He hitched forward and slapped his backside. "It's *gone!*"

I pulled his wallet out of my pocket and threw it over to him. "Don't get excited. I pinched it when we saw the rat.

It was hanging out a mile — I figured you might lose it."

The explanation upset him. He checked to see that all the money was there, then tucked the wallet inside his blazer. "So it *was* a rat."

"Well — " I started, and tried to laugh, but at that moment Mr. Sim came through the door with Betty, who was carrying a tray with two beers and some cold towels on it.

"Hi, sugar," I said.

The nutcracker, I called her, because her legs were shaped exactly like that instrument; she was not simply bowlegged — her legs had an extraordinary curvature, and the way they angled into the hem of her skirt gave no clue to how they could possibly be hinged. Her legs were the kind a child draws on the sketch of a girl, a stave at each side of a flat skirt.

Betty poured the beers and handed us each a cold towel with a pair of tongs. She took a seat next to the feller and waited for him to wipe his face with the towel and have a sip of the beer before she put her brave hand casually into his lap. The feller clutched his blazer, where he had stuck the wallet.

"You like *boochakong?*" asked Betty.

The feller looked at me. "They understand that my ship is leaving at six-twenty?"

"She know," said Mr. Sim. "I tell her. Betty very nice girl. She . . . *good.*"

"She's a sweetheart. She'll really go to town on you," I said to the feller; and to Betty, "You take good care of him — he's an old pal of mine." I stood up. "Well, nice meeting you."

"You're not going, are you?" said the feller. He plucked Betty's hand out of his lap and stood up.

"Things to do," I said, burying my face in the cold towel. "I've got to get some rest — the fleet's in this week. Those fellers run me ragged."

"I'll never find my way back."

125

"Can ring for a taxi," said Mr. Sim. "Where you are dropping?"

The feller was beside me. "Stay," he whispered, "please. I'll pay for your trouble."

"No trouble at all," I said. "I just wanted to help you out. You looked lost."

"I'll treat you to one," he said confidentially.

"It doesn't cost me anything," I said.

"I thought maybe you were doing this for the money."

"I get my share from Mr. Sim," I said. "Don't worry about that."

"So there's no way I can get you to stay?"

"You can ask."

"I'm *asking*, for Pete's sake!"

"Okay, I'll hang on here," I said. "Take your time."

"Thanks a million," he said, and nodded in gratitude.

"What your name?" asked Betty, steering him out of the room, carrying his glass of beer.

"Oh, no you don't!" I heard the feller say to her on the stairs.

"He'll be back in ten minutes," I said to Mr. Sim.

"No, no!" said Mr. Sim. "Rich fella — old man. Half-hour or more-*lah*."

"Bet you a fiver."

"Bet," said Mr. Sim, eager to gamble.

We put our money on the table and checked our watches.

"Quiet tonight," I said.

"Last night! English ship! Fifty fella!" He shook his head. "All the girls asleeping now. Tired! You like my new wireless set?"

"Nifty," I said. "Nice tone. It's a good make."

"The fella come back, he want me to eat a mice?"

It was Mr. Sim's party trick. He ate live ones whole to astonish and mortify rowdy seamen; he appeared beside a feller who was getting loud and offered a handful of them.

126

When they were refused, Mr. Sim would dangle one before his mouth, allowing it to struggle, and then pop it in like a peanut, saying, "Yum, yum!" It was a shrewd sort of clowning, and it never failed to quiet a customer.

"I don't think so," I said. "Might give him a fright. He's scared of rats."

"Rats," Mr. Sim laughed. "During Japanese occupation we eating them."

"Rat *foo yong*," I said. "Yech."

"No," Mr. Sim said, seriously. "Egg very scarce. We make with *tow foo*, little bit chilies, and *choy-choy*." He wrinkled his nose. "We hungry-*lah*."

"I'm not scared of rats," I said. "But I really hate cockroaches. I suppose you could say I'm scared of them." And what else? I thought — odd combinations: locked rooms, poverty, embarrassment, torture, secret societies, someone in a club asking me "Who are you," death, sun-bathing.

"Aren't you scared of anything, Mr. Sim?"

"No," he said firmly, and he looked handsome.

"What about the police?"

"These Malay boys? I not scared. But they making trouble on me."

"Buy them off," I said.

"I buy-*lah*," he said. "I give *kopi*-money. Weekly!"

"So what's the problem?"

"These politics," said Mr. Sim. "The other year some fella in here shopping votes — 'Okay, Sim *Xiensheng*, vote for me-*lah*' — and now they wanting close up house. Pleh!" He laughed — the insincere, unmodulated Chinese cackle, the mirthless snort of a feller surprised by a strong dig in the ribs. It was brief, it had no echo. He said, "They close up house — where we can go? What we can do?"

"Go someplace where they can't find you," I said. "I know a few. I've been playing with the idea of starting up on my own, something really fancy." Mine would be at the

127

edge of town, a large house with stained-glass windows —
dolphins, lilies, and white horses — to keep the sun out; an
orchestra in the parlor — six black South Indians with brilliantined hair, wearing tuxedos, playing violins; silk cushions on the divans, gin drinks and sweet sherbets. "Jack's
place," they'd call it.

Mr. Sim laughed again, the same reluctant honking. "You
not start a house. You get trouble."

"Well, no more than you."

"More," said Mr. Sim, and he showed me his face, the
Hakka mask of a tough pug, the broad bony forehead, no
eyebrows, just a fold in the brow, the swollen eyes and lower
lip thrust out and the hard angular jaw. He said again,
"More."

The door opened.

"Hi there," said the feller, moving quickly toward us.
"Sorry to keep you waiting."

Mr. Sim looked at his watch and grunted.

"That's mine, I believe," I said, and scooped up the ten
dollars from the table.

The feller sat down. Betty brought him a glass of tea and
a hot towel. The feller wiped his hands thoroughly, then
started on his chin, but thought better of it and made a face;
he dropped the towel on the tin tray. "Shall we go?"

"I'll just knock this back," I said, showing him my glass
of beer. "Won't be a minute."

He had crossed his legs and was kicking one up and down
and attempting to whistle. What looked like impatience
was shame.

"Betty . . . *good*," said Mr. Sim.

"Very pleasant," said the feller. But he avoided looking
at Betty as he said so. To me, he said, "You must find Singapore a fascinating place. I wish we had more time here.
We've got three days in Colombo, then off to Mombasa —
a day there — then — "

"Nice watch," said Mr. Sim. "Omega. How much?"

"Thank you," said the feller, and pulled his sleeve down to cover it. "Er, shouldn't we be going?"

"Plenty of time," I said. "It's only a little after eleven. Say, how'd it go inside?"

"Not, um, too bad," he said, still kicking his leg. "Say, I really think we must — "

"Jack," said Betty.

"Yoh?"

"He got one *this big!*" She measured eight inches with her hands. It was a vulgar gesture — the feller winced — but her hands were so small and white, the bones so delicate, they made it graceful, turning the coarseness into a dancer's movement. Only her open mouth betrayed the vulgarity. I saw a tattoo on her arm and reached over to touch it.

"That's pretty," I said. "Where'd you get it?"

"No," she said. She covered it.

The feller coughed, stood up, and started for the door.

"See you next time," said Mr. Sim.

"Thanks a lot," I said.

"Don't mention. Bye-bye, mister," he called to the feller. Then Mr. Sim drew me aside. "You taking girls out to ships, some people they don't like this but I say forget it. Everybody know you a good fella and I say Jack my friend. No trouble from Jack. Two hand clap, one hand no clap. But you listen. You don't pay *kopi*-money. You don't start up a house, or — " He rubbed his nose with the knuckles of his fist and looked at the floor, saying softly, "Chinese fella sometime very awkward."

"Don't worry about me," I said.

"Would it be safe to take a taxi?" the feller asked when we got to the corner of Sultana Street.

"Oh, sure," I said, and flagged one down.

On the way to the pier I said, "It's rather late for intros, but anyway. My name's Jack Flowers — what's yours?"

"Milton," he said quickly. "George Milton. If you're

ever in Philadelphia it'd be swell to see you. I wish I had one of my business cards to give you, but I'm fresh out."

"That's all right," I said. He was lying about his name, which on the I.D. card in his wallet was W. M. Griswold; and his address was in Baltimore. It might have been an innocent lie, but it hurt my feelings: he didn't want to know me. I had rescued him, and now he was going away.

"The first thing I'm going to do when I get down to my cabin is brush my teeth," he said. The taxi stopped.

"I don't blame you, George," I said.

"Will you take twenty bucks?"

"Now?" I said. "Yes."

"Be good," he said, handing it over.

It was still early and I was within walking distance of the seafront bars. I strolled along the pier, stepping carefully so I wouldn't get my shoes dirty on the greasy rope that lay in coils between the parked cars and taxis. At Prince Edward Road, near the bus depot, two fellers were standing under a streetlamp trying to read what looked like a guidebook. They were certainly tourists, and probably from Griswold's liner; both wore the kind of broad-brimmed hat strangers imagine to be required headgear in the tropics. It gave them away instantly: no one in Singapore wore a hat, except the Chinese, to funerals.

I walked over to them and stopped, rattling coins in my pocket with my fist and negligently whistling, as if waiting for a bus. Their new shoes confirmed they were strangers. I could tell a person's nationality by his shoes. Their half-inch soles said they were Americans.

"Kinda hot."

They turned and enthusiastically agreed. Then they asked their reckless question in a mild way. I nodded, I whistled, I shook my jingling coins; I was the feller they wanted.

*

It was so easy I could not stop. I hustled at a dead run until the streets were empty and the bars closed. New to the enterprise, I had the beginner's stamina. It wasn't the money that drove me; I can't call it holy charity, but it was as close to a Christian act as that sort of friendly commerce could be, keeping those already astray happy and from harm, within caution's limits. I raided my humanity to console them with reminders of safety, while reminding myself of the dangers. I was dealing with the very innocent, blind men holding helpless sticks; their passions were guesses. It especially wounded me that Griswold had lied about his name: in my conscientious shepherding I believed I was doing him, and everyone, a favor.

Guiding rather than urging, I paid close attention to a feller's need and was protective, adaptable, and well-known for being discreet. In those days it mattered, and though I acted this way out of kindness, not to impress anyone as a smoothie, it won me customers. There were so many then, and so grateful. I shouldn't remember Griswold among them, for he was so typical as to be unmemorable — something about the very desire for sex or the illicit made a feller anonymous without trying. But Griswold had lied; the lie marked him and identified his otherwise nameless face and brought back that evening. His distrust made me relax my normally cautious discretion, and for years afterward if a feller said he was from Baltimore I replied, "Know a feller named Griswold there?" Some knew him, or said they did, and one night a feller said, "Yes, we were great friends. That was such a damned shame, wasn't it?" And I never mentioned him again, this man who had refused my grace.

6

THE HOUSE on Muscat Lane was one of several in Singapore that did business in the old way. Any port is bound to cater to the sexually famished, but the age and wealth of a city, until recently, could be determined by how central the brothels were. Once, in old and great cities, they were always convenient, off shady boulevards, a stone's throw from the state house; in the postwar boom they went suburban to avoid politicians and high rents; then they moved back to the center — Madam Lum's place was near a supermarket — and it was no longer possible to tell from their location the city's age, though prosperity could still be measured by the number of whores in a place: the poorest and most primitive, having none, made do with forced labor, blackmail, or unsatisfying casual arrangements in ditches and alleyways and in the rear seats of cars.

Singapore was very old then, not in years but in attitude and design because of the way the immigrants had transplanted and continued their Chinese cities, duplicating Foochow in one district, Fukien in another. As a feller who had seen Naples and Palermo duplicated down to building styles, hawkers' cries, gangster practices, and patron saints in the North End of Boston, I understood that traditional instinct to preserve. The completely Chinese flavor of vice in Singapore made it attractive to a curious outsider, at the same time releasing him from guilt and doubt, for its queer differences (Joyce Li-ho had the tattoo of a panther leaping up her inner thigh) made it a respectable diversion, like the erotic art anthropologists solemnly photograph, maharani and maharajah depicted as fellatrix and bugger on the Indian temple. The sequence of activities in a Chinese brothel parodied Oriental hospitality: the warm welcome — the host bowing from the waist — the smoke, the chat, the cold towel, then the girl — usually the feller chose from one in a parade; money changed hands in the bedroom when the feller was naked and excited; then the stunt itself, and afterward, a hot towel and a glass of cold tea on the verandah while some old *amahs* ironed bedsheets and yapped beyond the rail.

It was the Chinese host's puritanism, his ability to make pleasure into a ritual, that added so much enjoyable delay to it. And though the Chinese customers with a harelike speed treated the whole affair with no more concern than we would in popping out for a quick hamburger, the fellers I took along, mainly gawking travelers bent on carrying away an armload of souvenirs, welcomed the chance to enter, and more than enter — participate — in a cultural secret, to be alone with the exotic Oriental girl in a ceremonial state of undress, and later to have that unusual act of love to report upon. It was much appreciated because it was perfect candor, private discovery, the enactment of the white bachelor's fantasy, the next best thing to marrying a sweet obedient Chinese girl. I could provide, without danger, the ultimate souvenir: the experience, in the flesh, of fantasy.

By never putting a price on my services, and by joking

133

about the enterprise the feller would take so seriously — Americans treating it, they'd say, as part of their education, continentals looking on it as a kind of critical therapy, the English preferring not to discuss it — I always came out better. I was prompt and responsive; I didn't insist on my presence; and I had a sense of humor.

"That was quite an experience," the feller would say, his face flushed.

"Glad you approved," I'd say, hailing my trishaw for the ride home.

"You've been a great help. Really, I — "

"Don't mention it. It's just a question of mind over matter, ain't it?"

"How's that?"

"I don't mind and you don't matter — hyah!"

My dedication to these souls, whom anyone else would call suckers, was so complete it made me unselfish in a way that calmed and rewarded me, for paradoxically it was this unselfish dedication that was commercially useful — I was making money. I was not so much a fool as to think that the money had been virtuously earned — there was no brotherhood in a cash transaction; my small virtue was a fidelity to other people's passion, but I would not martyr myself for it, I expected some payment. I was not a pimp with a heart of gold; however, I knew and could prove that I had saved many fellers from harm and many girls from brutes — not only from greedy cabbies, but the curfew districts controlled by the secret societies, the streets where all the pretty girls were men with kukris in their handbags, the girls with pox, the sadists, the clip joints, the houses you came away from with the fungus on your pecker known as "Rangoon Itch." "I've saved a lot of fellers from Rangoon Itch in my time," is hardly a saintly testimony, but it might be the epitaph of a practical man who gave relief the only way he could, trusting instinct and operating in the dark. I took blame, I risked damnation, I didn't cheat: *A Useful Man,* my tombstone motto would go. I was a knowledgeable friend in a remote place, able to read obscure and desperate verbal signals; with a deliberately corny sense of humor — the undemanding comedy that relaxed the fellers by avoiding all off-color or doubtful jokes, specifically the ones relating to lechery, which in the circumstances could only annoy the fellers by mocking or challenging their heat.

And Singapore helped. It was that atmosphere that had been exported with the immigrants from China and the oldie-worldie style of the city's subdivision into districts. To say that there was only one street in Singapore where you could buy a mattress is to describe the rigidness of the pattern; ship chandlers occupied one street, coffin makers another, banks another, printeries another. Brothels took up a whole block, mixed higgledy-piggledy with Chinese hotels, from Muscat Lane to Malacca Street, and the area was self-contained, bordered on one side by bars and noodle shops and on the other by laundries and pox doctors.

"It's like something out of a myth," Griswold had said. Without fuss, the excesses of Shanghai were available in the dream district — opium dens here, brothels and massage parlors and cockfights there — constructed by the wishful immigrant who in his homesick fantasy remembered a childhood longing for wealth and provided for his pleasure with the tourists' subsidy. An American appropriately complimented the unreality of it by saying, "It's just like a movie!"

"Jack, I want to tell you I feel very lucky," the same feller went on. "Give them a few years and they'll pull this all down and build over it — apartment houses, car parks, pizza joints, every lousy thing they can think of. Tokyo's already getting commercialized."

We were on Sago Lane, near Loon's Tip-Top; through the upstairs window of Loon's we could see two Chinese girls in red dresses, one smoking and looking out at the sky, the other combing her long hair.

"They'll put a gas station there or some dumb thing. It gives me the creeps to think about it," he said. "It'll just ruin it."

"It makes my blood boil," I said. But I could not match his anger.

Then he said something I have thought of many times since: "I feel damned lucky," he said. "At least I can say I knew what it was like in the old days."

Nineteen fifty-nine! The old days!

But he was right; it *was* pleasant then, and it changed. Answering the squalor of the city were the girls; noiseless and glittering and narrow as snakes, they looked like anyone's idea of the Oriental concubine. That was theatrical, a kind of costuming: the whore's mask depicted the client's sexual ideal — they were expected to pose that way, as in white shoes, I was expected to look like a pimp. It was the nearest word, but it didn't describe me: I was gentle. The girls were practical and businesslike. Their obsession was with good health, and they treated their tasks like ritual medicine or minor surgery, assisting like sexy nurses, those dentist's helpers who worked on complicated extractions, bending over a feller's open mouth, making him comfortable and being quick when he grunted unusually. They believed in ghosts and had a horror of hair and kissing and stinks and dirt, and complained we smelled like cheese. Some didn't feel a thing, but just lay there sacrificed and spread and might say, "You are finished, yes?" before a feller had hardly started. Most had the useful skill of the reliable worker, the knack of being able to do their job convincingly and well without having the slightest interest in it, and all had the genius to be remote at the moment of greatest intimacy, a contemplative gift. They were sensationally foul-mouthed, but they swore in English, and I was

136

certain from the soft way they spoke to each other in Chinese that they seldom swore in their own language, and had that learner's curious habit of finding it easy to say "fuck" in another tongue, for a foreign swearword is practically inoffensive except to the person who has learned it early in life and knows its social limits.

Dirty talk stimulated a lot of fellers, but left others cold. I remember a feller demanding to leave the Honey Bar, and as we left, saying disgustedly, "I could never screw a girl that said bullshit. Bullshit this, bullshit that. I'm not a machine. I like a girl I can talk to, a little human warmth."

Many of the girls were modest in a conventional way, which even as a pretense was a compelling sexiness in a whore: "I couldn't get the little doll to take her dress off," was a frequent comment from the fellers, and as no tipping was allowed in the houses, no amount of money could persuade the girls to disrobe. Yet far from diminishing their effectiveness it made them sought-after; any variation increased desire and the silk dresses gave these cold quick girls an accidental allure, titillating by flouncy mystification, partly concealing the act in the dark, keeping enough of it quaintly secret for a feller's interest to be provoked. A girl stark naked was not sexy. Hing was driven wild by even a clothed woman on all fours — as long as she was Australian and large; Ogham said the finest pleasure was to stick an ice pick into a woman's bloomered bottom; and once in the Bandung, when we were on the subject, Yardley said with awful sincerity, "Jesus, I love to see a woman with her mouth hanging open."

I knew the girls too well to think of them as kindly and cheerful, but they understood their cues and were dependable. Observe what virtue was in them: obedience, usefulness, reliability, economy — not mortification and solitary prayer. On one occasion, boarding a launch for a run out to a ship, Doris Goh (never absent, never late) stumbled

137

and fell into the water at the quayside. She could not swim and went rigid as soon as she went under. I hauled her out; soaking wet, her dress stuck to her, her make-up was streaked, and her nice hairdo became a heavy rope of loose braid. I told her she could go home if she wanted to, but she said no and soldiered on, earning forty dollars in the wheel house while her dress dried on a hanger in the engine room. They were unambitious in some ways, but not at all lazy and didn't steal.

So it surprised me — my amusement crept upon by an old slow fear — when I opened the *Straits Times* and saw, under ISLAND-WIDE VICE RING BROKEN — JOO CHIAT RAID NETS 35, a photograph of five girls being dragged by the arms toward a police van while grim Malay policemen watched, sturdily planted on widely spread bandy legs, holding trucheons and riot shields. The girls' faces were very white from the flash bulb's brightness and their astonished eyebrows were high and black, their objecting mouths in the attitude of shouting. That they were objecting did not surprise me — they were indignant, an emotion as understandable in them as in any harmless lathe operator yanked from his machine. But that particular raid was a great surprise: the Joo Chiat house was thought to be safe, with a Chinese clientele, protected by the fierce Green Triangle secret society whose spiderlike and pockmarked members could be seen at any time of the day or night playing cards by the back entrance, their knives and bearing scrapers close to hand. The article in the paper said this was "the first raid in an all-out campaign launched by the P.A.P. to rid the island of so-called massage parlors."

There were two raids the following day. One at an opium den resulted in the arrests of seven elderly men, six of whose worried, sunken-eyed faces appeared in the paper; the seventh was pictured on a stretcher with his hands clasped — he had broken his leg when he slipped trying to escape across

138

a steep tile roof. The second raid was at a massage parlor very close to Muscat Lane where all the girls, and the décor, were Thai. The raids disturbed me, but the picture I made of it in my mind was not of the girls — it was the terrifying vision of the old addict being hounded in his pajamas across a clattering rooftop.

I decided to lie low that night at the Bandung. "You don't understand the political background, Jack," Yates said. "I'd steer clear of Chinatown if I were you."

"Don't say we didn't warn you," said Yardley.

"I never go to Chinatown," said Froggett. "Bloody waste of time."

"Harry Lee's putting the boot in," said Smale. "I hate that little sod."

"I was just wondering what was going on," I said.

"Nothing that concerns you," said Yardley. "So keep out of it."

The next morning I went to see Mr. Sim. He seemed suspicious at my arriving so early, and reluctantly let me in. I asked him about the raids.

"Must be careful," he said. "How Kheng Fatt is keeping, okay?"

"Hing? He's doing all right. I'm only putting in a couple of hours a day, unless I've got business on a ship."

"So what you are worried? You got a job, neh?"

"If you want to call it that. Look, I earn peanuts there — little-little money. I can't bank on it. If they go on closing the houses down and arresting the girls I'm going to be out of luck. And so are you!"

"Better than in jail."

"What are you going to do?"

He didn't look at me, but he showed me his face. He said, "Funny thing. You know new wireless I got? Yes? It don't work now. I *enjoy* that wireless set, but it need repair."

"Where are you planning to go?" I asked.

He discovered his shirt and smoothed the pockets.

"They say a lot of the cops are plainclothes men," I said. "You know, Special Branch fellers wearing shirts like mine and plain old pants, pretending they want a girl. They pay up and just before they get into the saddle they say, 'Okay, put your clothes on — you're under arrest.' I think that's terrible, don't you?"

Mr. Sim twisted the tail of his shirt, and he worked his jaw back and forth as he twisted.

"I'll level with you, Mr. Sim. The reason I came over is I've got a plan. We know they're trying to close things up — they've already nabbed about a hundred people. So why wait? Why not just put our heads together and set up somewhere safe. Like I was telling you. We'll go where they least expect us, rent a big house up on Thomson Road or near a cemetery, get about ten girls or so and run a real quiet place — put up a sign in front saying 'The Wongs' or 'Hillcrest' or 'Dunroamin.' What do you say to that?"

"It is a very hot day." He went imbecilic.

"Come on, we haven't got much time. Are you interested or not?"

"It is a hot day," said Mr. Sim. "I am expecting my auntie."

"No taxis allowed — only private cars, no *syces*. Girls by appointment. If you think the Dunroamin idea is silly we can put up a sign saying 'Secretarial School — Typing and Shorthand Lessons.' No one'll know the difference."

He had twisted his shirttail into a hank of rope and now he was knotting it. "My auntie is very old. I tell her to stop so much smoking — forty-over sticks a day! But old peoples. Kss!"

"Okay, forget it." I stood up.

Mr. Sim let go of his shirt and leaped to the door. "Bye-bye, Jack. See you next time. Don't mention."

That night I brought a feller to Muscat Lane. I had met

him in a bar on Stamford Road. He had asked me if I knew a good "cathouse," and I told him to follow me. But the house was in darkness, the shutters were closed, and the red light over the altar was turned off. I rapped the lock against the gate bar, but no one stirred. Mr. Sim had run out on me.

"This looks like a washout," the feller said. "I'm not even in the mood now."

"They're worried about the cops. There's a political party here that's putting the heat on — trying to close down the whole district. They've got everyone scared. It didn't use to be this way, but maybe if we walk over — "

"I don't know why it is," said the feller, "but people are always saying to me, 'You should have been here last year.' It really burns me up."

"That's natural," I said. "But you gotta understand the political background, you see."

"Political background is crap," he said. "I'm going back to the ship."

"If there's anything *else* you want, anything at all," I said. "I could find you a gal easy enough. Fix you up in a hotel. Bed and breakfast."

He shook his head. "I had my heart set on a cathouse."

"We could try another one," I said. "But I don't want you to get in dutch. How would it look if you got your picture in the papers — cripe!"

"Makes you stop and think, don't it?" he said.

"Sure does," I said. "But if there's anything else — "

"Naw," he said, but saying so, he laughed and said again, "Naw," as if he was trying to discourage a thought. I was hoping he didn't want a transvestite — it would be hours before they'd be on Bugis Street.

"What is it?" I asked in a whisper. "Go ahead, try me. God, you don't want to leave empty-handed, do you?"

"Naw, I was just kicking around an idea that popped up,"

he said, laughing down his nose. "I don't know, I've never seen one."

"Seen what?"

He stopped laughing and said gravely, "Back home they call them skin flicks."

The room was stifling with all the shades drawn, and the screen was a bedsheet, which struck me as uniquely repellent. We sat, six of us, wordlessly fixed on the blue squares jumping and flickering on the screen while the rattling projector whirred: the countdown — a few numbers were missing; the title — something about a brush salesman; the opening shot — a man knocking at a door. We fidgeted when the man knocked; no knock was heard. It was a silent film.

The absence of a soundtrack necessitated many close-ups of facial expressions; and a story was attempted, for both characters — salesman and housewife — were clothed, implying a seduction, the classic plot of conquest with a natural climax — an older concept of pornography. The salesman wore a tweed double-breasted suit and his hair was slick and wavy. I guessed it was late forties, but what country? The housewife wore a long bathrobe trimmed with white fur, and when she sat down the front flapped open. She laughed and tucked it back together. The salesman sat beside her and rolled his eyes. He took out a pack of cigarettes and offered one, a Camel. So it was America.

He opened his case of samples and pulled out a limp contraceptive and made a face ("Oh gosh!") and shoved it back. Then there was an elaborate business with the brushes, various shapes and sizes. He demonstrated each one by tickling the housewife in different places, starting on the sole of her foot. Soon he was pushing a feather duster under her loosening bathrobe. The housewife was laughing and trying to hold her robe shut, but the horseplay went on, the robe slipped off her shoulders.

I recognized the sofa, a large prewar claw-foot model with thick velvet cushions, and just above it on the wall a picture of a stag feeding at a mountain pool. The man took off his shoes. This was interesting: he wore a suit but these were workman's shoes, heavy-soled ones with high counters and large bulbs for toes — the steel-toed shoes a man who does heavy work might wear. His argyle socks had holes in them and he had a chain around his neck with a religious medal on it. His muscled arms and broad shoulders confirmed he was a laborer; he also wore a wedding ring. I guessed he had lost his job; as a Catholic he would not have acted in a blue movie on a Sunday, and if it was a weekday and he had a job he would not have acted in the movie at all. Out the apartment window the sun shone on rooftops, but I noticed he did not take his socks off. Perhaps it was cold in the apartment. Afterward he walked back to his wife through some wintry American city and said, "Hey honey, look what I won — twenty clams!"

The housewife was more complicated. Judging from her breasts she had had more than one child. I wondered where they were. There was a detailed shot of her moving her hand — long perfect fingernails: she didn't do housework. Who looked after her kids? From the way she sat on the sofa, on the edge, not using the pillows, I knew it was not her apartment. She took off the fancy bathrobe with great care — either it was not hers (it was rather big) or she was poor enough to value it. She had a very bad bruise on the top of her thigh; someone had recently thumped her; and now I could see the man's appendix scar, a vivid one.

Two details hinted that the housewife wasn't American: her legs and armpits were not shaved, and she was not speaking. The man talked, but her replies were exaggerated faces: awe, interest, lust, hilarity, pleasure, surprise. She kissed the man's lips and then her head slid down his chest, past the appendix scar — it was fresh, the reason he was out of a job: he had to wait until it healed before he could go back to any heavy work. The housewife opened her mouth; she had excellent teeth and pierced ears — a war bride, maybe Italian, deserted by her GI husband (he thumped her and took the children). The camera stayed on her face for a long time, her profile moved back and forth, and even though it was impossible now for her mouth to show any expression, as soon as she closed her eyes abstraction was on her face — she was tense, her eyes were shut tight, a moment of dramatic meditation on unwilling surrender: she wasn't acting.

Mercifully, the camera moved to a full view of the room. On the left there was a wing chair with a torn seat, a coffee table holding a glass ashtray with cigarette butts in it (they had talked it over — *Are you sure you don't mind?* — perhaps rehearsed it), and on the right, the face of a waterstain on the wall, a fake fireplace with a half-filled bottle on the mantlepiece — the Catholic laborer had needed a drink to go through with it. There had been a scene. *If you're not interested we'll find someone else.* And: *Okay, let's get it over with.* It was breaking my heart.

There was a shot of the front door. It flew open and a large naked woman stood grinning at the pair on the floor — this certainly was the owner of the fancy bathrobe (the cameraman's girl friend?). She joined them, vigorously, but I was so engrossed in the tragic suggestions I saw in their nakedness I had not questioned the door. It was a silent movie, but the door had opened with a bang and a clatter. The feller beside me had turned around and was saying, "What do we do now?"

144

7

WITH SOME kidding fictor's touches, by changing the time of day and my tone of voice to make the story truer, by intensifying it to the point of comedy where it was a bearable memory, my escape from the blue movie raid became part of my repertoire, and within a year I was telling it at the bar of my own place, Dunroamin: " — Then the Chief Inspector, a Scotty, says to me, 'Have I not seen you somewhere before?' and I says, 'Not the club, by any chance?' and he says, 'Jack, I'll be jiggered — fancy finding you in a place like this!' 'I can explain everything,' I says. 'Confidentially, I thought they were showing *Gone with the Wind*,' and he laughs like hell. 'Look,' he says in a whisper, 'I'm a bit short-staffed. Give me a hand rounding up some of this kit and we'll say no more about it.' So I unplugged the projector and carried it out to the police van and later we all joked about it over a beer. And to top it off I still haven't found out which club he had in mind!"

I walked through the bar at Dunroamin all night, chatting fellers up, introducing the girls, and settling arguments.

"If you've got a certain attitude toward cats, you're queer they say. Ain't that right, Jack?"

"Sure. If you want to bugger a male cat, that means you're queer, prih-hih!"

As always, my clowning went over well, but like my new version of the blue movie story it was the clowning that worried me — the comedy struck unexpected notes of despair. I turned my worst pains into jokes to make myself small and to obscure my sick aches; it was my fear of being known well and pitied — my humor was motivated by humility. I sang songs like "What Did Robinson Crusoe Do with Friday on a Saturday Night?" and saying, "I wouldn't have anyone here that I wouldn't invite into my own home," I treated Dunroamin — where I had moved in with my *amah* and pets — as another joke. But it was no laughing matter. I had plowed my whole savings into it. My refusal to admit I took it seriously was my way of guarding against anyone feeling sorry for me if it failed.

It didn't fail; and the feature of it that I had conceived as a joke of last desperation was what saved the house from collapse. The house itself was not large, but it was walled in and set back from the road. I picked it for its high wall and rented it cheap from a superstitious *towkay:* it was on Kampong Java Road and the rear opened on to the Lower Bukit Timah Road cemetery. Those several acres of tombstones and the fact of the house being associated with some Japanese atrocities accounted for the low rent, but gave me headaches when it came to getting girls to live in. The joke was the Palm Court orchestra: fellers often came and paid my slightly higher bar prices to sit and listen.

Finding girls who didn't believe in ghosts was very difficult — the house was haunted; finding South Indian violinists was easy — many were looking for work. Mr. Weerakoon was my first violinist; he was backed up by Mr. ("Manny") Manickawasagam and Mr. Das. Albert Ratnam played the piano, Mr. ("Subra") Subramaniam the cello, Mr. Pillay the clarinet. Manny, an impressive baritone,

146

sometimes sang, and Subra switched to the accordian for the faster numbers. They turned up punctually at six every evening in their old-fashioned tuxedos and bow ties, smelling of Indian talcum, breathless after their hike from Serangoon Road. Their hair was neatly parted in the middle, making two patches of brilliantined waves which shook free to glistening black springs as soon as they began playing. Weerakoon, who had a severely large handlebar mustache, made them practice until seven, and he interrupted them constantly, saying, "No, no, no! — Take that from the top again," while looking at me out of the corner of his eye.

He refused praise. I would say, "A very nice rendition of 'Roses from the South.' "

"Hopeless. But what to do? Ratnam can't read music."

"It was very bouncy. I've never heard it played bouncy before."

"Fast tempo — I think it suits your house. But Pillay was dragging his feet. We need much practice." And pinching the waxy tails of his mustache, he'd add, "We shall have umple of trouble with more tricky numbers."

Weerakoon persuaded me to redecorate the front lounge and turn it into a music room. He had me print a concert card with the selections and intervals listed on it, menu fashion: he propped this on a music stand at the door. The orchestra had the effect Mr. Sim obtained by swallowing live mice — it fixed restless seamen into postures of calm, and later they told me Dunroamin had class. I could see them from the bar, where I stood to greet fellers arriving: a row of rough-looking men with sunburned arms, sitting and listening attentively on the folding chairs. And all night the *scree-scree* from the music room took the curse off the banging bedroom doors and the noisy plumbing, the creaky bedsprings and quacking fans, and that loud way the girls had of washing, sluicing themselves with dippers and gargling at the same time.

The Singapore residents, clubbable ones especially, flattered themselves that the Palm Court orchestra was for them, though some complained, calling Weerakoon and the others "greasy babu fiddlers." Some said I should sack them and get a couple of girls to put on a show. But I resisted these suggestions — sex exhibitions saddened me nearly as much as blue movies: this panicky nakedness was desire's dead end. The Palm Court orchestra, central to what I came to think of as my little mission station — a necessary comfortable house on the island outpost — was for the seamen. I had discovered something about them that I had been too obtuse or distracted to grasp on the *Allegro:* most men who go to sea are quiet and conservative by nature, an attitude that is fostered by the small protected community on a ship where the slightest disorder can be fatal; even the youngest have elderly cautious tastes — pipe-smoking and hobbies — and few read newspapers; most are anxious in the company of women and very shy on land, natural drunkards and rather unsociable. It was for them that Mr. Weerakoon practiced the waltz from *Swan Lake,* and he encouraged them to make requests after he finished the selections listed on the concert card. Then, a seaman with a ruined face would lean over, making his wooden chair squawk, and in a gravelly voice ask for "Brightly Shines Our Wedding Day" or "Time on My Hands."

My girls passed out cold towels from trays or leaned against the walls with their thin pale arms folded, or scuffed back and forth in the flapping broken slippers they always wore. In many ways, though it was not my wish — I was still groping to understand my job — Dunroamin was a traditional establishment, with cold towels, hot towels, glasses of tea, offering a massage at five dollars extra and all drinks more expensive than in a downtown bar; the oldest and frailest *amahs* did the heaviest work — yoked themselves to buckets of water and tottered upstairs to fill the huge stone shower jars, scrubbed sheets on the washboards out back, or boiled linen, which they stirred with wooden paddles, in frothy basins of hot evil-smelling water on the kitchen stove. In those same basins, after a quick rinse, they made *mee-hoon* soup and ladeled it out to the customers who demanded "real Chinese food."

Dunroamin worked smoothly, but it was older than my devising: the system of payment — the chit pads in the bar, the shakedown in the bedroom — the *jaga* at the front gate (Ganapaty, who said, "I am a dog, only here to bark"), the thickly waxed oxblood-colored floors in the graceful white house, camouflaged by vast Angsana trees that dripped tiny yellow blossoms, flanked by servants' quarters and a carriage shed; sloping rattan chairs with leg rests on the top floor verandah, the light knock on my back room and (though I insisted they call me Jack) the soft cry of *"Tuan"* with the morning tea, the skill of the Indian musicians and Weerakoon's habit of saying "Blast" when he played a wrong note — it was all a colonial inheritance, and it had fallen to me. But if my whorehouse was a scale model of the imperial dream, I justified my exploitation by adding to it humor and generous charity, and by making everyone welcome.

What Chinese fellers visited, mostly embarrassed businessmen with names like Elliot Ching and Larry Woo, did so for the same reason the rest of the Chinese stayed away — because my girls made love to redheads. I watched from my corner of the long bar, near the telephone and Ganapaty's emergency buzzer, greeting arrivals with, "Glad you could make it — what can I do you for?" and later watched them go down the gravel drive, each one depleted, rumpled from having dressed hurriedly — their ties and sometimes their socks stuffed in their back pockets — and wearing the pink face people associate with outrage but which I knew to be the meekness that comes after spending energy in a harmless way. It was pleasant to see them leave with new faces and I was flattered and reassured by their promises of generosity: "If there's ever anything I can do for you, Jack —"

But I was the host. "Just settle your bar bill at the end of the month, thank you, and a very good night to you all."

I got up early. In my pajamas at a sunny desk I totaled the previous night's receipts and checked to see that the bar was well stocked and the rooms were clean — in each room a girl would be brushing her hair before a mirror, a houseful of girls brushing: it cheered me. It was a strenuous round of ordering and overseeing, making sure the laundry was done, the pilferage recorded, the grass cut, the house presentable; then, I took my shower, cut across the cemetery to Lower Bukit Timah Road and caught the number 4 Green Line bus to Beach Road, and climbed onto the stool in my little cubicle and took orders from Hing.

In the days when I had hustled on the street and in bars, saying "Kinda hot" to likely strangers, I was glad of the safety of Hing's. I knew my job as a water clerk well enough to be able to do it easily. And though the money was nothing (any of my girls earned more in a week), the stool where I hooked my heels and pored over the shipping pages of the *Straits Times* was important. It was the basis for my visa, a perfect alibi, and a place to roost. But the success of Dunroamin made me consider quitting Hing's.

I continued to get friendly promises of attention from the fellers who came to Dunroamin, yet my relationship with them remained a hustler-client one. I was a regular visitor to the clubs and knew most of the members; in the shipping offices of the Asia Insurance Building and in the Maritime Building, fellers called me by my first name and said how nice it was to see me. But they never stopped to pass the time of day. The talks I had with them took place at prearranged times and for a specific purpose; and I was seldom introduced to their friends. I was careful not to remind them that

I knew more about them than their wives — and seeing them with their wives, by chance after a movie or at a cricket match at the Padang, it amazed me that the fellers came to Dunroamin: their wives were beautiful smiling girls (it was about this time that I had my fling with the Tanglin Club wife whom I reported as being "ever so nice"). My quickness might have disturbed the fellers. My attention to detail in arranging for girls to be sent out to ships or for club members to make a discreet visit in a trishaw for a tumble at Dunroamin could have been interpreted as somewhat suspicious, a kind of criminal promptitude, I think, the blackmailer's dogged precision. Still, most of the fellers insisted I should get in touch if I ever had a problem.

Once, I had one. It was a simple matter. Mr. Weerakoon said he needed new violin strings and could not find any in the shops. I knew the importer; I had fixed him up on several occasions. I gave him a telephone call.

"Hi, this is Jack Flowers. Say, I've got a little problem here — "

"I'll ring you back," he said quickly, and the line went dead.

That was the last I heard from him. I asked about him at his club.

"Why don't you leave the poor chap alone," one of his pals — also a customer of mine — said. "You've got him scared rigid. He's trying to make a decent living. If you start interfering it'll all be up the spout."

That was the last I heard from the pal, too. I got the message, and never again asked for a favor. But they continued to be offered. They sounded sincere. Late at night, after the larking, the contented pink-faced fellers were full of gratitude and good will. I had made them that way: I was the kind of angel I expected to visit me. They said I should look them up in Hong Kong; I should stop over some day and see their ships or factories; I should have lunch with them one day — or the noncommittal, "Jack, we must really meet for a drink soon." The invitations came to nothing; after the business about the violin strings I never pursued them. So I stayed at Hing's, as his water clerk, both for safety and reassurance: it was the only job I could legally admit to having — and soon I was to be glad I had it.

A young Chinese feller came in one evening. It was before six, the place was empty, and I was sitting at the bar having a coffee and reading the *Malay Mail*.

"Brandy," he said, snapping his fingers at Yusof. "One cup."

Yusof poured a tot of brandy into a snifter and went back to chipping ice in the sink.

I knew from his physique that the Chinese feller did not speak much English. The English-educated were plump from milk drinking, the Chinese-educated stuck to a traditional diet, bean curd and meat scraps — they were thin, weedy, like this feller, short, girlish, bony-faced. His hair was long and pushed back. His light silk sports shirt fit snugly to the knobs of his shoulders, and his wrists were so small his heavy watch slipped back and forth on his forearm like a bracelet. He kept looking around — not turning his head, but lowering it and twisting it sideways to glance across his arm.

"Bit early," I said.

He looked into his drink, then raised it and gulped it all. It was a stagy gesture, well executed, but made him cough and gag, and as soon as he put the snifter back on the bar he went red-faced and breathless. He snapped his fingers again and said, *"Kopi."*

"No coffee. Cold drink only," said Yusof.

The feller frowned at my cup. Yusof reached for the empty snifter. The feller snatched it up and held it.

I heard footsteps on the verandah and went to the door, thinking it might be Mr. Weerakoon. I faced three Chinese who resembled the feller at the bar — short-sleeved shirts, long hair, sunglasses, skinny pinched faces. One was small enough to qualify as a dwarf. He swaggered over to a barstool and had difficulty hoisting himself up. Now the four sat in a row; they exchanged a few words and the one who had come in first asked for a coffee again.

Yusof shook his head. He looked at me.

"We don't serve coffee here," I said.

"That is *kopi*," the feller said slowly. The others glared at me.

"So it is," I said. "Yusof, give the gentlemen what they want."

At once the four Chinese raised their voices, and getting courage from the little victory, one laughed out loud. The dwarf hopped off his stool and came over to me.

"You wants book?" he asked.

"What kind?"

"Special." He unbuttoned his shirt and took out a flat plastic bag with some pamphlets inside.

"Don't bother," I said. "Finish your coffee and hop it."

"Swedish," he said, dangling the plastic bag.

"Sorry," I said. "I can't read Swedish."

"Is not necessary. Look." He undid the bag and pulled one out. He held it up for me to see, a garish cover. I could not make it out at first, then I saw hair, mouths, bums, arms.

"No thanks," I said.

"Look." He turned the page. It was like a photograph of an atrocity, a mass killing — naked people knotted on a floor.

"I don't need them," I said. He shook the picture in my face. "No — I don't want it. Yusof, tell this creep I don't want his pictures."

"*Tuan* —" Yusof started, but the dwarf cut him off.

"You buy," said the dwarf.

"I *not* buy."

Now I looked at the three fellers near the bar. The first had swiveled around on his stool. He held the brandy snifter out at arm's length and dropped it. It crashed. Upstairs, a giggle from a girl in a beaverboard cubicle.

"How much?" I asked.

"Cheap."

"Okay, I'll take a dozen. Now get out of here."

The dwarf buttoned the pamphlets into his shirt and said, "You come outside. Plenty in car. You choose. Very nice."

I shook my head. "I not choose. I stay right here."

Glass breaks with a liquid sound, like the instantaneous threat of flood. One feller shouted, *"Yoop!"* I saw Yusof jump. The mirror behind him shattered, and huge pieces dropped to the floor and broke a second time.

"Tell them to stop it!" I said, and went to the door. "Where's your lousy car?"

A black Nissen Cedric was parked on Kampong Java Road, just beyond the sentry box where Ganapaty was hunched over a bowl of rice. He busily pawed at the rice with his fingers.

"In there," said the dwarf, opening the trunk.

There were torn newspapers inside. I turned to object. My voice would not work, my eyes went bright red, and a blood trickle burned my neck; I seemed to be squashed inside my eyeballs, breathing exhaust fumes and being bounced.

Believe any feller who, captive for a few days, claims he has been a prisoner for months. My body's clock stopped with the first sharp pain in my head, then time was elastic and a day was the unverifiable period of wakefulness between frequent naps. Time, like pain, had washed over me and flooded my usual ticking rhythm. I swam in it badly, I felt myself sinking; pain became the passage of time, pulsing as I drowned, smothering me in a hurtful sea of days. But it might have been minutes. I ached everywhere.

For a long time after I woke they kept me roped to a bed in a hut room smelling of dust and chickens and with a corrugated iron roof that baked my broken eyes. This gave my captors problems: they had to feed me with a spoon and hold my cup while I drank. They took turns doing this. They untied me, removing everything from the room but a bucket and mattress, and they brought me noodles at regular intervals. My one comfort was that obviously they did not plan to kill me. They could have done that easily enough at Dunroamin. No Chinese will feed a man he intends to kill. Anyway, murder was too simple: they didn't want a corpse, they wanted a victim.

"Money? You want money? I get you *big* money!" I shouted at the walls. The men never replied. Their silence finally killed my timid heckling.

Grudgingly, saying "Noodoos," banging the tin bowls down, they continued to feed me. Now and then they opened the shutters on the back window to let me empty my bucket. They didn't manhandle me — they didn't touch me. But they gave me no clue as to why they were holding me.

Confinement wasn't revenge for fellers who lingered at a murder to dig out the corpse's eyes or cut his pecker off, and risking arrest by wasting getaway time, dance triumphantly with it. I guessed they had kidnaped me, but if so — time and pain were shrouding me in the wadded gauze of sleep — something had gone wrong. Often I heard the Cedric start up and drive away, and each time it came back they conversed in mumbles. The Singapore police were poor at locating kidnapers. Even if the police succeeded, what rescue would that be? It would mean my arrest on a charge of living off immoral earnings. Some friend would have to ransom me. In those days wealthy *towkays* and their children lived in fear of kidnapers; they were often hustled away at knifepoint, but they were always released unharmed after a heavy payment. Who in the world would pay for my life?

A memory ambushed my hopes. On the *Allegro* a feller had told me a story I remembered in the hut. A loan shark had worked on a freighter with him. He called the feller a loan shark, but his description of the feller's loans made them sound like charity of the most generous and reckless kind, and eventually everyone on the ship owed him money, including the skipper. One day at sea the loan shark disappeared, just like that. "We never found him," said the feller on the *Allegro,* and his wink told me no one had ever looked.

The remembrance scared me and made me desolate, and I believed I would stay that way, in the misery that squeezes out holy promises. But that loneliness was electrified to terror the day my Chinese captors had a loud argument outside my hut. I had felt some safety in their mutters, in the regular arrivals of meals and in the comings and goings of the Cedric; and I had begun to pass the time by reciting my letters of glad news and my litany, *Sir Jack, President Flowers, King John, Bishop Flowers.* I drew comfort from the predictable noises of my captors and their car. My comfort ended with the arguing — that day they didn't bring me food.

I heard it all. The dwarf's name was Toh. He fretted in a high childish voice; the others bow-wowed monotonously. I listened at a crack in the wall, as my empty stomach scolded me and the argument outside grew into a fight. It had to concern my fate — those whinnyings of incredulity and snuffling grunts, smashings and bangings, and Toh's querulousness rising to an impressively sustained screeching. Then it was over.

That night they put the bed back into my room, but I was so hungry and disturbed I couldn't sleep. I was drowsy hours later when I heard the door being unlocked. The morning dazzle of the sun through the door warmed my face. I started to rise, to swing my feet off the bed.

"You stay," said Toh.

Two fellers began tying me up.

"What's the big idea?" I said. "You want money? I get you money. Hey, not so tight!"

I considered a fistfight, working myself into a fury sufficient to beat them off and then making a run for it. I decided against it. Any rashness would be fatal for me. They were small, but there were four of them, and now I looked up and saw a fifth. I had survived so far by staying passive; I was sensible enough to prefer prison to death — to surrender anything but my life. Something else stopped me: I was in my underwear and socks — they had taken my shoes. I wouldn't get far. If I had been dressed I might have taken a chance, but seminaked I felt particularly vulnerable. I let them go on tying me.

They roped my ankles to the end of the bed, and then put ropes around my wrists and made me fold my arms across my chest. I was in a mummy posture, bound tightly to the bed. The fifth man was behind me. I rolled my eyes back and saw that he was stropping a straight razor, whipping it up and down on a smacking tongue of leather.

"Who's he?" Numbness throttled my pecker.

Toh was checking the knots, hooking a finger on them and pulling. *Smick-smack,* went the razor on the strop. Toh pushed at my arms, and satisfied they were tight, said, "That Ho Khan."

"Just tell me one thing," I said in a pitifully unfamiliar voice. "Are you going to kill me? Tell me — please."

Toh looked surprised. "No," he said, "we not kill you."

"Why the razor?"

"Shave," he said.

The other fellers erupted into yakking laughter. I tried to shift on the bed to see them. It was impossible. I couldn't move.

"You're trying to scare me, aren't you?" I heard *smick-smack-smuck.*

Toh leaned over and nodded, smiling. His dwarf's face

made the smile impish. "Scare you," he said, "and scare udda peoples, too."

"What do you mean by that?" *Smuck-smuck.* "Come on, this is silly. I'm an American, you know. I am! The American consulate is looking for me!"

"*Mei-guo ren,*" someone said, "an American." Another replied in Chinese, and there was laughter.

"Now I give you but," said Toh. He scrubbed the backs of my arms with a soapy cloth. The others leaned over for a good look. One was holding a bowl, eating noodles as he watched, gobbling them in an impatient greedy way, smacking his lips and snapping at the noodles like a cat, not chewing. He peered at me over the rim of his bowl. He gave me hope. No one would eat that way in the presence of a person about to be slashed.

Ho Khan fussed with the razor. He braced his elbows, one against my throat, one on my stomach; and then, scraping slowly, shaved the hairy parts of my arms that Toh had soaped, from my elbow to the rope at my wrists. To my relief he put the razor aside.

My relief lasted seconds. Ho Khan fitted a pair of wire glasses over his eyes and took a dart-shaped silver tool which he dipped into a bottle of blue liquid. He leaned on me again and with the speed of a sewing machine began jabbing the needle into the fleshy part of my arm. He was tattooing me — biting on his tongue in concentration — and behind him the others shouted, bursts of Chinese, seeming to tell him what to write in the punctures.

8

AT NEWTON CIRCUS, by the canal, they pushed me out of the car and sped away, yelling. I found a few wrinkled dollars in the clothes they had handed over, enough for a pack of cheroots and a meal of mutton chops at a Malay gag stand on the corner. I was grateful for the night, and glad too for the incuriousness of the Chinese who wolfed food noisily at tables all around me and didn't once look at me. My arms appalled me; I examined them in the light of the stall's hissing pressure lamp. The shaven backs of my arms were swollen and raw, the fresh punctures tracking up and down from elbow to wrist, the small half-exploded squares of Chinese characters, perhaps fifty boxes puffed up and blue and some still leaking blood. I felt better after a meal and a smoke, and left, swinging my arms, so that no one could see their disfigurement, down the canal path, past the orphanage, in the direction of Dunroamin.

I smelled the acrid wood smoke, the stink of violence, before I saw the damage; the strength of it, at that distance, telegraphed destruction. The house was gutted. The tile roof had fallen in and the moon lighted the two stucco roof peaks, the gaping windows, the broken and burned verandah chicks. The abandoned black house looked like an old deserted factory; the fire had silenced the insects and killed the perfume of my flowering trees. No crickets chirped in the compound, a smell of burning hung in the still air. Torn mattresses were twisted and humped all over the driveway and lawn. I was about to go away when, feeling the fatigue and pause of melancholy, I decided that I would enter the house, to try to find something in the ruins that belonged to me, anything portable I could recognize to claim as a souvenir, maybe a scorched clock or the German metronome Mr. Weerakoon kept in a cupboard drawer: *There's an interesting story behind this little thing* . . .

I stumbled in the driveway, and stumbling felt like an intruder. Stepping over the splintered front door, I passed through the bar. Broken glass littered the floor. I balanced on fallen timbers, tiptoed into the music room, and there I stood, in the decay the fire had made, not wanting to go upstairs to see what had happened to my cats. The staring shadows of the overturned chairs stopped me. I could feel the tattoos aching on my arms.

Then I saw the candle burning in the kitchen, and near it a crouching man, his face lighted by the yellow flame.

The eeriest thing about him, this old scarecrow in the burned-out house, was that he was imperturbably reading a folded newspaper. I would leave him in peace. I started toward the front door and kicked a loose board with my first step. *Bang.* The candle flame flickered and went out.

"Don't worry," I called to him. "I'm not going to hurt you."

I made my way into the kitchen, found the candle and lit it. The old man had run to the wall where a blanket was spread. He was Chinese and had the look of a trishaw driver, the black sinewy legs and arms, close-cropped hair, a small dark reptile's face. He wore a blue jacket and shorts, and on his feet were rubber clogs cut from tires.

"You know me, eh? Me Jack." I laughed. "This my house!" In that dark smelly place every sound was weird and my laugh was ghoulish. "You want smoke?" I threw him a cheroot. He cowered when I brought the candle over for him to light it.

"Me Jack," I said. "This my house — Dunroamin."

He blinked. "You house?"

"Yeah," I said. "All finished now."

He cackled and said something I couldn't make out.

"You live here now?" I asked. "Sleep here, eat here — *makan* here, eh?"

"*Makan, makan,*" he said, and picked up a small bowl. He offered it to me. "You *makan.*"

There were lumps of rice inside, with two yellow pork rinds on top of the rice. I took it and thanked him and choked back one of the rinds. It was a sharing gesture and it worked. The poor man was calmed. He went to a tin lunch pail and spooned some more rice into the bowl.

"No," I said.

"*Makan,*" he said, and smiled.

I took the bowl and ate a few grains, chewing slowly. I pointed to the newspaper. "You read, eh? *Sin Chew Jit Poh?*" Naming the paper was like conversation. I thought of another. "*Nanyang Siang Pau,* eh?"

He nodded eagerly and handed me the paper.

I put the bowl down and unfolded the paper, looked at it, said, "Yes, yes," and gave it back.

He didn't respond. He was looking at my arms. He put a skinny finger on one row of tattoos, and tapping each character, worked his way down, tracing the vertical column. He frowned and tapped at another column, but faster now.

"Chinese," I said. "Chinese tattoo."

I grinned.

He backed away, holding an outstretched palm up to ward me off; he groaned distinctly, and he ran, kicking over the tin lunch pail, and tramping the broken boards of the music room, and howling down the drive.

That night I slept on the old man's blanket and breathed the fumes from his crudded lunch pail.

"Curse of Dogshit," said Mr. Tan, translating in the Bandung the next day. He read my left arm. *"Beware Devil, Whore's Boy, Mouth Full of Lies, Remove This and Die.* Very nasty," said Mr. Tan. "Let me see your other arm." The right said, *Red Goatface, Forbidden Ape, Ten Devils in One, I Am Poison and Death, Remove This and Die.*

After that, Mr. Tan was included in the conversations Yardley had with the others when my tattoos were mentioned. For years, Mr. Tan had sat every afternoon alone with his bottle of soybean milk. Now he was welcome. Yardley couldn't remember all the curses and he called upon Mr. Tan to repeat them.

"Incredible," Yardley said. "There, what about that one?"

"Forbidden Ape," said Mr. Tan promptly.

"Can you imagine," said Yardley. "And that one — 'Monkey's Arse' or something like that?"

"Dogshit," said Mr. Tan.

"All right," I said. "That's enough."

"Remember old Baldwin, the chap that worked for Jardine?" asked Smale. "He had tattoos all over the place. Birds and that."

"You going to keep them, Jack?" asked Coony. "Souvenir of Singapore. Show 'em to your mum."

"You think it's a joke." I said. "These things *hurt.* And the doctor says I have to wait till they heal before I can get them off."

"You'll never get them buggers off," said Yardley.

"The doctor says — "

"They can graft them," said Smale.

"Acid," said Yates. "They burn them off with acid. I read

about this somewhere. It leaves scars — that's the only snag. But scars are infinitely preferable to what you've got there, if you ask me."

"Maybe they used some kind of Chinese ink," said Coony. "You know, the kind that never comes off."

"Balls!" said Smale. "If it was Chinese ink he'd be able to wash the flaming things off with soap and water. No, that there's your regular tattooing ink. You can tell."

"*Monkey's Arse,*" said Yardley, laughing. "Christ, be glad it's not in English! What if it was and Jack was in London, on a bus or something? 'Fares please,' the conductor says and looks over and sees *Monkey's Arse, Pig Shit,* and all that on Jack's arm."

"He'd probably ride free," said Frogget.

"No, I've got a better one," said Smale. "Let's say Jack's in church and the vicar's just given a little sermon on foul language. The lady next to Jack looks down and — "

"Lay off," I said, rolling down my sleeves to cover the scabrous notations. "How would you like it if they did it to you?"

"No bloody fear," said Coony. "If one of them little bastards — "

"Shut up," said Yardley. "They'd tattoo the same thing on your knackers before you could say boo." Yardley turned to me and said, "Don't get upset, Jacko. They got ways of getting that stuff off. But I'll tell you one thing — you'd be a fool to try it again."

"What are you talking about?"

"That whorehouse of yours," said Yardley. "You were asking for it. Any of us could have told you that. Right, Smelly?"

"Right," said Smale.

"So you're saying I deserved it."

"What do *you* think?"

I said, "I was making a few bucks."

"Where is it now?" Yardley nudged Frogget.

"None of your business," I said.

"Jack thinks he's different," Yardley said. "But the trouble is, he's just the same as us, living in this piss hole, sweating in a *towkay's* shop. Face facts, Jack, you're the bleeding same."

"Really?" I said, wondering myself if it was true, and deciding it was not.

"Except for that writing on his arms," said Coony.

Macpherson, an occasional drinker at the Bandung, came through the door. He said, "Good evening."

"Hey, Mac, look at this," Yardley said. He grabbed my arm and spoke confidentially. "This is nothing compared to what they do to some blokes. You learned your lesson. From now on, stick with us — we'll stand by you, Jack. And just to show you I mean what I say, the first thing we'll do is get that put right."

"What's it supposed to say?" asked Macpherson.

Mr. Tan cleared his throat.

Weeks later, Yardley found a Chinese tattooist who said he knew how to remove them. We met at the Bandung one evening and he looked as if he meant business. He was carrying a doctor's black valise. But he never opened it; he took one look at the tattoos, read a few columns, and was out the door.

"Look at him go," said Smale. "Like a shot off a shovel."

"A Chink won't touch that," said Coony.

"So we'll find a Malay," said Yardley.

The Malay's name was Pinky, and his tattoo parlor was in a *kampong* out near the airport. He was not hopeful about removing them, though he said he knew the acid treatment. But no matter how much acid he rubbed in, he said, I would still be left with a faint but legible impression. And grafting took years.

"Why don't you just cut your arms off and make the best of a bad job?" said Smale.

"Isn't there anything you can do?" I asked Pinky.

164

"Can make into something else," said Pinky. "Fella come in. He tattoo say 'I Love Mary' but he no like. So I put a little this and that, sails, what. Make a ship, for a sample."

"I get it," I said. He could obliterate the curse but not remove it.

"He puts a different tattoo over it, apparently," said Yates.

"Only the one on the bottom stays the same," said Frogget.

"It's better than leaving them like they are," said Yardley.

The walls of Pinky's parlor were covered with sample tattoos. Many were the same design in various sizes. *Death Before Dishonor,* Indian chiefs, skulls, eagles and horses, *Sweet-Sour, Cut Here,* tigers and crucifixes, *Mother,* bluebirds, American flags, and Union Jacks. Behind Pinky, on a shelf, were many bottles of antiseptic, Dettol, gauze, aspirin, and rows and rows of needles.

"You'll have a hard job making those into ships," said Yates, tapping my blue curses.

"Do you fancy a dagger?" asked Smale. "Or what about the old Stars and Stripes?"

"That's right," said Coony. "Jack's a Yank. He should have an American flag on his arm."

"Fifty American flags is more like it," said Smale.

"Hey, Yatesie," said Coony, pointing to the design reading *Mother,* "here's one for you."

My arms were on Pinky's table. "Chinese crackter," he said. "I make into flowers."

So I agreed. But on each wrist the wide single column — *Remove This and Die* — was too closely printed to make into separate flowers. Pinky suggested stalks for the blossoms on my forearms. I had a better idea. I selected from the convenient symbology on the wall: a dripping dagger on my left wrist, a crucifix on my right.

I went back to Hing's. I was thankful to climb onto my stool and pick up where I'd left off: vegetables for the *Vidia,* stirrup pumps for the *Joseph B. Watson,* new cargo nets for the

165

Peshawar. It was as if I had never been away. But what counted as an event for the fellers at the Bandung and gave the year I was tattooed the same importance they had attached to the year Ogham left and the year the bees flew through the windows — an importance overshadowing race riots, bombings, Kennedy's death, and the threat of an Indonesian invasion — went uncommented upon by Hing. Gopi said, "Sorry mister."

Hing's lack of interest in anything but his unvarying business made him doubt the remarkable. He refused to be amazed by my survival or by the motley blue pictures that now covered my arms. He did not greet me when I came back. He refused to see me as I passed through the doorway. It was his way of not recognizing my long absence: no explanation was necessary. Though he was my own age, his years were circular, ending where they began. He turned the tissue leaves of a calendar that could have been blank. His was the Chinese mastery of disappointment: he wouldn't be woken to taste it, he wouldn't be hurt. Some days I envied him.

I moved into the low sooty semidetached house on Moulmein Green, an uninteresting affair which the washing on the line in front gave the appearance of an old becalmed boat. My aged *amah* found me and turned up with a bundle of my clothes and two of the cats. She wouldn't say what happened to the others; she reported that no one had been injured in the fire at Dunroamin. My tattoos intrigued her and when her mahjong partners came over she asked me if they could have a look. My kidnaping and tatoos raised her status in the neighborhood. Now and then, for pleasure I had a flutter at the Turf Club, and it was about this time that I persuaded Gopi to be fitted for the brace, but that came to nothing. I slept much more, and on weekends sometimes slept throughout the day, waking occasionally in a sweat and saying out loud, *It's still Sunday,* and then dozing and waking and saying it again.

I did no hustling. Every evening I drank at the Bandung and I became as predictable in my reminiscences as the other fellers; the re-creation of what had gone, a continual re-hearsal of the past in anecdotes, old tales sometimes falsified to make the listener relax, made the present bearable. I told delighted strangers about "Kinda hot," the *Richard Everett,* Dunroamin, and my tattooing. "And if you don't believe it, look at this — "

My fortunes were back to zero, but as I have said, it was desolation of this sort that gave me more hope than little spurts of success. However uncongenial poverty was, to my mind it was like the explicit promise of a tremendous ripen-ing. I hadn't regretted a thing. But there was something that mattered more than this, to which I was the only wit-ness. My stories glamorized the terror and often I brooded over my capture to look for errors or omissions. I had proved my resoluteness by surviving the torment without denying what I had done — my house, my girls — and at no moment had I gone down on my knees and said a prayer. It wasn't that I didn't think I ought to be forgiven. Forgiveness wasn't necessary. I had nothing to live down. The charitable loan shark, pitched overboard by his furious debtors, had swum to shore.

9

"You don't know me," said the foxy voice at the other end of the phone. "But I met a good pal of yours in Honolulu and he — well — "

"What's the feller's name?" I asked.

He told me.

"Never heard of him," I said. "He's supposed to be a friend of mine?"

"Right. He was in Singapore a few years ago."

"You don't say! His name doesn't ring a bell," I said. "What business was he in? Where did he live?"

"I can't talk here," he said. "I'm in an office. There's some people."

"Wait," I said. "What about this feller that knows me? Did he have a message for me or something like that?" *Brace yourself. I've got some fantastic news for you. Ready? Here goes . . .* I braced myself.

"Maybe you don't remember him," he said. "I guess he was only in Singapore one night."

"Oh."

"But that was enough. You know?"

"Look — "

"He, um, *recommended* you. Highly. You get what I'm driving at?"

"What's on your mind?"

"I can't talk here," he said. "What are you doing for lunch?"

"Sorry. I can't talk here either," I said. How did *he* like it?

"A drink then, around six. Say yes."

"You're wasting your time," I said.

"Don't worry," he said. "Let's have a drink. What do you say?"

"Where are you staying?"

"Something called the Cockpit Hotel."

"I know where it is," I said. "I'll be over at six. For a drink, okay? See you in the bar."

"How will I recognize you?"

I almost laughed.

"So-and-so told me to look you up." He was the first of many. He didn't want much, only to buy me a drink and ask me vulgarly sincere questions: "What's it really like?" and "Do you think you'll ever go back?" I used to say anything that came into my head, like "I love lunchmeat," or "Sell me your shoes."

"What made you stop pimping?" a feller would ask.

"I ran out of string," I'd say.

"How long are you going to stay in Singapore?"

"As long as my citronella holds out."

"What do you do for kicks?"

"That reminds me of a story. Seems there was this feller — "

In previous years the same fellers would have wanted to visit a Chinese massage parlor; now they wanted to see me. The motive had not changed: just for the experience. And evidently stories circulated about me on the tourist grape-vine: I had been deported from the States; I was a pederast; I had a wife and kids somewhere; I was working on a book; I was a top-level spy, a hunted man, a rubber planter, an in-former, a nut case. The fellers guilelessly confided this gos-sip and promised they wouldn't tell a soul. And one feller said he had looked me up because "Let's face it, Flowers, you're an institution."

I didn't encourage them. If they wanted a girl I sug-gested a social escort who, after a tour of the city — harbor sights, Mount Faber, Tiger Balm Gardens, Chinese temples, War Memorial, Saint Andrew's Cathedral — would ama-teurishly offer "intimacy," as they called it. Politics hadn't stopped prostitution; it had complicated it, taken the fun out of it, and made it assume disguises. The houses had moved to the suburbs — Mr. Sim operated on Tanjong Rhu, in an innocuous-looking bungalow near the Swimming Club. Many had gone to Johore Bahru, over the Causeway, and all paid heavily for secret-society protection. There were two brothels in town, Madam Lum's, behind the supermarket, and Joe's in Bristol Chambers, across from the Gurkha's sen-try box on Oxley Rise: they were characterless apartments, unpersuasively decorated, and they relied on taxi drivers to bring them fellers.

Oddly enough, the fellers who looked me up were seldom interested in girls. They were tourists who fancied them-selves adventurers, bold explorers, and they had two opposing wishes: to be the very first persons to reach that faraway place, and to be seen arriving. They thought it was quite a feat to fly to Singapore, but they needed a reliable native witness to verify their arrival. I was that witness, and the routine was always the same — a drink, a stroll around the seedier parts of town; then a picture — posed with me and snapped by the Indian with the box camera on the Espla-nade. All these fellers did in Singapore was talk, remarking on the discomfort of their hotels, the heat, the smells, their fear of contracting malaria. And when I told my heavily embroidered tales they said, "Flowers, you're as bad as me!" Sometimes, with wealthy ones, I wanted to lean across the table and plead, *"Get me out of here!"* But that was the voice of idleness, the one that screamed prayers at the Turf Club and hectored the fruit machines for a jackpot. I did my best to suppress it and listened to the travelers chuntering on about their experiences. I wish I had a nickel for every feller who told me the story about how he had picked up a pretty girl and taken her back to his hotel, only to find ("I was flabbergasted") that she was really a feller in a swishy dress; or the story, favorite of the fantasist, beginning, "I used to know this nympho — "

For me these were not productive years. The longer I stayed at Hing's the more I participated in the fellers' conversations at the Bandung: "My *towkay* says — " The Sunday curry was the only event in the week I viewed with any pleasure. Though Singapore was awash with tourists, and, for the first time, American soldiers on leave from Vietnam, I did very little hustling. The attitude toward sex was changing in the States and I found it hard in Singapore to keep pace with the changes; the new attitudes arrived with the tourists. Fellers were interested in exhibitions of one sort or another, Cantonese girls hanging in back rooms like fruit bats and squealing "Fucky, fucky" to each other, sullen displays of gray anatomy on trestle tables; off the Rochore Canal Road there were squalid rooms where a dozen tourists sat around a double bed, like interns in a clinic, and applauded cucumber buggeries. The feller who said "I do it with mirrors" or that he was in love with a slip of a girl meant just that; and one joker implored me to get a young Chinese boy to (I think I've got this right) stand over him and, as he put it, "do number two — oh lots of it — all over me."

"Now, you're going to think I'm old-fashioned," I said to

171

this dink. "And I know nobody's perfect. But — "

I could see nothing voluptuous about being recumbent under a Chinese and shat upon, something I went through, in a sense, every day at Hing's. I would fall into conversation with a tourist and hear myself saying, "That's where I draw the line." My notion of sex, call me old-fashioned, was a satisfying and slightly masked and moist surprise, unhurried, private, imaginative, and inexpensive, as close to passion as possible; neither businesslike nor over-coy, maintaining the illusion of desire with groans of proof, celebrating fantasy, a happy act the price kept in perspective: give and take, no lies about love.

The anonymous savagery of the new pornography might have had something to do with the change in the tourists' attitude. I had always considered myself a reasonable judge of pornography, but I was out of my depth with the stuff that came in on the freighters and was good-naturedly handed over to me by the mates responsible for the provisioning. It was as unappealing as a pair of empty rubber gloves. I refused to sell it, though I still sold decks of photographic playing cards. I didn't know what to do with the new cruel sort; I had too much of it to burn discreetly, and someone would have found it if I had thrown it in a trash barrel. I kept it at the Bandung, behind the bar. At the Bandung I was able to confirm that I was not alone in finding it grotesque.

"It's useless," said Yardley. "They don't have expressions on their faces."

"She got *something* on her face," said Frogget. "Sickening, ain't it?"

"That's what I always look at first," said Smale. "Their faces."

"Do you suppose," said Yates, selecting a picture, "that she expects that bulb to light up if she does *that* with it?"

"Maybe she blew a fuse," said Frogget.

172

"Yeah," said Smale, "here she is blowing a fuse."

" 'orrible," said Coony. "A girl and a mule. Look at that."

"Let's see," said Yates. "No, that's no mule. It's a donkey, what you call an ass."

"Oh, that's an ass," I said. "Oh, yes. Broo-hoo-hoo!"

"Do herself a damage," said Smale.

" 'orrible," said Coony.

"This one's all blokes," said Yardley. "All sort of connected up. I wonder why that one's wearing red socks."

"Are there names for this sort of thing?" asked Yates.

"I'd call that one 'The Bowling-Hold,' " said Frogget.

"Hey, Wally, come here," said Yardley.

"Leave him alone," I said.

"See what he does," said Yardley.

Wallace Thumboo came over, grinning; he glanced down at the pictures, then looked away, into space.

"What do you think of that, Wally old boy?"

"Nice," said Wally. He looked at the ceiling.

"Cut it out," I said. "He doesn't like them. I don't blame you, Wally. They're awful, aren't they?"

"Little bit," he said, and screwed up his face, making it plead.

"You said they were *nice,* you lying sod!" Yardley shouted. Wally wrung his hands. Yardley turned to me. "You're a bloody hypocrite, Jack."

"These photographs are shocking," said Yates. "What kind of people — "

"And he's the one who sells this rubbish!" said Yardley.

"Not this stuff," I said. "The other stuff, but only if they ask."

Edwin Shuck asked. He phoned me one morning at Hing's and said, "You don't know me — "

"Yes, I do," I said, snappishly. I had wanted for a long time to put one of these yo-yos in his place, and this was the day to do it: out in the van a consignment of frozen meat for the *Strode* was going soft in the sun. Little Hing was double-parked on Beach Road and beeping the horn. The *Strode* had a right to refuse the meat if it wasn't frozen solid, which meant we would have to sell it cheap to a hotel kitchen. "You met a horny feller somewhere who said he was a pal of mine, right?" I accused. "And he told you to look me up, right? You don't want to take too much of my time, just have a drink, right? And after that — "

"Not so fast," he said.

"Friend," I said, "the only thing I don't know about you is your name."

"Why don't we have lunch? Then I can tell you my name."

"I'm busy."

"After work."

"For Christ's sake, don't you understand? My meat's getting all thawed out!"

"What's *that* supposed to mean?"

"My meat's in the van," I said.

"I won't argue about it," he said.

"So long, then," I said.

"Give me a chance," he said. "Surely the Bandung can spare you for one night."

The Bandung was my private funk hole: "What *is* your name, friend?"

And: "Eddie Shuck, pleased to meet you," he said that evening in the floodlit garden of the Adelphi. I had just come from the *Strode,* where I had spent the whole afternoon on a shady part of the breezy deck playing gin rummy with the chief steward.

"Hope I haven't kept you waiting," I said.

"Not at all," said Shuck. "What'll you have?"

"I usually have a pink gin about this time of day."

"That's a good navy drink," he said, and he called out, "Boy!" to the waiter.

174

I found that objectionable, but something interested me about this Edwin Shuck. It was his lisp — not an ordinary lisp, the tongue lodged between the teeth, that gives the point to the joke about the doctor who examines the teen-age girl with a stethoscope and says, "Big breaths"; Shuck's was the parted fishmouth: his folded tongue softened and wetted every sibilant into a spongy drunken buzz. He prolonged "Flowers" with the buzz, and what was endearing was that his lisp prevented him from saying his own name correctly.

"Got some homework, I see."

"This?" I had a thick envelope on my lap, pornography from the *Strode,* a parting gift from the friendly steward. I said, "Filthy pictures."

"Seriously?" Buzz, buzz; he lisped companionably.

"The real McCoy," I said.

"Can I have a look?"

We were the only ones in the garden. I put the envelope on the table and pulled out the pictures. I said, "If anyone comes out here, turn them over, quick. We could be put in the cooler for these."

"You've sure got enough of them!"

"They're in sets. Get them in sequence. Ah, there we are. Starts off nice, all the folks in their skivvies having a cozy drink in the living room."

"What's the next one?" Shuck was impatient.

"Now we're in the bedroom. A few preliminaries, I guess you could call that."

"Kind of a group thing, huh? That gal — "

The waiter came over with our drinks. I flipped the large envelope over the pictures. I wasn't afraid of being arrested for them, but the thought of that old polite Chinese waiter seeing them embarrassed me. Pornography affected me that way: I could not help thinking that whoever looked at the stuff was responsible for what was happening in the picture. That girl, that dog; those kneeling men and vaulting women;

175

those flying bums. A single look included you in the act and completed it. Until you looked it was unfinished.

"Down the old canal," said Shuck, guzzling his fresh lime. "Hey, is that the guy's arm or what?"

"No, that's his bugle."

"His *what?*"

"Pecker, I think." I turned it over. "Here are your Japanese ones."

"You can't see their faces," he said. "How do you know they're Japs?"

"By their feet. See? That's your Japanese foot."

"It's in a damned strange position."

"This one's blurry. Can't make heads or tails of it."

"Wise guy." Shuck laughed. "What else have you got?"

"I've seen this bunch before," I said. "From some hamlet in Denmark."

"I wonder why that guy's wearing red socks?"

"Search me," I said. "Got some more — here we are. God, I hate these. I really pity those poor animals."

"Labrador retriever," said Shuck. "Foaming at the mouth."

"Poor bugger," I said. "Well, that's the lot."

"Huh?" Shuck was surprised. He didn't speak at once. He frowned and said thoughtfully, "Haven't you got any where the guy's on top and the girl's on the bottom, and they're — well, you know, *screwing?*"

"Funnily enough," I said, "no. Not the missionary position."

"That's a riot," said Shuck.

"It's pitiful," I said. "There's not much call for that kind. Here, you can have these if you want. My compliments. Strictly for horror interest."

"That's mighty neighborly," said Shuck. "Shall we eat here?"

"Up to you," I said. "What time is your plane leaving?"

176

"I'm not taking any plane," said Shuck. "I live here."

"What business are you in? I've never seen you around town."

"This and that," he said. "I do a lot of traveling."

"Where to?"

"K.L., Bangkok, Vientiane," he said. "Sometimes Saigon. How about you? How long do you aim to stay in Singapore?"

"As long as my citronella holds out," I said. "What's Saigon like?"

"Not much," said Shuck. "I was there when the balloon went up."

I didn't press him. He was either a spy and wouldn't admit to it, of course; or he was a businessman who was ashamed to say so and took pleasure in trying to give me the impression he was a spy. In any case, hemming and hawing, a mediocre adventurer.

We had a meal at the Sikh restaurant on St. Gregory's Place and then went on to a nightclub, the Eastern Palace, where Hing had taken me in my *Allegro* days. Shuck fed me questions — about hustling, the fantastic rumors (a new one: was I the feller who appeared in What's-his-name's novel?), the "meat run," Dunroamin, short-time rates, all-nighters. It was the same interview I got from other fellers, the gabbing that was like a substitute for the real thing.

The Eastern Palace had changed. "Years ago, this place had a bunch of Korean chorus girls, and a little Chinese orchestra. It wasn't as noisy as this. There was even a dance floor."

"Tell me a little bit more about this Madam Lum," said Shuck. "How does she get away with it in town?"

"Good question. She — " But I could not be heard over the roaring of a machine offstage. The curtains parted and in the center of the stage a girl crouched on a black motorcycle. The back wall slipped sideways — it was a moving landscape, a film of trees and telephone poles shooting past. By concentrating I could imagine that stationary girl actually speeding along a country road.

She flung off her goggles and helmet. A fan in the wings started up and blew her long hair straight back. She wriggled out of her leather jacket and let that fly. The music became louder, a pumping rhythm that emphasized the motorcycle roar.

"I don't like this," I said.

Shuck frowned, as he had when he had said, "Haven't you got any where the guy's on top — ?"

The girl stood up on the motorcycle saddle and kicked off her boots and tore off her britches. She was buffeted by the wind from the fan; she undid her bra and squirmed out of her pants — they sailed away. Then she hopped back onto the seat, naked, and pretended to ride, bobbing up and down, chafing herself on the saddle.

"I'm shocked," said Shuck.

I liked him for that. I said, "Isn't that a Harley-Davidson?"

The film landscape was moving faster now, the music was frenzied, the engine screamed. The girl started doing little stunts, horsing around on the motorcycle, lifting her legs, throwing her head back.

She bugged out her eyes and shrieked; she covered her face with her hands. There was a terrific crash. The landscape halted, the motorcycle tipped over, the naked girl took a spill and sprawled across the machine in the posture of an injured rider, her legs spread, her head awry, her arms tangled in the wheels.

Around us, Chinese businessmen, *towkays* in immaculate suits, applauded wildly and shouted, *"Hen hao!"* which meant "very good" and sounded like "And how!"

"This is where I draw the line," I said. "Let's get out of here." The act had disturbed me — what fantasy did such violence promote? — and I avoided mentioning it to Shuck. Walking down Orchard Road, past Tang's, and confounded by what to say, I asked him again about his business.

"You might say Asian affairs," said Shuck.

"Well," I said, "how do you expect to know anything about Asian affairs if you've never had one?"

Madam Lum greeted me as an old friend, with an affectionate bear hug, and with her arms around me she turned to Shuck and said, "Mr. Jack a very nice boy and he my best brother, no, Jack?"

"She's a real sweetie," I said.

"You want Mona?" asked Madam Lum. "She free in a coupla minutes — hee hee!"

"Who's Mona?" asked Shuck.

"One of the fruit flies," I said. "Rather athletic. She's got a nine-inch tongue and can breathe through her ears."

"Just my type," said Shuck, looking around. "Cripe, look at all the broads."

Over by the window, three girls were seated on a sofa, languidly reading Chinese comic books; one in a chair was buffing her fingernails, and another was eating pink prawns off a square of newspaper. No towels, no tea. It would never have happened at Dunroamin: no girls sat down if two fellers had just come through the door. "This is your newer sort of wang house," I said to Shuck. "Not my style at all." One of the girls put down her comic and sauntered over to Shuck, smoothing her dress.

"What your name?" she asked.

"Shuck."

"Twenty-over dollar."

"No, no," said Shuck, wincing, setting his mouth so as not to lisp. "*Me* Shuck."

"*Me* shuck you," said the girl, pointing.

"Forget it," I said. But I had recorded the exchange; it was 'material,' and it bothered me to acknowledge the suspicion that very soon, chewing the fat with an admiring stranger who had looked me up, I would be saying, "Funny thing happened the other day. I know a feller with the unfortunate name of Shuck, and we were goofing off in — "

"Mona coming," said Madam Lum.

"Not tonight," I said. "But my buddy here might be interested. What do you say, Ed?"

"I'm just window-shopping," he said. Buzz, buzz. "What was the name of that other place you mentioned?"

"Bristol Chambers," I said. "But, look, they don't like people barging in and out if they're not serious about it."

"You're a funny guy," said Shuck. "I used to know a guy just like you."

That annoyed me. It was presumptuous; he didn't know me at all. I could not be mistaken for anyone else. The half-baked whoremonger in the flowered shirt, with the tattoos on his arms, hamming it up on Orchard Road ("How do you expect to know anything about Asian affairs if you've never had one?") — that was all he saw. I resented comparisons, I hated the fellers who said, "Flowers, you're as bad as me!" They looked at me and saw a pimp, a pornocrat, an unassertive rascal marooned on a tropical island, but having the time of his life: a character. I said, "I don't want to hurt their feelings."

"That's what I mean," said Shuck.

"Well, what the heck's wrong with that?"

"The next thing you'll be telling me is that they've got hearts of gold, like these strippers that say they do algebra in their dressing rooms. They're better than we are or something."

"Not on your life," I said, and feeling the prickly sensation that his judgment on them was a judgment on me, added, "But they're no worse."

"I guess you're right. We're all whores one way or another," said Shuck, with a hint of self-pity. "I mean, we all sell ourselves, don't we?"

"Do we?"

"Yeah. We all sell our souls."

"Those girls don't sell their souls, pal. There's no future in that."

"You know what I mean. Holding a job, people climbing all over you. It's a kind of screw. I do it for fifteen grand."

"Madam Lum does it for fifty," I said, trying to wound him. "Tax free."

Walking down Mount Elizabeth I said, "Years ago, it was better, with the massage parlors and all that. There are still some in Johore Bahru. Madam Lum's place always reminds me of a doctor's office. Did you notice the potted plants and magazines? The only good thing about it is that it's convenient. The number twelve bus stops here and that supermarket over there is very good, probably cheaper than cold storage. I usually pick up half a pound of hamburg and some frozen peas before I nip over to Madam Lum's. You can't beat it for convenience."

"You really are a funny guy," said Shuck.

"Thanks," I said.

"I mean it in the good sense," he said.

"I'll take you to the Bristol," I said. "It's not far. But you can't go inside unless you want some action."

"If I must," said Shuck, buzzing. "What's the attraction?"

"The guy that runs it isn't very friendly," I said. "And the girls are nothing to write home about. It's a pretty run-of-the-mill sort of place, except for one thing."

"Spit it out."

"One of the bedrooms — the air-conditioned one — faces the Prime Minister's house. Some afternoons you can see him on his putting green. At night, around this time, you can get a look at him through the window. While you're in the saddle, you know? Strictly for laughs. But since you're interested in Asian affairs — "

"I think I saw him," Shuck said later at the Pavilion where we had agreed to meet for a drink. "He was talking to a guy with a goatee and a shirt like yours. That takes the cake," he said, smiling to himself. "But the hooker kept telling me to hurry up. Is that the usual thing? God, it put me off."

"It's a popular room," I said.

"Vientiane," said Shuck, using the monotone of reminiscence. "That's a wide-open place. Lu-Lu's, The White Rose. First-class hookers. They do tricks with cigarettes. 'Hey, Joe, you wanna see me smoke?' I had the strangest experience with a broad there — at least I *thought* it was a broad."

"But it wasn't."

"No, but that's not the whole story," said Shuck.

"I have to go," I said.

"Wait a minute," said Shuck. "I'm not finished."

"I've heard it before."

"No, you haven't."

"About the bare-assed waitresses in The White Rose in Vientiane, and the girl that was really a feller, and the nympho you used to know? I've heard it before. Now, if you'll pipe down and excuse me — "

"Jack," said Shuck, "sit yourself down. I've got some good news for you." Buzz, buzz.

10

Sex I had seen as a form of exalted impatience, trembling as near to hilarity as to despair — just like love — but so swift, and unlike love, it happily avoided both; that was a relief, grace after risk. And the strangest part of the sex wish: you wore all of it on your face. This assumption had been the basis of my whole enterprise. Paradise Gardens, Shuck's good news, made me change my mind about this.

"Here she comes," I said, and Ganapaty scrambled to his feet. I was standing in bright sunshine at the end of the cinder drive by his sentry box, squinting down Adam Road where, at the junction, the shiny bus had stopped at the lights. I folded my arms. The first fellers were arriving. Behind me, glittering, was Paradise Gardens, known in District Ten as a private hotel.

It was a new three-story building, long and narrow, white stucco trimmed with blue, and with a blue square balcony and a roaring air conditioner attached to every room. The usual high whorehouse fence, this one strung with morning-glories and supporting a hedge of Pong-Pong trees, concealed it from Dr. B. K. Lim's bungalow on one side and a row of semidetached houses (each with a barbed-wire fence and a starved whimpering guard dog) on Jalan Kembang Melati on the other side. On our cool lawn there were mimosas and jasmine and the splendid upright fans of three mature traveler's palms. In the secluded patio out back we had a small swimming pool.

The idea of Paradise Gardens was Shuck's, or perhaps that of the United States Army, who employed him and now me. The design was my own; I had supervised the construction. The catering contract was Hing's, and the glass-fronted shops in the arcade — the entire ground floor — were run by Hing's relations: a tailor (I was wearing one of his white linen suits that first day), a photographer, a curio seller (elongated Balinese carvings, *wayang* puppets, and a selection of Chinese bronzes ingeniously faked in Taiwan), a druggist with a RUBBER GOODS sign taped to his window, a barber, and a news agent. My orders had been to design a place that a guest — Shuck told me ours would be GIs when it was done — would check into and stay for five days without having to leave the grounds. It was an early version of the tropical tourist hotel which, more than a place to sleep, contains the country, a matter of size, food, décor, and entertainment. I had a vision of luxury hotels underpinning the rarest and most exotic features of a people's culture, the arts and crafts surviving in the Hilton long after they had ceased to be practiced in the villages. Tourism's demand for atmosphere and authentic folklore would force the hotel to be the country. So I made it happen. We had Malay and Chinese dances every night, and traditional food, and we were scrupulous about observing festivals. It took two days for our Mr. Loy to cook a duck; outside Paradise Gardens the Chinese ate hamburgers standing up at lunch counters or in their parked cars at the A & W drive-in. Once a week we put on a mock wedding in the Malay style. It had been years since anyone had seen something like that in Singapore.

"The bus coming," said Ganapaty.

"She's full up," I said.

Ganapaty came to attention, a crooked derelict figure with a beautiful white caste mark, a finger's width of ashes between his eyes. It pleased me that at Paradise Gardens I was able to employ everyone I owed a favor to: Yusof tended the big bar, Karim the smaller one; the room Shuck called "your theaterette" was run by Henry Chow, a blue-movie projectionist who had been out of work since the raids; Mr. Khoo, my old boatman, I employed as a mechanic, Gopi picked up the mail — though the post office was only across the street, his limp made what I intended as a sinecure for him a tedious and exhausting job. And the girls; the girls were no problem — fruit flies from Anson Road, floaters and athletes from the shut-down massage parlors, the sweet dozen from Dunroamin, and Betty from Muscat Lane — all my quick and limber daughters.

Shuck wanted to see their papers: "We're not taking any chances." He made me fire three who had been born in China, one with a sore on her nose, and a Javanese girl, a willowy fellatrix with gold teeth, reputedly a mistress of the late Bung Sukarno.

Every five days, as on that first day, the bus swayed into the driveway and I could see the young faces at the green-tinted windows. I waved. They did not wave back. They stared. I learned that unimpatient stare. It was a look of pure exhaustion focusing on the immediate, fastening to it, not glancing beyond it. It was new to me. Once, I had been able to spot a likely client thirty yards off by the way he watched girls pass him, the face of a feller running a temperature, wearing helpless lechery on his kisser; with that telling restive alertness as, turning around with tensed arms and eager hands, sipping air through the crack of a smile starting to be hearty, he looks as if he is going to say something out loud. Each fidget was worth ten dollars. But the faces of the boys

185

on the buses that deposited them for what Shuck called "your R and R" were expressionless and kept that bombed uncritical stare until they boarded the same bus five days later. The boys sat well back in their seats; they didn't hitch forward like tourists, and they didn't chatter.

I expected uniforms the first day. Shuck hadn't mentioned that they would be wearing Hawaiian shirts, but here they were getting off the bus with crew cuts, bright shirts, the white socks that give every American away, and staring with tanned sleepy faces.

"Jack Flowers," I said, stepping forward. "Glad you could make it, fellers."

"It's sure as hell — " a feller began slowly.

"Excuse me, sir," another butted in. "Are those girls — "

"The girls," I said, raising my voice, "are right over there and dying to get acquainted!"

Florence, May, Soo-chin, Annapurna, and nutcracker Betty, hearing me, responded by ambling into the sunlight on the arcade's verandah. The other girls moved behind them. The fellers carried their duffel bags and handgrips over to the verandah and dropped them, and almost shyly walked over to the girls and began pairing off.

"We're in business," said Shuck.

Later they walked in the garden, holding hands.

The soldiers' five-day romance was a rehearsal of innocence, and then they went back to Vietnam. This all-purpose house was the only gentle shelter, halfway down the warpath, with me at the front gate saying, "Is there anything — ?" My mutters made me remember: in the passion that caged us the issue was not escape — it was learning gentleness to survive in the cage, and never loutishly rolling against the bars.

"For some of these guys it's their first time with a whore," said Shuck. "What do you tell them?"

"Don't smoke in bed."

Was I serving torturers? I didn't feel I had a right to ask. I believed in justice. The torturer slept with harm and stink, the pox would eat him up, his memory would claw him. I wanted the others to wrestle in their rooms until they were exhausted beyond sorrow — a happy bed wasn't everything, but it was more than most worthy fellers got.

I write what I never spoke. Conversation is hectic prayer; it deprived me of subtlety and indicated time passing. It didn't help much. At Paradise Gardens, by the bar, showing my tattoos and joshing the girls and soldiers, I was a noisy cheerful creature. But the mutters in my mind told me I was Saint Jack. Edwin Shuck, saying so casually, "We're all whores one way or another," was parodying an enormous possibility that could never be disproved until we had rid ourselves of the habit of slang, the whore's own evasive language, a hard way to be honest and always a mockery of my mutters. I simplified, I used slang; I was known as a pimp, the girls as whores, the fellers as soldiers: none of the names fits.

I kept Paradise Gardens running smoothly, and what made me move was what had stirred me for years, my priestly vocation, my nursing instinct, my speedy hunger and curiosity, my wish to head off any cruelty, my singular ache to be lucky; and I did it for fortune. I had seen a lot of fellers come over the hill, and as I say, the drift then was away from all my old notions of sex. In Singapore my suggestions had long since been overtaken by wilder ideas, pictures, movies, devices, potions, acrobatics, or complete reticence; my vocabulary was obsolete and words like "torrid," "fast," "daring," and "spicy" meant nothing at all. What had once seemed to me as simple as a kind of ritual corkage became a spectator sport or else an activity of nightmarish athleticism. It made me doubly glad for Paradise Gardens. The soldiers were happy with a cold beer and the motions of a five-day romance. I made sure the beer was so cold their tonsils froze and had Karim put four inches of ice in every drink. All afternoon we showed old cowboy movies in the theaterette. Some of the fellers taught the girls to swim. Every five days the bus came, and for five days most of the fellers stayed inside the gates. When they wandered it was up to the university, close by, to try out their cameras.

One group of GIs bought me a pair of binoculars, expensive ones with my initials lettered in gold on the leather case, and a little greeting card saying *To a swell guy*.

"Now I can see what goes on in your rooms," I said.

They laughed. What went on in those rooms, anyway? *Aw honey*, the purest cuddlings of romance, pillow fights; they tickled the girls, and they never broke or pilfered a thing.

"You won't see much in Buster's," one said.

I turned to Buster. "That right? Not interested in poontang?"

"I can't use it," Buster said, with a lubberly movement of his jaw.

"Buster's married." The feller looked at me. "You married, Jack?"

"Naw, never got the bug — ruins your sense of humor," I said. "Marriage — I've got nothing against it, but personally speaking I'd feel a bit overexposed."

"Where's your old lady, Buster?" the feller asked.

"Denver," said Buster, shyly, "goin' ape-shit. How about a hand of cards?"

"Later," a tall feller said. "My girl wants a camera."

My girl. That was Mei-lin. They all wanted cameras; they knew the brands, they picked out the fanciest ones. When the fellers boarded the bus for the ride back to the war the girls rushed to Sung's Photo in the arcade and sold them for half price.

"Used camera," said Jimmy Sung, when I challenged him.

"Cut the crap," I said. It was a shakedown. From a two-hundred-dollar camera Sung made a hundred and the girl made a hundred; the soldier paid. But Sung ended up with the camera, to sell again.

"Full prices for the cameras," I said to Sung, "or I'll toss you out on your ear."

In the kitchen Hing made up huge deceitful grocery lists which he passed to Shuck without letting me see, and he got checks for items he never bought. The arcade prices were exortionary, the girls were grasping. No one complained. On the contrary: the fellers often said they wanted to marry my girls and take them back to the States, "the world," as they called it.

I did what I could to reduce the swindling. The arcade shopkeepers saw it my way and "Sure, sure," they'd say, and claw at their stiff hair-bristles with their fingers when I threatened.

In Sung's, on the counter, there was an album of photographs, a record of Paradise Gardens which thickened by the week. Many were posed shots Sung had snapped, tall fellers embracing short dark girls, fellers around a table drinking beer, muscle-flexers by the pool, group shots on the verandah, candid shots — fellers fooling with girls in the garden. There were many of me, but the one I liked showed me in my linen suit, having my late-afternoon gin, alone in a wicker chair under a traveler's palm, with a cigar in my mouth; I was haloed in gold and green, and dusty beams of sunlight slanted through the hedge.

Shuck was right: the news was good, almost the glory I imagined. I was surprised to reflect that what I wanted had taken a war to provide. But I didn't make the war, and I would have been happier without the catastrophe. In every picture in Sung's album the war existed in a detail as tiny and momentous as a famous signature or a brace of well-known initials at the corner of a painting: the dog tag, the socks, the military haircut, the inappropriate black shoes the fellers wore with their tropical clothes, a bandage or scar,

189

a particular kind of sunglasses, or just the fact of a farm boy's jowl by the pouting rabbit's cheek of a Chinese girl. In the lobby it was a smell, leather and starch and after-shave lotion, and a nameless apprehension like the memory of panic in a room with a crack on the ceiling that grows significant to the insomniac toward morning. "Saigon, Saigon," the girls said; we didn't talk about it, but the fellers left whispers and faces behind we could never shoo away.

And Sung's photograph album, the size of a family Bible and bound with a steel coil, was our history.

A sky of dazzling asterisks: the Fourth of July. The fellers set off rockets and Roman candles in the garden with chilly expertness, a sequence of rippling blasts that had Dr. B. K. Lim screaming over the hedge and all the guard dogs in the neighborhood howling. The fellers ate wieners and sauerkraut, had a rough touch football game; that night everyone jumped into the pool with his clothes on.

Mr. Loy Hock Yin holding a huge Thanksgiving turkey on a platter. Fellers with napkins tucked in at the throats of their shirts. I was at the head of the table, and the feller next to me said, "How'd you get all those tattoos, Jack?" The fans were going, the table was covered with food, I had a bottle of gin and a bucket of ice beside my glass. "What I'm going to tell you is the absolute truth," I said, and held them spellbound for an hour. At the end I showed my arm to Betty.

"What's underneath that flower?" I asked.

She squinted: *"Whore's Boy."*

Me as Santa Claus, with a sack. Late Christmas afternoon we ran out of ice. I drove downtown in Shuck's Toyota with four uproarious soldiers and some squealing girls. I was still wearing my red suit, perspiring in my cotton beard, as we went from shop to shop saying, "Ice for Santy!" On the way back, in traffic, we sang Christmas carols.

Gopi with an armful of mail. He said, "Nice post for you." Postcards of Saigon I taped to my office wall. Messages: "It's pretty rough here all around — " "When I get back to the world — " "Tell Florence my folks don't care, and I'll be down in September — " "We could use a guy like you, Jack, for a few laughs. This is a really shitty platoon — " "The VC were shelling us for two days but we couldn't even see them — " "Richards got it in Danang, but better not tell his girl — " "What's the name of that meat on sticks Mr. Loy made — ?" "I had a real neat time at Paradise Gardens — How's Jenny?" "It's fucken gastly or however you write it — I know my spelling is beyond the pail — "

A Malay orderly in a white smock tipping a sheeted stretcher into the back of an ambulance.
"Fella in de barroom no come out."
I knocked. No answer. We got a crowbar and prized the lock apart. The feller had hanged himself on the shower spout with a cord from the Venetian blind. A whiskey bottle, half-full, stood on the floor. He was nineteen years old, not a wrinkle on his face.
"It was bound to happen," said Shuck. What certainty! "But if it happens again we'll have to close this joint."
No one would use the room after that, and later the door grew dusty. All the girls played that room number in the National Lottery.

Flood. When a strong rain coincided with high tide the canal swelled and Bukit Timah Road flooded; muddy water lapped against the verandah. The photograph was of three girls wading to Paradise Gardens with their shoes in one

191

hand and an umbrella in the other, and the fellers whistling and cheering in the driveway.

The theaterette. Audie Murphy in a cowboy movie. "He's a game little guy," I said. "He won the Medal of Honor." A feller to my right: "Fuck that."

A group photograph: Roger Lefever, second from the left, top row.
"What's the big idea, Roger?"
"I didn't mean it."
"She came down crying and said you slugged her."
"It wasn't hard. Anyway, she pissed me off."
"I got no time for bullies. I think I could bust you in the mouth for that, Roger. And I've got a good mind to write to your C.O. You wouldn't do that back home, would you?"
"How do you know?"
I slapped his face.
"Smarten up. You're on my shit list until you apologize."

A group photograph: Jerry Waters, on the end of the middle row, scowling.
"You're lucky, Jack. You were fighting the Nazis."
"I didn't see any Nazis in Oklahoma."
"You know what I mean. It helps if the enemy's a bastard. But sometimes we're shooting the bull at night, tired as shit, and a guy comes out and says, 'If I was a Vietnamese I'd support the VC,' and someone else says, 'So would I,' and I say, 'That's for sure.' It's unbelievable."

The curio shop. After a while the carvings changed. Once there had been ivory oxen and elephants, teakwood deer, jade eggs, and lacquer jewelry boxes. Then we got bad replicas, and finally obscene ones — squatting girls, heavy wooden nudes, carvings of eight-inch fists with a raised middle finger, hands making the *cornuto.*

The Black Table.

"I'd like to help you, George, but it's against the rules to have segregated facilities."

"We don't want no segregated facilities *as such,* but what we want's a table to sit at so we don't have to look at no Charlies. And the brothers, they asked me to spearhead this here thing."

"I don't think it's a good idea," I said.

"I ain't asking you if you think it's a good idea. I'm telling you to get us a table or we'll waste this house."

"You only have three more days here. Is it too much to ask you to simmer down and make friends?"

"We got all the friends we want. There's more brothers coming next week, so if you say no you'll have to negotiate the demand with a real bad ass, Baraka Johnson."

"*Haraka-haraka, haina baraka,*" I said. "Swahili. My ship used to stop in Mombasa. *Nataka* Tusker beer *kubwa sana na beridi sana.*"

"Cut the jive, we want a table."

"What if everybody wanted a table?"

"That's the nitty-gritty, man. Every mother *got* a table except us. You think them Charlies over in the corner of the big bar want us to sit with them? You ever see any brothers sitting along the wall?"

"Maybe you don't want to."

"Maybe we don't, and maybe them Charlies and peckerwoods don't want us to. Ever think of that?"

"What you're saying is there are already white tables, so why not have a table for the colored fellers?"

"What *colored fellers?*"

"Years ago — "

"We are *black* brothers and we wants a *black* table!"

"The point is I didn't know there were white tables. I would have put my foot down."

"Go ahead, mother, put your foot down, you think I care? I'm just saying we want a table — now — and if we don't get it we'll waste you. Dig?"

It was true. Yusof said so: we had a wall of "white" tables. I gave in. Sung's photograph showed smiling and frowning faces, all black, and the girls — the only ones they would touch — long-haired Tamils, because they were black, too.

"Give them what they want," said Shuck.

"Up to a point," I said, "that's my philosophy."

Me, in my flowered shirt, having a beer with three fellers. A middle-aged sentence recurred in my talk. "That was a lot of money in those days — "

A group photograph: Bert Hodder, fifth from the end, middle row. He got tanked up one night and stood on his chair and sang,

> *"East Toledo High School,*
> *The best high school in the world!*
> *We love East Toledo,*
> *Our colors are blue and gold — "*

Neighborhood kids from the block of shophouses around the corner. They were posed with their arms around each other. They lingered by the gate, calling out "Hey Joe!" Ganapaty chased them with an iron pipe. The fellers chatted with them and gave them errands to run. They came to my office door.

"Ten cents, mister." This from one in a clean white shirt.

"Buzz off, kid, can't you see I'm busy?"

"Five cents."

"Hop it!"

Edwin Shuck. His blue short-sleeved shirt, freckled arms, and narrow necktie; clip-on sunglasses, sweat socks, and loafers.

"Got a minute?" he asked.

I was with Karim. "The cooler's on the fritz. I'll be with you in a little while."

"That can wait," he said. "I've got to see you in your office."

"Okay," I said, and wiped my greasy hands on a rag.

Shuck poured himself a drink at my liquor cabinet. He closed the door after me.

"I spent yesterday afternoon with the ambassador."

"How's his golf game?" I took a cigar out of the pocket of my silk shirt.

"He spent yesterday morning with the army."

"So?"

"I've got some bad news for you."

"Spill it," I said. But I had an inkling of what it would be. A week before, a Chinese feller named Lau had come to me with a proposition. He was from Penang and had twenty-eight girls up there he wanted to send down. He expected a finder's fee, bus fare for all of them, and a job for himself. He said he knew how to do accounts; he also knew where I could get some pinball machines, American sports equipment, a film projector, and fittings for a swimming pool, including a new diving board. I told him I wasn't interested.

"They're closing you up," said Shuck.

"That's one way of putting it," I said. "Who's *they?*"

"U.S. government."

"They're closing *me* up?" I snorted, "What *is* this?"

"It's nothing personal — "

"You can say that again," I said. "This isn't my place — it's *theirs!* So I suppose you mean they're closing themselves up."

"In a manner of speaking," said Shuck. "Officially the U.S. Army doesn't operate cathouses."

"If you think this is a cathouse you don't know a hell of a lot about cathouses!"

"Don't get excited," said Shuck, and now I began to hate his lisp. "It wasn't my decision. The army's been kicking this idea around for ages. I've got my orders. I'm only sorry I couldn't let you know sooner."

"Do me a favor, Ed. Go down the hall and find Mr. Khoo. He's just bought the first car he's ever owned — on the strength of this job. He's got about ninety-two more payments to make on it. Go tell him the Pentagon wants him to sell it and buy a bike. See what he says."

"I didn't think you'd take it so hard," said Shuck. "You're really bitter."

"Go find Jimmy Sung. He's paying through the nose for a new shipment of Jap cameras. Tell him the ambassador says he's sorry."

"Sung's a crook, you said so yourself."

"He knew what he was doing," I said. "I shouldn't have stopped him. I was getting bent out of shape trying to keep this place honest, and then you come along and piss down everyone's shoulder blades."

"Everyone's going to be compensated."

"What about Penang? You screwed them there."

"That's classified — who told you about Penang?"

"I've got information," I said. "You're ending the R and R program there. They're all looking for jobs, and you know as well as I do they're not going to find them. It's not fair."

"Jack, be reasonable," said Shuck. "We can't keep half of Southeast Asia on the payroll indefinitely."

"Why put them on the payroll in the first place?"

"I suppose it seemed like a good idea at the time," Shuck said. "I don't know. I don't make policy."

"I can't figure you out," I said. "You're like these fellers from the cruise ships that used to come to Singapore years ago, dying to get laid. Money was no object, they said. Then

196

when I found them a girl they'd say, 'Got anything a little less pricy?' And you! You come in here with an army, making promises, throwing money around, hiring people, building things, and — I don't know — *invading* the frigging place and paying everyone to sing "God Bless America." And then you call it off. Forget it, you say, just like that."

"Maybe it got too expensive," said Shuck. "It costs — "

But I was still fulminating. "Play ball, you say, then you call off the game! You call that fair?"

"I never figured you for a hawk."

"I'm not a hawk, you silly bastard!"

"Okay, okay," said Shuck. "I apologize. What do you want me to say? We'll do the best we can for the people here — compensate them, whatever they want. You're the boss."

"Oh, yeah, I'm the boss." I was sitting behind my desk, puffing on the cigar, blowing smoke at Shuck. Briefly, it had all seemed real. I had a notebook full of calculations: in five years I would have saved enough to get myself out, quietly to withdraw. But it was over, I was woken.

Shuck said, "You don't have anything to worry about."

"You're darned tootin' I don't," I said. "I had a good job before you hired me. A house, plenty of friends." Hing's, my semidetached house on Moulmein Green, the Bandung. *There's Always Someone You Know at the Bandung.*

"I mean, I've got a proposition for you."

"Well, you can roll your proposition into a cone and shove it. I'm not interested."

"You haven't even heard it."

"I don't want to."

"It means money," said Shuck.

"I've seen your money," I said. "I don't need it."

"You're not crapping out on us, are you?"

"I like that," I said. "Ever hear the one about the feller with the rash on his arm? No? He goes to this skin specialist who says, 'That's a really nasty rash! Better try this powder.'

The powder doesn't work. He tries ointment, cream, injections, everything you can name, but still the rash doesn't clear up. Weeks go by, the rash gets worse. 'It's a pretty stubborn rash — resisting treatment,' says the doc. 'Any idea how you got it?' The feller says he doesn't have the foggiest. 'Maybe you caught it at work,' the doc says, 'and by the way where *do* you work?' 'Me?' the feller says, 'I work at the circus. With the elephants.' 'Very interesting,' says the doctor, 'What exactly do you do?' 'I give them enemas — but the thing is, to give an elephant an enema you have to stick your arm up its ass.' 'Eureka!' says the doc. 'Give up your job and I guarantee the rash on your arm will clear up.' 'Don't be ridiculous,' says the feller, 'I'll never give up show biz.' "

Shuck pursed his lips. I didn't blame him: I had told the joke too aggressively for it to raise a laugh.

"Do you know the one about Grandma's wang house? Seems there was this feller — "

"I've heard it," said Shuck. " 'You've just been screwed by Grandma.' "

"That's how I feel," I said. I split a matchstick with my thumbnail and began picking my teeth.

"Just listen to my proposition, then say yes or no."

"No," I said. "Like the feller says, it's a question of mind over matter. You don't mind and I don't matter. Get it?"

"You're being difficult."

"Not difficult — impossible," I said, and added, "Mr. Shuck," lisping it with the same fishmouth buzz that he gave his name. I regretted that, and to cover it up, went on, "Now, if you'll excuse me, I think I'll go break the news to Hing. I get the feeling Hing and I are on our way back to Beach Road. I'm not really a pimp, you know. That's just talk." I puffed the cigar and grinned at him. "I'm a ship chandler by profession, and it's said that at ship chandling I'm a crackerjack."

I winked.

Shuck glumly zipped his briefcase. "If you ever change your mind — "

"Never!"

At lunchtime it rained and the rain quickly developed into a proper storm, a Sumatra of the same velocity I had weathered in the harbor on Mr. Khoo's launch when we towed that lighterful of girls to the *Richard Everett*. Ever since then, storms excited me: I could not read or write during a storm, and for the duration of the rain and wind my voice was louder; I found it easy to laugh, and I drank more quickly, standing up, peering out the window. I couldn't turn my back on a storm. I switched off the radio and watched this one from my office at Paradise Gardens. It grew as dark at half past twelve as it was at nightfall — not sunset, but after that, dark sunless evening. I threw the windows open to hear the storm; it was cool, not raining yet, but very dark, with leaves turning over and stiff tree branches blowing like hair.

The lower part of the sky was lighted dully and all the pale green grass and the palm leaves turned olive, and tree trunks blackened. The birds disappeared: a last blown one straggled over Dr. Lim's hedge. The fronds of the traveler's palms parted and the larger trees swayed, and in the darkness the widely spaced drops began, as big as half dollars, staining the driveway. There was a rumble of faraway thunder. At the beginning it was still dark, but with the torrent it grew silvery, the air brightened as the rain came down, and softened to daylight as the larger clouds collapsed into the dense glassy streaks of the downpour flooding the garden. Soon it was all revolving sound and water and light; the trees that had thrashed grew heavy, the drooping leaves seeming to force the branches downward. Water foamed and bubbled down the roof tiles and flooded the gutters of Dr. Lim's bungalow.

It continued for less than an hour, and before it was over the sun came out and made the last falling drops and the mist from the hot street shine brilliantly. Everything the rain touched glistened and dripped, and afterward all the houses and trees and pushcart awnings and bamboo fences were changed. The wetness gave everything in the sun the look of having swelled, and just perceptibly, buckled.

Some months later, in the old shop on Beach Road, Gopi the *peon* sidled into my cubicle, showed me two large damp palms and two discolored eyes, and said, "Mr. Hing vaunting Mr. Jack in a hurry-*lah*." You know what for.

Part Three

Part Three

1

THE SMOKE behind me — Leigh combusted — as I drove
from the crematorium with Gladys, was the same pale color
as the mid-morning Singapore cloud that sinks in a steamy
mass over the island and grows yellow and suffocating throughout the afternoon, making the night air an inky cool surprise. I felt relief, a springy lightness of acquittal that was
like youth. I was allowed all my secrets again, and could
keep them if I watched my step. It was like being proven
stupid and then, miraculously, made wise: a change of air.

Leaving, I was reminded of the chase of my past, my sea-
son of flights and reverses; and I began to understand why
I had never risen. The novelist's gimmick, the dying man
seeing his life flash before him, is a convenient device but
probably dishonest. I had once been clobbered on the head:
my vision was an unglued network of blood canals at the back
of my eyes and the feeble sight of the sausage I'd had for
breakfast. Pain made my memory small, and Leigh had
looked so numb and haunted I doubt that he had remembered his lunch. A life? Well, the dying man risks pain's
abbreviations or death's halting the recollection at a mis-

leading moment. The live glad soul I was, bumping away from the crematorium, had access to the past and could pause to dwell on the taste of an ambiguity, or to relish an irony: "Let's face it, Flowers," the feller had said, "you're an institution!" I was rueful: feeling chummy I had helped so many, stretching myself willingly supine on the rack of their fickleness — any service short of martyrdom, and what snatchings had been repeated on me! But, ah, I wasn't dead.

Leigh was dead. He had told me his plans, everything he wanted. It amounted to very little, a quiet cottage on that rainy island, a few flowers, some peace — an inexpensive fantasy. He had got nothing. His example unsettled me; and as death rephrases the life of everyone who's near, I felt I was reading something new in my mind, an altered rendering of a previous hope. It was a correction, needling me to act. It worried me. My resolution, inspired by his death, was also mocked by his death, which appeared like an urging to hope at the same moment it demonstrated the futility of all hope. His life said: *Act soon.* His death said: *Expect nothing.* My annoyance with him as a rude stranger who messed up my plans was small compared to my frustration at seeing him dead — there was no way to reply. And worse, his staring astonished look had suggested the unexpected, the onset of a new vision irritatingly coupled with an end to speech. Behind me, clouding Upper Aljunied Road, was the smoke of that dumb prophet, made private by death, who had stared at an unsharable revelation, which might have been nothing at all.

"Where I am dropping?" Gladys's voice ended my reverie.

"Palm Grove."

"Air-con?"

"I wouldn't be a bit surprised."

"I *like* Palm Grove." Gladys hugged herself. Her skinny hands and the back of her neck were heartbreaking.

"Good for you," I muttered.

"You sad, Jack. I know. You friend dead," said Gladys. "He was a nice man, I think."

"He wasn't," I said. "But that's the point, isn't it?"

"Marry with a wife?"

"Yeah," I said. "In Hong Kong. The cremation was her idea. She chose the hymn. The ashes go off to Hong Kong in the morning, by registered mail. She thought it would be better that way." I could see the mailman climbing off his bike and pulling a brown paper parcel out of his knapsack. Your husband, one pound, eight ounces; customs declaration and so forth: *Sign here, missy.*

"Why you not marry?"

"That's all I need." Marriage! Any mention of the Chinese gave me a memory picture of a caged shop near Muscat Lane, the family seated grumbling around a table (Junior doing his homework), beneath an unshaded bulb of uselessly distracting brightness; I couldn't think of the Chinese singly — they lived in gangs and family clans, their yelling a simulation of speech. The word marriage gave me another picture, a clinical American bathroom, locked for the enactment of marriage: Dad shaving, Mom on the hopper with her knees pressed together, the kids splashing in the tub, all of them naked and yakking at once. It was unholy, safety's wedded agony; I had been tempted, but I had never sinned that way. I said to Gladys, "What about you?"

"Me? Sure, I get marry every night!" She cackled. My girls were always asked the same questions — name, age, status — and they built a fund of stock replies. It was possible for me to tell by the speed and ingenuity of the reply how long a girl had been in the business. *I get marry every night:* Gladys was an old-timer.

In the lobby of the Palm Grove Hotel a huddle of tourists gave us the eye as we walked toward the elevator. If I needed any proof that there was no future in hustling for tourists there it was: two wizened fellers gasping on a sofa, another propped on crutches, a vacant wheelchair, a white-haired man asleep or dead in the embrace of a large armchair. Struldbrugs. Like the joke about the old duffer who says he has sex fifty weeks a year with his young wife. "Amazing," says a youngster, "but what about the other two weeks?" The old duffer says, "Oh, that's when the feller that lifts me on and off goes on vacation."

Gladys was no beauty, I wasn't young; the tourists were watching, trying to determine the relationship between the red-faced American and the skinny Chinese girl. I hooked my arm on hers like a stiff old-fashioned lover and began remarking loudly on the tasteful décor of the lobby and the thick carpet, pleased that the suit I was wearing would deflect some of the scorn. *Who does that jackass think he is?*

Upstairs, the feller answered the door in his bathrobe.

"My name is Flowers."

He looked at Gladys, then at me.

"We spoke on the telephone about a month back, when you were passing through on the *Empress*."

"That's right," he said. "I thought maybe you'd forgotten."

"I made a note of it here," I said, tapping my desk diary. "Anyway, here she is, skipper."

Now he leered. Gladys nodded and looked beyond him into the cool shadowy room.

"Thanks very much," he said. He opened the door for her, then fished five dollars out of his pocket and handed the money to me.

"What's this?"

"For your trouble."

"That doesn't exactly cover it," I said.

"It'll have to."

"Hold your horses," I said. "How long do you want her for?"

"We'll see," he said.

Gladys was in the room, looking out the window.

"Gladys, don't let — "

"Leave her out of this," the feller said.

I wanted to sock him. I said, "Until tomorrow morning is a hundred and twenty bucks, or sterling equivalent, payable in advance."

"I told you *we'll see*," he said. "Now bugger off."

"I'll be downstairs."

"That won't be necessary."

"It's my usual practice," I said. "Just so there's no funny business."

"Suit yourself," he said, and slammed the door.

At half past three Gladys was nowhere in sight. I was standing by the elevator, afraid to sit in the main lobby and get stared at by the Struldbrugs who would know what I was up to as soon as they saw me alone. Until Leigh came I had never found that embarrassing.

Next to the elevator there was a blue Chinese vase filled with sand, and bristling from the sand were cigarette ends, crumpled butts, and two inches of what looked to me like a good cigar. I was anxious, and I quickly realized that the source of my anxiety was a longing to snatch up that cigar, dust it off, and light it. What troubled me was that only the thought that I would be seen prevented me from doing it.

A fifty-three-year-old grubber in ashtrays, standing in the shadows of the Palm Grove lobby. Downtown, on Beach Road, a *towkay* hoicked my name and kicked his dog and demanded to know where I was. Between the cremation of a stranger and the session of hard drinking that was to come, I had obliged a feller with a Chinese girl and been handed five bucks and told to bugger off. I had kept the five bucks. I waited, doglike but without a woof, and I went on swallowing self-pity, hugging my tattoos and watching Chinese hurry through air remarkably like the smoke their own ashes would make. I knew mortality, its human smell and hopeless fancies. What was I waiting for?

"She's not down here, skipper," I said over the room phone. "You're overtime."

"You're telling me!"

"Where is she?"

"Take a wild guess."

"I'll inform the management," I said. "You leave me no other choice."

"I'll inform the management about *you*. Moo-wah!"

"Be reasonable, skipper. I don't find that funny."

"Stop pestering me. You her father or something?"

"Guardian you might say."

"Is *that* what they call it these days!"

"I've just done you a big favor, pal!" I shouted. "And this is what I get for it, a lot of sass!"

"I don't owe you a thing."

"You owe me," I said, "a great deal, and you owe Gladys — "

"Go away."

"I'm staying put."

"You should be ashamed of yourself," the feller said, and hung up.

In the basement corridor I passed a fire alarm; the red spur of a switch behind glass, with a handy steel mallet hanging next to it on a hook. The directions shouted to me. I waited until the corridor was empty, then sprang to it and followed the clear directions printed on the black label riveted to the wall. I smashed, I pulled. A bell above my head rapped and rang and lifted to a scream.

2

AN HOUR LATER, in a phone booth, that alarm was still screaming in my ears, turning my recklessness into courage as I
dialed the American embassy. I held the receiver to my
mouth like an oxygen mask; I was out of breath, and panting, felt incomplete — rushed and unimaginative. The
phrases I was prepared to use, urgent offers of service my
canny justifications, you might say, had once mercifully
blessed, struck me as whorish. They had not troubled me
before — "Anything I can do — ," "Just name it — ," "Leave
it to me — ," "An excellent choice: couldn't have done better
myself — ," "No trouble at all — ," "It was a pleasure — ,"
"That's what I'm here for — ," "What are friends for — ?"
But that was when I had a choice. This phone call was no
decision. It was hardly my choice; it was the last plea possible. I was on my back. I needed a favor. *Is there anything
— anything at all — you can do for me?*

"Ed, remember — "

"Flowers, is that you?" It was a relief to hear Shuck's
jaws, the familiar and endearing buzz as he casually moistened my name with the kiss of his fishy lisp. "Where have
you been hiding yourself?"

"Had my hands full," I said.

"It's good to be busy."

"It was driving me bananas," I said.

"Nice to hear your voice."

"Same here," I said. "I thought I might drop around sometime. Chew the fat. Maybe this afternoon if it's okay with you. Things are pretty quiet at the office. I could hop in a taxi and be over in a few minutes, or — "

"I'd really like that," Shuck said. "But I'm tied up at the moment."

For pity's sake, I was going to say. I resisted. "Some other time then. It's just that I'm free this afternoon, and, ah, I don't know whether you remember, but we've got some unfinished business."

Shuck hummed. He said, "Jack, to tell the honest truth I didn't think I'd hear from you again. You know?"

"That's what I want to explain."

"Don't get me wrong, I'm glad you called," he said. "I'm *damned* glad you called."

"How about a drink?"

"Sorry," he said.

"What about after work? What time do you knock off?"

"I'll write you a letter," Shuck said quickly.

"A *letter*? What if it gets lost in the mail?"

"You're a card," said Shuck. "Hey, heard any good ones lately?"

"Gags? No, nothing." I thought of my double, the hilarity and malice he provoked, the embarrassment of his presence which was the embarrassment of a comic routine ("Does this establishment — ?"), fumblings which circumstances twisted into laughless gestures of despair, the alien clown killed by tomfoolery. At a distance, as a story — with death absent — it was a joke I could enter into. But death turned the shaggy-dog story into tragedy by making it final. If Leigh had survived I would have found it all screamingly funny; I could have kicked his memory with a mocking story at the Bandung. But it was different, I was on the phone; the memory of smoke stopped my mouth.

"You'll get the letter tomorrow," said Shuck. "Stay loose."

It was delivered to Hing's by an embassy *peon*. I signed for it and took it into my cubicle to open. It was a limp envelope of the sort that just squeezing it in my fingers I knew contained nothing important. I slit it open and shook out a brown coupon and a small memo. The coupon said, HARBOUR TOUR — ADMIT ONE ADULT $3.50; the memo specified a day and time, and bore Edwin Shuck's squinting initials.

"We can talk better here," said Shuck on the launch *Kachang*. We climbed the ladder to the cabin roof and took up positions some distance from the tourists. Shuck looked back and said, "Hold the phone."

A feller in a straw hat had crawled up behind us. He said, "Hi! Do me a favor? Take a picture of me and my wife? That's her down there, with the hat. All you have to do is look through here and snap. I've set the light meter. Swell."

"It's not usually this crowded," said Shuck, aiming the camera at the man and wife on the afterdeck.

"Thanks a lot," said the feller, retrieving his camera. "How about a snap of you two? I'll send you a print when we get back to the States."

"No," said Shuck sharply, and turned away and closed his eyes in an infantile gesture of refusal.

The *Kachang's* engine whirred and pumped, and she leaned away from the quay steps. All around us a logjam of bumboats and sampans began to chug and break up, bobbing across our bow. Waiting behind a misshapen barricade of duffel bags and cardboard suitcases at the top of the stairs were six sunburned Russians, two stocky women with head scarves and cotton dresses, four men with Slavic lips, blond crew cuts, transparent nylon shirts, and string vests. One smoked a tubelike cigarette.

"Russkies," I said.

"What do *they* want?" muttered Shuck.

"Going out to their ship," I said. "Next stop Bloodyvostok, heh."

Gray sluggish waves, streaked with garter snakes of oil slick, sloshed at the cement stairs, lapped at an upper step, then subsided into rolling froth, depositing a crushed plastic bottle on a step halfway down. A new wave a second later lifted the bottle a step higher. I watched the progress of this piece of flotsam traveling up and down the stairs — the stairs where small-toothed Doris Goh had stumbled and soaked herself, where my handsome girls boarded sampans in old pajamas and overalls and giggled all the way to the freighters.

It was late afternoon; the sun behind the customs house and maritime building put us in shadow that made the inner harbor all greasy water and dark vessels. But farther out, where the water was lit, purest at the greatest distance, ships gleamed and made true reflections in the sky-blue sea mirror.

"See that little jetty?" I said. "Years ago, I used to take gals out from it in little boats. There, where that old feller's in the sampan."

The old man in flapping black pajamas, his foot braced against a plank seat, stirred his long oar pole back and forth on its crutch, rocking the sampan through the continual swell.

"I used to worry. What if a storm comes up and blows us out to sea? We're set adrift or shipwrecked. Makes you stop and think. You'd probably say, 'Great, alone with some hookers on a desert island.' But it would be fatal — you'd croak or turn cannibal. You'd be better off alone."

"You'd still croak," said Shuck.

"But you wouldn't turn cannibal," I said.

"I'm glad you made it today," said Shuck.

"So am I," I said. "God, I'm tickled to death."

Shuck pulled a sour face. "The way you talk," he said. "I can never make out if you're putting me on."

"Cut it out," I said. "I wouldn't do that."

"At Paradise Gardens I used to see you rushing around, getting into a flap and think, *Can he be serious?*"

"I worried about those fellers," I said. The *Kachang* was a hundred yards out; the tour guide had started his spiel. "That gray stone building over there is the general post office. One Christmas eve, about eleven o'clock, I stopped in to send a telegram for Hing. There were three Marines in there sending telegrams — to their folks, I suppose. I followed them out, and down the street. They headed over Cavanagh Bridge at a pretty good clip and I went after them. At Empress Place I was going to say something, wish them a Merry Christmas, offer them a drink, or take them around. I had some dough then — I could have shown them a real good time. But I didn't do a thing. They went off with their hands in their pockets. I felt like crying. I'd give anything to have that chance again."

The story made Shuck uneasy. "I thought you were telling a joke," he said. "Don't sweat it, Jack. The military takes good care of themselves."

"It wasn't that they were soldiers," I said. "They were strangers. I had the feeling that after they turned the corner something awful happened to them. For no good reason."

"You would have made a good — what's the word I'm looking for?"

"I know what you mean," I said. "There isn't one. Anyway, what's on your mind?"

"Hey, *you* called *me,* remember?"

"This harbor tour wasn't my idea," I said. "I just wanted to shoot the bull in your office."

"You said we had some unfinished business."

"Did I? Oh, yeah, I guess I did." I tried to laugh. Shuck's silence prompted me. I said, "I'm looking for work."

"What makes you think I can help you?"

"You said you had a proposition. I told you I wasn't interested. Now I am."

"I remember," said Shuck. "You told me to roll it into a cone and shove it."

"A figure of speech," I said. "I got a little hot under the collar — can you blame me?" I leaned close. "Ed, I don't know what you had in mind, but I could be very useful to you."

If he laughs I'll push him overboard, I thought.

Shuck said faintly, "Try me."

I was trembling. I was prepared to do anything, say anything. "See that channel?" I said. "Well, follow it far enough and you come to Raffles Lighthouse. Go a little beyond it and you're in international waters. You don't know what goes on there. I do."

"What does that prove?"

"Listen," I said, "smugglers from Indonesia sink huge bales of heroin in that water and then go away. Skindivers from Singapore go over and dredge it up. That's how the stuff's transferred — underwater. You didn't know that."

"That's the narcotics division. Dangerous drugs," said Shuck. "Not my bag."

"Commies your bag? How about the Goldsmiths and Silversmiths Union on Bras Basah Road — what do you know about them?"

"We've got a file on them."

"I know a feller who's a member — pal of mine, calls me Jack. He makes teeth for my girls. I could show you the teeth."

"Making gold teeth doesn't count as subversion, Jack."

"He's a Maoist," I said. "They all are. What I'm trying

214

to say is I'm welcome in that place anytime. I could get you names, addresses, anything."

"That stuff's no good to us."

"I'll buy that — I'm just using it as an example," I said. "Don't forget, I've been hustling in Singapore for fourteen years. What I don't know about the secret societies isn't worth knowing. See those tattoos? I've learned a trick or two."

Shuck smiled.

"You look suspicious," I said.

"You're too eager," said Shuck. "We get guys coming into the embassy every day with stories like that. They think we'll be interested. Lots of whispering, et cetera. The funny thing is, we know most of it already."

I tried a new tack. "Tell me frankly, what's the worst job you can imagine?"

"Frankly, yours," said Shuck. "I think hustling is about as low as you can go."

"Fair enough," I said. "Now, who's the straightest feller you know?"

"I used to think it was you."

"Why don't you think so now?"

"You're coming on pretty strong, Jack."

"I'm looking for work," I said. I was getting impatient. "You told me you had a proposition. All I want to know is — is it still on? Because if it is, I'm your man."

The *Kachang* was speeding alongside a wharf where a high black tanker was tethered. The tour guide was saying, " — fourth largest port in the world — "

"It was just an idea," said Shuck finally. "And the whole thing's pretty unofficial. I mean, it's *my* baby, not Uncle Sam's."

"All the better," I said. "So it's just between us two."

"There's someone else," said Shuck. "But he doesn't know a thing." Shuck spoke slowly, teasing me with lisps and pauses. "Let's call this guy Andy Gump. He comes to Singapore now and then. From Saigon. Is there anyone behind me? No? Andy Gump doesn't do much here — probably picks up a hooker and rips off a piece of ass. That's not news to you. In Saigon, though, it's a little bit different. He makes policy there."

"How high up is he?"

"High," said Shuck. "Now this is the crazy thing. No one finds fault with what he does there, but they'd shit if they knew what he did here. I'm talking about pictures and evidence."

"Can we be a little bit more concrete?"

"I'm just sketching this thing out," said Shuck. "Take a guy that's got the power to keep a whole army in Vietnam. He says he's idealistic and so forth. Everyone believes him, and why shouldn't they? He's got some shady sidelines, but he's a family man, he's fair to his troops — more than fair, he covers up for them when they kill civilians. He does his reports on time and flies to Washington every so often to explain the military position. So far, so good. Now, let's say we know this guy is screwing Chinese whores — maybe slapping them around, who knows? Ever hear of a credibility gap?"

Even in the stiff sea breeze my hands were slippery. I said, "For a minute I thought you were going to ask me to kill him."

"You're not *that* desperate for work," said Shuck. "Are you?"

"In despair some fellers contemplate suicide," I said. "I'm different. I contemplate murder."

"From what we hear, the same might be true of Andy Gump."

I said, "You want something on him?"

"That would be nice," said Shuck, squashing "nice" with a buzz.

"A few years ago," I said, "you would have been pimping for him. With a smile."

216

"That was a few years ago," said Shuck. "Now *you're* going to pimp for him. You know all the girls, you've got friends in the hotels. It should be easy."

"I don't monkey around with a feller's confidence," I said. "This is pretty nasty."

"It *stinks*," said Shuck. "I wouldn't do it myself. But you might think it over and if it interests you — you say you're looking for work — maybe we can talk about the details."

"There's only one detail I'm concerned about," I said. "Money."

"You'll be paid."

"Who names the price?"

"Good question," said Shuck. "Tell me, in your business who does that?"

"With hustling?" I said. "The gal does."

"The whore?"

"Yeah," I said. "The one that does the work."

"So what's your price?"

I scratched my tattoos; the tourists hooted in the cabin below; the breeze on my face was so warm it made me gasp, and when I looked at the *kampong* on stilts we were passing I saw some children swimming near the hairy bobbing lump of a dead dog. I said, "I won't lift a finger for less than five grand."

Shuck didn't flinch.

"And another five when I finish the job."

"Okay," said Shuck. Was he smiling, or just making another fishmouth?

"Plus expenses," I said.

"That goes without saying."

"I could use a drink."

"They pass out Green Spot when we get to the model shipyard in Kallang Basin," Shuck said. "What's wrong?"

"I was just thinking about Andy Gump," I said. "How old would you say he is?"

"Mid-fifties."

217

I shook my head. "I might have known."

"I'll tell you a couple of stories," said Shuck, "just so you don't go and get a conscience about him."

3

"AND GET THIS — " Shuck rattled on, itemizing Andy Gump's waywardness with such gloating and sanctimonious fluency he could have been lying in his teeth. Still, the image of the man, whose proper name was Andrew Maddox, rank major general, was a familiar one to me — so familiar that twice I told Shuck I had heard enough to antagonize me: it was not the man I was after, but the job. I did not need convincing; my mind was made up. This effort of mine, a last chance to convert my fortunes in a kind of thrusting, mindless betrayal, had required a number of willful deletions in my heart.

But Shuck was unstoppable. He ranted, pretending disgust, though the man he described was of a size that every detail, however villainous, enhanced. Shuck's accusations were spoken as the kind of envious praise I always thought of when I overheard someone in a bar retailing the story of a resourceful poisoner.

"You name a way to make a fast buck, and he's tried it," said Shuck. And he added in the same tone of admiring outrage that General Maddox had a yacht, smoked plump cigars, sported silk shirts, went deep-sea fishing off Cap St. Jacques, and stayed in expensive hotels.

"I know the type," I said.

The stories were not new — the fellers at Paradise Gardens had told me most of them without naming the villain, and Shuck had alluded to him before. But while I had taken all of it seriously, none of it had given me pause. I had lived long enough to know how to translate this bewilderment. I heard it as I heard most human sounds — Leigh's pastoral retirement plans, Yardley's jokes, Gunstone's war stories, my old openers (*Years ago* — and *I once knew a feller* —), and especially the exultant woman's moan of pleasure and pain, half sigh, half scream, while I knelt furiously reverent between her haunches — all this I heard as a form of prayer.

Vietnam stories throbbed with contradiction, but were as prayerful and pious as any oratorio. Like the tales of murder and incest associated with Borgia popes — horror stories to compliment the faith by supposing to prove the durable virtue of the Church — the song and dance about corruption in Vietnam never intended to belittle the bombings and torturings or the fact of any army's oafish occupation (the colonial setup, with Maddox as viceroy), but were meant as a curious sidelight on a justly fought war in which Shuck maintained, and so did some of the fellers, we had already been rightfully victorious: "But human nature being what it is — "

"I'll tell you another thing about him," said Shuck. He screwed up his face. "He's got a finger in the B-girl rackets."

"So he can't be all bad," I said. The *Kachang*, turning to port, pitched me close to Shuck's face. "Ed, I've got a whole *arm* in those!"

"He's a general in the U.S. Army," said Shuck. "You're not."

Shuck then set out to describe what he took to be the darkest side of General Maddox, his operating a chain of Saigon brothels, and his involvement with the less profitable skin-trade sidelines — which I knew to be inescapable — wholesaling massages, pornography, exhibitions; forging passports, nodding to con men, and smuggling warm bodies over frontiers — for the servicemen. Without wishing to, Shuck convinced me that, murder apart, this general was a more successful version of myself, his charitable carnal felony a fancier and better-executed business than "Kinda hot," the meat run, or Dunroamin. I hadn't bargained on this; warm wretchedness thawed my resolve.

"I don't get it," I said. "Your objection to this feller is that he's ungallant."

"He's a creep," said Shuck. "A disgrace."

"Tut tut, you're flattering yourself," I said, and went on, "Still, he's no stranger to me. If you called him a hero I'd find him ten times harder to understand."

"That's what *you* say."

"Heroes aren't my department," I said. "You want to end the war, so you try to unmask the villain. Me, I'd unmask the hero — he's your feller. Especially war heroes. If I was in charge I'd have them shot."

"You've got some screwy ideas," said Shuck.

"I haven't had your advantages," I said. "See, I don't know very much about virtue."

"*I* do," said Shuck.

"Good for you," I said. "Virtue is the distance that separates you from your favorite villain, right? It's an annual affair — every year there's a new American villain. Ever notice that? Virtuous people like you elect him, and then stone him to death. It's a sign of something."

"Maybe it's because we're puritanical," said Shuck.

"I was going to say bankrupt, and pretty fickle."

Shuck gave me a sour laugh. "So Maddox is an angel."

"Maddox is a hood, obviously," I said. "But you think he has a complicated motive. I know lots of fellers like him who behave that way because they're middle-aged and have bad teeth."

"Suppose he really *is* evil," said Shuck. "Think what a service you'll be doing by nailing his ass to the wall."

"Don't give me that," I said.

"You know what I think?" said Shuck. "I think you don't want to do this."

"I don't always want what I need," I said. "Why else would I have so little?"

"You're losing your nerve."

"Only when you try to justify this lousy scheme."

"Who's justifying? I told you the whole thing stinks."

"Now you're talking!" I said.

Not a job — an exploit, blackmail, an irrational crime with an apt rotten name; it was what I needed, the guarantee of some evil magic I didn't want to understand. Like a casual flutter at the Turf Club with an unpromising pony, and then a big payoff; the single coin in the fruit machine for the bonus jackpot; anything for astonishment, no questions asked. Then I understood my fantasies — they were a handy preparation for making me bold; little suggestions made my tattooed bulk jump to oblige. As a young man I often dreamed of a black sedan pulling up beside me as I sauntered down an empty street, the door swinging open, and the exquisite lady at the wheel saying softly, "Get in."

My fantasies provided something else: method, and a means of expression.

So: *"Follow that car,"* I said to the taxi driver at the airport. The fantasy command, immediately suspicious to any native English speaker, I could use in Singapore. I had wormed a copy of the passenger list from May Lim, a fruit fly turned ground hostess. From behind a pillar near the Customs and Immigration section, not far from the spot where I had first recognized Leigh, I watched the general arrive — a tanned, well-shod, barrel-chested man who walked with the easy responsible swing of a man accustomed to empty hands. He strode past me, followed by a laden porter, and got into a waiting taxi. Now, in my own taxi, I was saying, "Don't lose him — *keep on his tail*."

At the Belvedere I stood next to him while he checked in. He signed the register with a flourish, then straightened up. He untangled the springy wire bows of his military sunglasses from his ears and glanced around the lobby: that look of lust, the prompt glee of the man about to deliver a speech. I caught his eye.

"Kinda hot."

He agreed. "Muggy."

"This way, sir," said a costumed porter to him. He said, "See you around," and overtook the porter with long scissor steps.

I scribbled my name in the register, noting that Maddox had omitted his rank, that he was in room 913 and was staying for a week.

"Here I am again," I said to the Chinese clerk. "Remember me?"

"Oh, yes," he said, without looking up. He was scribbling on a pad. "So you like Singapore? Clean and green."

"A great little place," I said.

"Don't mention," he said, still scribbling.

"And this is a mighty fine hotel," I said. "I wouldn't stay anywhere else. I got sorta attached to that room you gave me before — nine-fifteen. Can you put me in the same one?"

"If it is empty."

"I'll make it worth your while," I said softly.

"Can," he said, glancing at the pigeonholes behind him.

I congratulated myself on knowing that odd-numbered rooms were on one side of the corridor, evens on the other. After all, it had only been a matter of weeks since I had fixed up Gunstone with Djamila here; over there, in the bar lounge, I had pretended to be Bishop Bradley.

223

"This way, sir," said the porter, at the elevator door.

"Put my suitcase in the room," I said, when we got to the ninth floor. "I'm just going to have a word with my friend here."

The elevator operator's face creased with terror. He shut his mouth.

"You look like a smart feller," I said. "Do you know how to keep your eyes open?"

"Do," he said, and widened his eyes.

"That's it," I said. "You're destined for big things. If you want to make a little extra money, just listen — "

After an hour my buzzer rang.

"Yoh?"

It was the elevator operator, grinning. "I take him down to lobby. He walk outside. I come straight back."

"Beautiful," I said, handing him five dollars. "Keep up the good work."

"Okay boys, this is it," I said into the phone, and five minutes later, Mr. Khoo, Jimmy Sung, and Henry Chow were in my room, sitting on the edge of the bed, straining to understand the plan. *The boys, the room, the plan:* the labels had an appealing sound.

What was most touching was the way the patient fellers listened, gaunt, threadbare, unblinking: my shabby gang of Chinese commandos. It was pleasing to conspire with a makeshift army, skinny sharpshooters in cast-off clothes. I had always served the rich by depending on such people, putting trust in the only helpers I could afford, the irregulars, the destitute, the socially famished — silent Karim, crooked Ganapaty, limping Gopi, the whispering urchins who stood sentry duty outside the blue-film sheds off Rochore Road, my girls. Poverty made them invisible, and I saw how much their devious skills resembled mine. I picked them for cunning and loyalty. I liked the drama: the rumpled middle-aged blackmailer in the elegant but smoke-fouled hotel room, saying, "Okay, boys — " to his team of ragged disciples who might have had nicknames like Munkypoo, Broomface, and The Ant.

In his lap, Mr. Khoo cradled an electric drill, like a nickel-plated Tommy gun; Jimmy Sung held a tape recorder, Henry Chow a camera. They hadn't asked why, and wouldn't — Chinese: the people with no questions.

"You know what you're supposed to do," I said. "Let's get moving."

Henry Chow flipped the lever on the camera; he had removed the ratchet from the spools: it wound noiselessly. Mr. Khoo speedily drilled and reamed a hole through the baseboard, into the next room, just under the general's bed. We took the additional precaution of disguising the microphone as a light socket. The positioning of the camera was next. Henry took a bucket and window washer's squeegee and crawled from my balcony to the general's, and giving the glass doors a good splash, estimated the angle for a shot at the bed. He returned, white-faced and shuddering, heaving himself slowly over the parapet, holding lightly to the balcony rail.

"Can we sling a camera up?"

"Can," he said, "but curtains — "

"It's no good," I said. "If he goes out to the balcony he'll see it and the jig's up. We can't do it that way." I was stumped. How *did* you take pictures in a feller's room without his knowing it? After I had spoken to Shuck I imagined myself, tape recorder slung over one shoulder, camera over the other, in a blackmailer's crouch, by a keyhole or window, listening, watching, pressing buttons, and then hopping away on tiptoe with the damning evidence.

The simplicity of that had struck me as cruel, but it wasn't so simple. This was a technical problem, a dilemma which in the solving made the cruelty slight, and as an executioner might think of himself as an electrician, absorbed in the study of watts and volts, a brainwasher a man concerned with candlepower, my sense of betrayal was soon forgotten in my handyman's huffing and puffing over the matter of wires, lenses, drilling, and testing — so complicated the general no longer seemed vulnerable. He was safe; I was the victim.

"Now, let's see here," I said. "We can't put the camera on the balcony. What about in his air conditioner? Make it look like a fuse box." My boys were silent. I replied to my own question. "That means we have to get into the room."

"Get a key," said Jimmy Sung.

"If only the bed was on the other side of the room," I said. "Then we could cut a hole up there, stick the camera through, and bingo."

"Move the bed," said Henry.

"He'll see the mike if we do that," I said. "Gee, this is your original sticky wicket."

Jimmy Sung suggested an alternative. He had once been hired to spy on a *towkay*'s wife, to get evidence of adultery. He followed the wife and her lover to a hotel. He bribed the cleaning woman to give him a key and had simply burst through the door at an opportune moment, taken a lightning shot of the copulating pair, and run.

"That's okay if you want one picture," I said. "But one's not enough. There must be another way."

I paced the room. "Henry says the general's room is just like this one, right? Bed here, chair there — " The three men looked from object to object as I named — "bureau there, desk over there — *wait!*"

Over the desk was a large rectangular mirror, reflecting the room; Mr. Khoo, Jimmy Sung, Henry Chow, seated uneasily on the bed. A mirror, distracting for anyone using the desk, made it useful as a woman's dressing table.

"We can't photograph the bed," I said, "but we can make a small hole in the wall and aim the camera at that mirror. It's right across."

226

"Wide-angle lens," said Jimmy.

Henry Chow smiled.

This time Mr. Khoo used his drill like a chisel, to loosen plaster and scoop out brick from our side of the wall. He made a niche for the camera and punched a small lens hole through to the other side. Jimmy Sung fitted the camera with a plunger on a long cable, and fixed the camera against the hole, bandaging it into the niche with adhesive tape.

"I guess that wraps it up," I said.

Mr. Khoo wiped his drill with a rag.

"This calls for a drink."

Henry said no. Mr. Khoo shook his head. Jimmy Sung scratched his head nervously and said he had to take his wife shopping.

"Come on, I'll treat you," I said. "They've got everything at this hotel. We could have lunch sent up. Anything — you name it. No charge!"

Mr. Khoo muttered something in Chinese. Henry looked embarrassed. Jimmy said, "Seng Ho want money," and winced.

"Anything you say." I paid them off, and when I did they edged toward the door. I said, "What's the rush? It's early. Stick around."

There is a Chinese laugh that means "Yes, of course!" and another that means "No, never!" The first is full of sympathy, the second is a low mirthless rattle in the throat. They gave me the second and were gone.

"So long, boys." I was alone. It was bright and noisy outside, but waiting I felt caged in the dim cold room of the Belvedere's ninth floor. On the far wall was the print of an old water color, Fort Canning, ladies with parasols, children rolling hoops, the harbor in the distance. I became aware of the air-conditioner roar, and shortly it deafened me and gave me goose flesh. In my bedroom in Moulmein Green I had a friendly fan that went *plunk-a-plunk* and a scented mosquito coil; a fig tree grew against the window.

An old phrase came to me, my summing up: *Is this all?* I looked at the completed handiwork and hated it. The problem of eavesdropping had been complicated and nearly innocent. The solution was simple and terrible, the sticky tape, the wires, the mirror, the black contraptions, the violated wall.

4

CRASH, BANG. The general went to his room after lunch, and my tape recorder amplified the racket of his entry to a hurried blundering. The door banged, the fumbled bolt was shot. Footsteps and belches and undressing noises, the flip-flap and yawn of a shirt being stripped off, coins jingling in lowered trousers, the bumps of two discarded shoes. Then bedsprings lurching, sighs, yawps. I stood on a chair and peeked through the camera's view finder. No girl; he napped alone, his arms surrendering on his pillow. He slept, snorting and shifting, for over an hour, awoke, changed into a green bathing suit, scratched his chest, made a face at me in the mirror, and went out in clunking clogs, with a towel scarflike around his neck — I guessed he was going to the swimming pool on the roof.

He needed tempting. But I had a sprat to catch this mackerel.

"Madam Lum? Jack here. Thelma busy? Yeah, right away. You're a peach — "

Thelma Tay goggled at the room. "Smart," she said, pronouncing it *smut*. She tossed her ditty bag on the bed and went over to the window. She worked the Venetian blinds and said, "Cute."

"It's great to see you," I said, giving her cheek a pinch. "I've been going out of my gourd."

She glided up and down, sniffing, touched the ashtray, turned on the bedside lamp, felt the curtains. She was no beauty, but I knew she was capable and had the right enthusiasm. Her glossy black hair was carefully set in ringlets and long curls and crowned with a small basket of woven plaits; she had the lovely hollows in her face that indicate in a Chinese girl small high breasts. She kicked off her shoes and smoothed her shiny belted dress. She posed and said, "Wet look."

"It's catching on," I said. "Very classy."

She undid the belt and pulled the dress over her head, and then, in her red bra and red half-slip, walked over to me and leaned her soft stomach into my face. "You ready?"

"Wait a sec, Thelma," I said, looking up. "It's next door."

She stepped back. "You not want?"

"Not me — the feller in there," I said, pointing to the broken wall. "He just stepped out, but he'll be back pretty soon."

"Oh," she said. She sat on the edge of the bed and found something on her elbow to pick.

"How's Madam Lum?"

"Is okay. Not so busy."

"It's hard all around," I said. "Not like it used to be. These people from the package tours — they're all ninety years old. God knows why they come here."

Thelma wasn't listening. She made a meowing sound in her nose — a Chinese pop song.

"Seen any good films lately?"

"Dracula," she said. "At Cathay."

"How was it?"

"I was scared-*lah!*" She laughed.

I poured myself a neat gin. "You want one?"

"Soft drink," she said. "Got Green Spot?"

"Thelma, anything you want — "

Crash, bang.

"It's him," I whispered. "Wait here. The lift boy's going to introduce you." I tiptoed over to the chair and looked through the viewfinder.

A dark Chinese girl in a frilly bikini walked past the mirror. The door banged, and my tape recorder spoke: *No, really, I think you were getting the hang of it. You've just got to remember to keep your legs straight and kicking and paddle like this —*

"You dirty devil," I mumbled, fiddling with the volume knob.

"I go now?" asked Thelma. She held her shiny dress up.

I drew her over to the bed. "Apparently," I said, "it's all been fixed."

— no, keep your fingers together. That's right. Here, hop on the bed and I'll show you —

"I'm sorry about this," I said. "Wait a minute. I'll explain." I grasped the plunger and snapped a picture, then went back and sat on the bed next to Thelma. "It looks like I got you up here for nothing."

"You no want fuck?"

"I've got my hands full," I said. "Don't worry, I'll pay you just the same. In the meantime let's watch our language?"

"Mushudge?"

"Oh, I don't know," I said.

— lift those arms up! Like this — keep kicking! Sort of move your head —

Thelma started kneading my shoulders, working her way down, and then pinching my backbone. It was soothing. I got down on the bed and she took my shirt off and straddled me, hacking at my shoulders and back with the sides of her

231

hands, rubbing, clapping, like someone preparing a pizza.

"Gosh that feels good." I closed my eyes, enjoying it, feeling my muscles unknot.

— *breath control's very important. Take a deep breath — way down. Beautiful. Now let it out real slow, and twist —*

"Hop off, Thelma," I said. I went over and looked through the view finder. The general crouched next to the girl in the bikini who was stretched out and making loud sounds of breathing. I snapped two pictures.

Thelma had stripped, and bare, seemed serious and businesslike, her nakedness like a uniform. She saddled herself on the small of my back and dug her knuckles against my ribs, and then went through the kneading and pinching routine again, neck, shoulders, and spine, warming me all the way down to my kidneys.

"Gorgeous," I said. Her knees were tight against my ribs, and still she rode me, jogging slightly as she massaged.

— *that's what we call the crawl. Now let me show you the breast stroke. This is a very useful one. All you have to do —*

"Picture," I said, and Thelma slid off. I wound the film and shot.

"Turn over," said Thelma when I crept onto the bed again.

"Hey, wait a minute — "

But she had already unbuckled my belt, and laughing softly, explored me as she shoved my trousers down to my ankles.

— *push those hands all the way out —*

"You say no, but he say yes."

"He? Who's *he?*" I looked at the tape recorder.

"This one," said Thelma. She gave my pecker a squeeze and made it look at me with the single slit eye on its rosy dome.

"Oh, I see," I said. "Our friend here."

— pretend you're flying. That's it —

I disengaged myself and hopped to the wall to take another picture.

"You very sexy, mister," said Thelma. "Look!"

"That's right," I said, "broadcast it."

"He *like* me, mister."

"Not so loud," I hissed.

"What style you wants?" She lay flat and put her hands behind her head, as if responding to the swimming lesson coming over the tape recorder's speaker: *Floating on your back is easy if you know how —* . Then Thelma did an extraordinary thing; she knelt in a salaaming position, an expressive and dainty obedience, and put her face against the pillow, and raised her buttocks into the air. She laughed and said what sounded like, "Woof, woof."

"Let's keep it simple," I said. I stood thoughtfully between the camera and the bed, holding my pecker the way a patient fisherman holds his pole. "And don't be surprised if I hop up in the middle of it. I've got a job to do, Thelma." I shuffled over to the bed, muttering, "And honestly it's a very ticklish business."

I embraced her, holding her tightly with my eyes shut; she rotated, helping me, and at once my engine began turning over, quietly rousing my body, warming old circuits in my belly and beyond. I had taught myself and shown others that love was the absence of fear; so this sexual veneration, pure joy, made the past accessible. I was raised up, a prince at the parapet of his castle tower, to look over a bright kingdom of memories. Today, without inviting him, I saw Roosevelt Rush, a black deck hand on the *Allegro*, who called me "Flahs" and slept with a nylon stocking drawn tight over his hair. One hot night, anchored in Port Swettenham, he stood in the engine room carefully pouring whiskey over his pecker. I remarked on the quality. "Black Label," he said: "Ain't nothing too good for this banana," and he kept pouring. He flicked drops from his business end and explained, "Think I got me some clap from a 'ho'." I'd had it myself seven times, and got used to the progress of the complaint I called a runny nose: the unusual sting on the third day, the sticky dripping, the pinching pain of leaking hot needles, and the itch that was always out of reach. I knew tropical pox doctors by the solidly painted windows of their storefront clinics, and was treated by men with degrees from Poona who jammed syringes into my arm as if they were celebrating Thaipusam, said "drink plenty bottles of beer," gave me capsules the size of Mexican jumping beans, and offered to waive the ten-rupee fee if I'd help them emigrate to Canada.

Thelma groaned; I rode her like a dolphin and plunged back into my memory: I was lying on Changi Beach eating a melting ice cream with Tai-ann and Choo-suat; in the Botanical Gardens hearing a smart Sikh regiment of bagpipers play, "Will You No Come Hame Again" — and I cried then into my hands; in my narrow back garden discovering with surprise and pleasure a wild orchid fastened to my elastic fig; in a cool bedroom in Queen Astrid Park with that beautiful woman who panted "Jim, Jim" into my ear, and then laughed; in that noisy little hotel on Prinsep Street one afternoon, where I held a short-haired girl from behind and was jerked from my towering reverie by a screech of brakes in the street below, a wicked bump, a howling dog that went on howling even after I stopped. That memory froze me today.

And of course there were the pictures.

Sexual desire, a molehill for a boy of twenty, gets steeper with age, and at fifty-three it is a mountain. You pant up slowly at a tricky angle; but pause once and you slide back to where you started and have to begin all over again. *You're learning real quick,* the general said; and *Try it this way — don't be shy;* and *Let me hold you.* The interruptions

234

of these three pictures almost undid me, and at the end Thelma said, "*Ai-yah!* Like Mr. Frank!"

"You've got the wrong end of the stick there, sugar," I said. Frank, one of the balding "eggs" from the Cricket Club, supported his lovemaking with an assortment of Swedish apparatus. The pesky things were always slipping or jamming and needed constant adjustment. One day I met the old feller on Bencoolen Street. He was smiling. He took an ugly little cellophane-wrapped snorkel out of his briefcase and said proudly, "I think this is the answer, Jack. She runs on batteries."

Thelma shook her head. She was amused but nevertheless disgusted.

"This is official business," I whispered. "You wouldn't laugh if you knew what."

"Like Mr. Frank!"

"Have it your way," I said, and paid her. "Feel like sticking around?"

She counted the money and put it into her purse. "Madam Lum say come back with legs on. If I late she scold-*lah*."

"Stay till six," I said. "For old times' sake."

She smiled. "For twenty-over dollar."

I considered this.

She said, "For twenty, can."

"Never mind," I said. I opened the door for her, and then I had the same feeling that worried me when the boys left: with no one else in the room I didn't exist, like an unwitnessed thunderclap in the desert. I sat down with a gin and read through the Belvedere brochures. They offered room service — "Full-course dinners or snacks served piping hot in the traditional Malay style." Also: "Relax at our poolside bar — or have a refreshing dip" and "Your chance to try our newly installed sauna" and "It's happening at our discotheque — the 'right now' sounds of The Chopsticks!" Another bar promised "alluring hostesses who will serve your every need." There were a 24-hour coffee shop, a secretarial service, French, Chinese, and Japanese restaurants, and a nightclub, "Featuring the Freddy Loo Dancers," a Japanese kick line and an Australian stripper. And mawkish suggestions: *No visit to Singapore is complete without* — and *You will also want to try* —

This *you* they kept addressing, was it me? I looked at the nightclub brochure again. The stripper was waving from the seat of a motorcycle. That finished me. I changed into my flowered shirt and started lacing my shoes.

— *You're sure I'm not hurting you?*
— *Sure.*

I wound the film. I closed my eyes. I snapped; and securing my room with a DO NOT DISTURB sign, fled down the fire stairs.

They were on the verandah of the Bandung, in the low wicker chairs with the swing-out extensions on the arms, all of them with their feet up, their heels hooked, as if they were about to be shaved. Yardley was reading the *Straits Times* to Frogget, who listened with a pint of beer resting on his stomach.

"That ghastly old sod got an O.B.E.," said Yardley. "Would you believe it? And guess who got an M.B.E.? This is ridiculous — "

"What's cooking?" I said, pulling out the arm extensions on a chair next to Yates and settling in. I put my legs up and was restored.

"Honors' List just published," said Yates. "Yardley's rather cross. He wasn't knighted."

"I'd send the bloody thing back," said Yardley. "I wouldn't be caught dead on the same list with that abortionist. Christ, why don't they give these things to people who deserve them?"

"Like Jack," said Frogget.

"Maybe Jack got an O.B.E.," said Smale.

"Very funny," I said.

"Let's have a look," said Yardley. He rattled the paper.

"Don't bother," I said. "Pass me the shipping pages."

"Aw, that's a shame," said Yardley. "They missed you out again."

"Where's Wally?" I asked.

"Wally!" shouted Smale. Once, a feller came to the Bandung and did that very same thing, shouted Wally's name from the verandah; and Smale said, "If you do that again I'll boot your rude arse." The feller was an occasional drinker; no one had ever spoken to him, and after Smale said that he never came again. Soon, each of us had a story, a reminiscence of his behavior, and Yardley finally arrived at the view that the feller was crazy.

Wally appeared at my elbow.

"A double pink gin with a squirt of soda," I said. "And ask these gentlemen what they'd like."

"Telephone for you, today morning," said Wally. "Mr. Gunstone."

It passed without a remark. I had just bought everyone a drink.

"What about you, Yatesie?" asked Smale. "When's your M.B.E. coming around?"

"It's just a piece of paper," said Yates.

"Listen to him," said Yardley. His legs clattered on the wooden rests as he guffawed. "When I came in here at half-five he was reading the paper, looking for his name."

"That is untrue," said Yates with a note of hurt in his voice that contradicted his words.

"He'd give his knackers for an M.B.E.," said Yardley, "and even the flaming Beatles got *that.*"

"I wouldn't mind," said Smale, and cursed under his breath. "I wouldn't complain if I got one of those things. Face it, none of you would."

There was a moment of silence then, the silence a bubble

of sheepishness, as mentally we tried on a title. Viscount Smale. Lord Yardley. Sir Desmond. Lord Flowers, I was thinking, Saint Jack.

"Who's on the list?" I asked. "Anyone I know?"

"Apart from Wally, who got a knighthood — right, Wally? Sure you did — only Evans, the twit that works in the Hong-kong and Shanghai Bank. M.B.E."

"Evans? Oh, yeah," I said. "I know him. He's in the Cricket Club."

"I wouldn't know about that," said Yardley.

"Or so I heard," I said.

"He makes a good screw," said Smale. "Him a banker."

"Rubbish," said Yardley. "Not more than three or four thousand quid."

"Call it four," I said. "It's ten thousand U.S. That's pretty good money."

"Pretty good money," said Yardley, mocking me. "Four thousand quid! That's not money."

"Ten thousand bucks would take you pretty far," I said. Frogget laughed uncertainly and looked at Yardley.

Yardley shifted in his chair. He said, "That's not money."

"No," said Smale. "Not *real* money."

"I suppose not," I said.

We stared into the garden. It was darkening; the garden became simple and orderly in the twilight, the elastic fig and the palm it strangled were one. The mosquitoes were waking, gathering at the verandah light and biting our exposed ankles. Frogget slapped at his bare arm.

"Say fifty or sixty thousand quid," said Yardley. "That's money."

Someone's wicker chair creaked.

"Or maybe a hundred," said Frogget.

"You could live on that," said Yardley.

"You certainly could," said Yates.

"Imagine," said Smale.

"Funnily enough," I said, "I can."

"So can I," said Frogget.

"The last time I was on leave," said Smale, "I took a taxi from Waterloo to King's Cross. Had a lot of baggage. I paid the fare and told the driver to keep the change. 'A bob,' he says, and hands it back to me. 'Fit it up your arse.' "

"That rosebush wants pruning," said Yates.

" 'Fit it up your arse'," said Smale. "A shilling!"

"It wouldn't fit," said Frogget.

"That reminds me," said Yardley. "The funniest thing happened today. It was at Robinson's. Jack, you're not listening."

"I'm all ears," I said.

5

My week was over, though it seemed like more than a week: it was very hard for me to tell how fast the time went with my eyes shut. It was the suspenseful captivity I had known with Toh's gang, the time no one ransomed me. I sat blinded by resolution in my luxurious armchair — luxury at that price now something like a penalty — and I recorded the general confirming his plane ticket, packing his bags, phoning for a taxi; I knew that I was listening to the end. Mr. Khoo came up and filled the holes in the wall. I checked out quietly and went back to Moulmein Green. It was three in the afternoon. I slept under the fan and woke up the next day to the squeals of children playing outside my window. They were comparing paper lanterns they had obviously just bought, squarish roosters in red cellophane, airplanes and boxy fish.

A few days later, at Hing's, I was standing in the shade of the portico, watching the traffic on Beach Road, my hands in my pockets.

"Sorry," said a voice behind me. I turned and saw Jimmy Sung unzipping a briefcase. "The pictures," he said, laughing, "no good, myah!" He passed me a thick envelope of pictures.

"If they're duds it's not your fault," I said. I flicked through the envelope and saw rippling water stains on an opaque background; some were totally black, others smirched and blurred. No human form was apparent. I was off the hook.

"Wrong esposure," he said.

"That's how it goes," I said. I wanted to hug him.

"And these," he said. He gave me a smaller envelope.

"What's this?"

"Some good ones."

"You said they were all dark."

"Not all." He nodded. "I make some estra print. Okay, Jack, I see you."

"Be good," I said. I took the envelope into my cubicle to open it, and with fingers slowed by dread I started shuffling. The swimming lesson was first, and though "swimming lesson" sounds like the euphemism for a pervert's crimp, this one looked genuine enough: the girl thrashed, the general stood at the end of the bed and coached, and in one he appeared to be giving the girl artificial respiration. Some showed the girl alone, or the general alone, and at the side of the picture the arm or leg of the other. Two I liked. In the first the general was wagging his finger at the grinning girl; in the second they were staring in different directions, the general vacantly at his watch, the girl at her splayed-out fingers. It was always the swimmer. One I treasured: the general's arms were folded around the dark girl who sat in his lap and held his head in her hands. He was a big man, his embrace was protective, and her posture replied to this. If the photograph of a posture could prove anything, this proved fondness, even if it was a hopeless flirtation like his own war.

As blackmail they were of no value — the opposite of incriminating. It might have been different; in the Belvedere that week a crime fantasy had sustained me. The blackmailer photographing what he thinks is an infidelity discovers that he is witnessing a murder; he hears the threats, he sees the violence, he springs into the room, a nimble rescuer in the nick of time. It would have made a good story. Mine was not so neat, but there in my cubicle I had my first insight into the whole business: betrayal may damn, or it may vindicate. It was, after all, revelation. I had spied on the general to find him guilty; I came away with proof of something ordinary enough to be blameless. I was as relieved as if it was an affirmation of whatever well-intentioned gesture I had made: that impulsive embrace when one can believe for a full minute that one is not alone. So I was saved, and I thought: might not some chilly gray intriguer, hard by an enemy window, watch sadness or love rehearsed and change his mind? Shuck held him responsible for a war. I could not speak for that outrage, but in one respect, the only one I had seen, the man was gentle. I had spied on innocence.

"You looked pleased with yourself," said Shuck in the Pavilion. Shuck had taken a corner table, and he looked around the bar as he spoke to me.

"I've got them." I patted my breast pocket. "He's in here."

"How about a drink first," said Shuck. "I'm just having a Coke."

"Gin for me," I said. "Well, here they are."

We were beside a ship's clock, under a long shelf of brassware, old pistols, sabers, and muskets. Shuck looked closely at the clock before he opened the envelope. He kept his poker face while he examined each picture, and when he finished and put them back he said, "Any others?"

"Nope."

He creased the envelope. "He's no Casanova, that's for sure. I wouldn't have believed it. But these'll be useful. I mean, he's with a Chinese girl, loving her up and so forth. He'll have a hard time explaining that to the Pentagon. You know the girl?"

"Swimming lessons," I said. "Can I see them a minute?"

Shuck palmed them and put them into my hand. I slipped the envelope into my pocket.

"What are you doing?"

"Keeping them."

"Maybe it's better that way, for the time being." Shuck was still looking around the bar, half covering his mouth when he spoke, though with his lisp I doubted whether anyone could have understood a word he said.

"For good," I said. "Until I burn them."

"Hey, not so fast," he said. "Those pictures are mine."

"I took them," I said. "They're mine."

Shuck laughed uncertainly. "I know your game," he said. "You want more money. Okay, I'll give you more — in addition to the ten grand we agreed on."

"It's not enough."

Shuck gripped his Coke; his face was malevolent. "Another five."

"No."

"Jack — "

"It's not enough."

"Six," he lisped, and his expression changed from malevolence to concern. "I understand. You're holding out for more and you think I have to give it to you because you've got something on me — because I put you up to this. I've got news for you — it won't wash. Now hand over the goods."

"It's not enough money, one," I said. "And, two, you're not getting them anyway."

"It figures," said Shuck. His smile was grim. "This happens with nationals all the time. Thais, say, or Cambodians. They agree on a price, usually peanuts — but they're Thais, so how do they know how much to ask? They deal in small figures, then later they want more. It always gets bigger. And then they really get expensive."

"So you tell them to get lost."

"Sometimes," said Shuck. "Anyway, as soon as you told me how much you wanted I knew you'd been out of the States for a long time. You really belong here. Ten grand! I couldn't believe it."

"I know," I said. "That's not money. I'm glad you didn't ask me to shoot him. I might have done that for fifteen."

"So what's your price?"

"No price."

"You're putting me on again, aren't you?"

"I'm not," I said. "No price, no pictures. I'm giving you back the five grand. No sale."

"You *did* lose your nerve after all," said Shuck.

"Not on your life," I said. "I've even got tapes of the guy — more graphic than the pictures in a way, but harder to visualize. Muffled noises, very touching really."

"Jack," said Shuck. "Are you going to the other side with them?"

"You're a tricky feller," I said. "Do you know that until now that possibility hadn't even occurred to me?"

"You're playing with dynamite."

"Dynamite," I said. "A feller kissing a girl. A girl saying fuck. A feller in bed. A girl doing the breast stroke. Dynamite!"

"He's a general!" said Shuck.

"He was out of uniform," I said. "I want to change the subject."

"I know you're going to the Russians," said Shuck. "Or is it the Chinese?"

"Neither."

"I'll tell you something," said Shuck. "They're not even good pictures. They're very amateurish."

"To me they're hopeful," I said. "I'd give them to you — for nothing — but you'd do the wrong things with them. You'd misuse them."

"Jack, I promise — "

244

"You'd put the wrong interpretation on them," I said. "That would kill me." And I wanted to say, but I couldn't phrase it, that the honor he talked about was a very arbitrary notion, as temporary as power, and would be out of fashion tomorrow, when the sides changed. I wanted no part of the graceless distortion. I was a person of small virtue; virtue wasn't salvation, but knowing that might be.

"I don't believe he's guilty," I said at last.

"How do you know?"

"Because *I'm* not."

"If you don't hand those over you are."

"If I give you these," I said, "I'm sunk."

"So you're trying to save yourself!"

"And you, too," I said.

Shuck appealed, but I was scarcely listening: "You'd never have to worry . . . I'm not talking about nickels and dimes . . . Blow the lid off this thing . . . only the beginning . . . everything you always wanted . . . *famous.*"

I was looking at the old waiter with the lucky moles on his face, the dusty sabers, the pots of beer; and I was thinking: *What a pleasant bar this is, what happy people.*

And I walked. Alone, leaving Shuck and my untouched gin, out the swinging doors, and stumping regally down Orchard Road, which was choked with traffic and the nighttime bustle of shoppers and late eaters; past the car dealers and the Istana Gardens, to Dhoby Ghaut, where a gigantic blood-flecked poster of a fanged and green-faced Dracula was suspended, garishly lit, over the Cathay marquee; past the secondhand bookshops on Bras Basah Road (*"Ksst.* Mistah, something special?"). I had panicked and acted. I shouldn't have panicked; but the act released me. I was a lucky feller.

"Hey Jack!" A nasal Chinese yell, the man's shyness causing him to scream. I saw a white shirt in a doorway, not a zombie — a friend with no face.

245

I waved to him and kept walking, cutting through the noise that was crowding me, liking the night air. I had had my nose pressed against two fellers, one dead, one alive. I knew them, and my betrayal, begun exclusively as a crime — I had insisted on that — ended as an act of faith, the conjuring trick that fails when you understand it. The Oriental Bookstore, Convent of the Holy Infant Jesus, Bamboo Bar, Goldsmiths and Silversmiths Union — mottled and beflagged — and down Victoria Street I could see children ducking into alleys, carrying flimsy red lanterns for the moon festival: colored lights jostling in the dark, illuminating shirtfronts and faces. I walked across the grassy *maidan,* past the War Memorial to civilians which looks like four enormous flood-lit chopsticks, and dodging traffic — pretty nimble for a feller my age — bounded to the steel rail on the harbor promenade. Out there, ship lights twinkled. This was the very edge of the island, on the thickest part of the world.

Not one life — I had had many. A memoir selects from the interruption of different fears. There had been others; I expected more, and I was calm, for I had had a death as well. But all I thought were preparations for flight had readied me for staying, a belonging the opposite of what I wanted: familiar, yes, and yet who would willingly die here? I was no exile. There were fast planes west, and I knew the cosiest ships. Being away can make you a stranger in two places, I thought; but it wasn't a country I needed, and not money, though I knew some cash would improve my backward heart. I had a ten-dollar win ticket on *Major General* in the fourth race on Saturday, and a lottery ticket — Toto Number 915. Fortune might be denied me, but that denial still held a promise like postponement. No drums, no trumpets; a love gallop thundered in my head, and the random sea splash quickened below me, signals of danger very much like the sounds of rescue.

I was tranquil enough at last to kill myself — to toss myself into the harbor; but I changed my mind and decided to live for a hundred years. So my life was only half gone. I would celebrate the coming glory with an expensive drink at Raffles, down the road, and, time permitting, do a spot of work before I put in an appearance at the Bandung. Children with bright lanterns moved along the promenade toward me, swinging their blobs of light. I blessed them simply, wishing them well with a nod.

There was another admirer. A woman in a white dress, with a camera slung over her shoulder, leaned against the sea rail twenty feet away. When the children passed by, she approached me, smiling.

"What beautiful children," she said. "Are they Chinese?"

"Yeah," I said. "But they should be in bed at this hour."

"So should I," said the woman, and she laughed gently. She was a corker. She looked across the street and held her fingers to her mouth and kissed them in concentration. "Oh, hell," she said, "I'm lost."

"No, you're not," I said.

"Hey, you're an American, too," she said. "Do you have a minute?"

"Lady, believe me," I said, and a high funny note of joy, recovered hope, warbled in my ears as I pronounced the adventurous sentence, "I've got all the time in the world."